KING'S G. MBIT

The Remarkable Life & Times
of George de Carteret
1609 - 1680

JOHN DANN

To The Société Jersiais, its Members & Staff.

ACKNOWLEDGEMENTS

I offer my thanks to the staff and officers of The Société Jersiais for their interest in this project, and the assistance provided. Grateful thanks also to Sue Hardy for introducing me to people and places, and offering invaluable advice concerning publication. Thanks are also due to Doug Ford for his advice concerning naval matters.

My special thanks to Charles Malet de Carteret, Seigneur de St. Ouen, for providing access to parts of the house once familiar to George de Carteret, and showing me Charters, manuscripts, and portraits related to my research.

The staff of the Essex County Record Office, Chelmsford, provided access to The Calendar of State Papers: Domestic, dictionaries of Oxford University Divines, Academics and Lawyers, which cast light on their professional involvement in the controversies of their time. These insights were essential for my understanding of the three families whose lives form the background of this book.

I also express thanks to Valerie Bixley and Bruce Hilton-Tapp for their endless pains in editing my text, and to David Spiller for designing the cover.

Finally, I offer gratitude to Simeon Dann seeing the manuscript through to publication.

John Dann is an academic and retired teacher. When not writing, he enjoys wandering around the countryside, making music and helping out in the small village where he lives. His historical interests include the Middle Ages in Europe and the Byzantine Empire. He has researched the Civil War in Great Britain for several years which led to a fascination with the part played by Jersey and its islanders in the events of that time. Several visits to Jersey over the years, led to his fascination with the direct effect of the conflict on island families. King's Gambit is the present result.

A select bibliography

Calendar of State Papers, Domestic Series 1600 – 1690

Aubrey, J. (1692). Brief Lives

Balleine, GR. (1976). All for the King. Jersey

Balleine, GR. (1976). A Biographical Dictionary of Jersey. London

Balleine, GR. (1950). A History of the Island of Jersey

Balleine, GR. (1951). The Bailiwick of Jersey

Dunton. (1637). True Journal of the Sallee Fleet

Carteret, G. (1633). The Chase of a Pirate

Carteret, G. (1639). Return to Africa

Falle, P. (1694). An account of the Island of Jersey.

Hakluyt, R. (1600). Navigations, Voyages, Traffiques and Discoveries.

Poingdextre, J. (1889). Caesarea, or a Discourse on the Island of Jersey

Padfield, P. (1999). Maritime Supremacy. London

Partlett, D. (1979) Card Games. London

Syvret. M and Stevens, J. (1981). Balleine's History of Jersey. Jersey: Phillimore & Co

The Diary of Samuel Pepys (full edition)

Wells, H.G. (1911) Floor Games. London

Facts are meaningless:

Art confers Reality

The Carterets

Rachel, nee Paulet: Mother of Elias and Philippe

Elie (Elias) de Carteret, b. 1585:   Attorney General for Jersey
Elizabeth, nee Demaresque: Wife of Elie, b. 1590
George de Carteret: Their eldest son, b. 1609
Philippe de Carteret: Their second son, b. 1612
Reginald de Carteret: Their third son, b. 1615
Anne de Carteret: Their elder daughter, b. 1615
Rachel de Carteret: Their daughter, b. 1617

Philippe de Carteret, b. 1583:   Seigneur de St. Ouen,
                                     Governor of Jersey
Amyas de Carteret: Brother of Philippe, b. 1587
Gideon de Carteret: Brother of Philippe, b. 1591
Anne, nee Dowse: His wife, b. 1585
Philippe de Carteret: Their eldest son, b. 1620
Elizabeth de Carteret: Their daughter, b. 1625
Amyas de Carteret: Their son, b. 1627
Francois (Francis) de Carteret: Their son, b. 1630

Amice de Carteret, b. 1559:   Seigneur de Trinité,
                                     Governor of Guernsey
Catherine, nee Lemprière: His wife, b. 1559
Dr. Philippe de Carteret, an M.D.   Their eldest son, b. 1608.
Joshua de Carteret, a lawyer: Their son, b. 1611

x

Chapter 1

Although it was early in the morning when George set out on the journey which could change his life, he did not to use the track to St Helier, not wishing to be distracted from his intention. Leaving the wagon track, he descended the steep slope beneath the Manor house bastion and slid down to the brook and the concealed pathways he and his friends had always used.

At once the sounds of early morning work in the stables and dairies ceased, and he heard nothing more than birds, rustlings in the undergrowth, and snapping twigs under his boots. He met no-one, although while ducking under low branches and avoiding tangled roots and mossy rocks he could hear cows going for milking, and the barking of dogs.

His path led him to the track to St Aubyn, and he passed early labourers going to work. Most exchanged nodded greetings, no doubt taking in his work clothes and backpack. They would know, if they thought about it, of his purpose. His appearance said it all.

Leaving the track again, he travelled over the more exposed land beyond St Peter's, and saw a glimpse of Mont des Vignes, his family home, where his mother would be preparing to wake his brothers and

1

sisters and see that they ate a good breakfast. He had said goodbye to them all two days before, wishing to avoid any last-minute precautions offered, and especially his mother's distress, which might disturb the small children. They knew he would be away from home for several months but was not leaving for ever, and, thank goodness, he was not leaving bad feeling behind him. Very close to his destination, his mind ran over the confusion and distress he had gone through until after Christmas, when his uncle and aunt had lent their support and helped him to convince his father that he had made a sound choice.

The smell of the harbour and strength of the breeze both told him that it was perfect sailing weather for setting out on a long voyage, and he had received his father's blessing, which only three months ago had seemed an impossibility.

* * *

It was the previous autumn when George had begun to have questions about his future and what life might offer him. For a boy in his early teens, he was energetic and optimistic, and his friends would have noticed no change in him or his generally sanguine and cheerful view of life. In that respect, he remained constant and had learned to control his easily roused anger, for the right moment. As the eldest son, he had always known that his parents expected much of him, which he was happy about, and his relationship with his parents and the younger members of the family was good. He learned from his friends that many of them were less fortunate, often quarrelling with their siblings.

As often happens, it was his progress in school which threatened this stability. Generally, he was not a problem pupil and the Regent of St Peter's School found him willing, one of several pupils who could be relied on. The Head teacher had, in fact ambitions in mind for him, and saw him as a future Oxford scholar, like several of his ancestors.

His father was a considerable landowner and lawyer, and inherited family responsibilities early, on the death of his father; an obligation he had never regretted. He was pleased that George showed academic promise, particularly in view of the disappointment his elder brother Philippe had experienced when their father died. He was a born academic and had matriculated for Pembroke College. The sudden death of their father, however, left him as guardian of his mother and nine siblings, and Seigneur of St Ouen! George nourished a growing suspicion that both brothers might see him as one to fulfil their frustrated ambitions.

Initially the thought amused him, and he was naturally pleased that he was held in such regard, knowing he was expected to set an example, this was not burdensome, since he enjoyed being with his siblings and finding things to amuse them. He was as much at home with the much younger children of his Uncle Philippe at the Manor. His two-year-old cousin, Philippe, worshipped the air he breathed, and little Lizzy was a smiley, chuckling baby still. He enjoyed the peace and quiet of the Manor and his uncle's humour and wit, in contrast with his father's restless activity, and reluctance to pause for conversation. When his uncle was away in London, which he often was, his Aunt and he had become close friends, and she was only about eight years his senior. She missed her brothers, left behind in England, and having no sisters, she had been taught by their tutors, reading their books when they went to boarding school and University.

Anne, his aunt, encouraged his interests in sciences and travel, since her brothers and father had all travelled in Europe. His Uncle had a large collection of books on many subjects, some almost 200 years old, and in classical languages. He especially enjoyed the large number on sea trade and fishing, both essential for their livelihood in Jersey. He also had a considerable collection of maps and sea charts, drawn by generations of island seafarers, and geographers and map makers from Antwerp and Boulogne. George was spending increasing amounts of time with his Uncle and Anne. The Manor came to be a refuge from incipient ill-feeling at home.

Once the Autumn Term had begun, the Regent took one or two of his pupils aside to provide extra coaching in Mathematics and Latin in preparation for matriculation. George was surprised to be asked, but enjoyed a challenge and, with strong support from his father, consented to the arrangement. He and his younger brother, Philippe, spent considerable time in each other's company, and George found explaining the lessons helped him to understand them. Philippe was an eager learner and, after a few weeks George began to feel that his brother was enjoying the work more than he did. Probably he would be offered coaching next year but he was already able to sort out the complexities of Caesar's addresses to his troops quite fluently.

Although George enjoyed study, he found he had had more pleasure in his uncle's library with the maps. He was aware of wanting something more and experienced feelings of restlessness. It was the accidental discovery of Hakluyt's Voyages that was a turning point. Here was a man who had travelled, and then spent many hours collecting and writing up the accounts written by sea Captains of their voyages, to lands previously unvisited by an Englishman. Their descriptions of unfamiliar coastlines, and remarkable weather conditions, and keeping up the morale of the seamen on whom their lives depended, was familiar to him from his own fishing experiences in local waters, and further south around Finisterre.

Often while working on geometry, he found himself gazing from the window noticing slight changes in the weather, or comparing the angles drawn on sea charts, using a headland by an alignment with the pole star, to provide directions at sea. In addition, he began to wonder how greater knowledge of Latin as a language, could play a part in his life. Above all, he felt a desire for fresh air and strenuous exercise, and second-guessing the unpredictable and subtle changes of tide or ocean currents, was a challenge he would enjoy. Chatting to the sons of fishermen, he shared their eager wish to follow their fathers into the family fishing trade, and heard more tales told by their elders of exciting and dangerous trips.

It seemed to him that his greatest enjoyment was to be at sea, in any capacity. He heard older boys wondering when they would be strong enough to join the crew of a fishing boat. Some knew that an elder brother was hoping to join the next fishing fleet, sailing next spring for Newfoundland. He began to hope that a Captain would suddenly ask him to join his crew next week, and his eager acceptance of the offer, but thought of his father's indignation if he dared to suggest it.

Matters came to a head one fine day in mid-October. He and Philippe had taken advantage of a brisk westerly to spend a day among the smaller islands, Les Ecréhous and Les Dirouilles, navigating hidden reefs was rewarded by crystal-clear swimming and sandy beaches. Once on their way, in companionable silence, Philippe broached a matter of concern. He asked whether his brother realised how much he enjoyed learning Latin: he was expecting to leave school in a year and would like to be a lawyer like their father. He hoped that George would not mind if he asked to study law. George wondered why his brother was asking him for permission, and realised that Philippe had assumed that, with him at University, he might be needed on the family boats. Before answering, George made an adjustment to the helm. He found that he could suddenly see a future before them which might solve their problems. Would they be permitted to express a preference? This was a new thought, and he saw their future in a new light.

5

"I know our uncle enjoyed Latin, bro, and would be pleased that you like it, but you might have to go to College in Coutance, or a University in England. Uncle Philippe finds Latin invaluable in London when he goes to the Privy Council to defend our interests. One day someone will have to take on those matters: perhaps it could be you!"

"Why not you, George?"

"I could not do it, Philip! I think I would go mad trapped in a law court, day after day."

"But you would be very good at the work. Nothing ever annoys you, and you make new friends, easily. Everyone would want you to defend them. You are very good at mathematics, too!"

"I will tell you something, Philippe, which I have told no-one. Promise not to mention it until I have decided how to raise it at home. It will not be easy. Promise not to repeat it until I have decided what to do."

Philippe made the required promise...

"I think Latin and Mathematics are matters for law courts and laboratories. I want to be in the open air, not shut up indoors. You have read some of Hakluyt's book, and Uncle Philippe showed me the charts we use for fishing in the Banks and Biscay. There are charts of our coasts and the shoals, some of them charts drawn in Dieppe a hundred years ago and showing parts of coasts and islands which are unexplored. Some of them were drawn by men in our family. I want to be a Merchant Venturer like Sebastian Cabot. Perhaps I might join the Royal Navy, if they would have me. I want to sail and be a Commander and visit China and the Pacific."

"What will our father say?"

"He won't approve. And there is something else, bro: I've been talking to some of our friends who will be going to the banks for the cod fishing next April and I am determined to go with them. Father, of course

6

is the organiser of the boats going from Jersey, and who sees that they have crew and provisions, and always captains a supply boat and sails with them. I don't know how to tell him."

"No-one else in the family has joined the King's Navy, George!"

"I know that, but few of the family have ever been to England either. I must see the world, bro! I don't expect to make a fortune, and from our trouble with pirates, I know I could never go robbing ships and selling their crew. Father wants me to go to University. I will have to try to persuade him and I don't know how. Father and the Regent both want me to go to Oxford."

"I'll back you up when you go to tell him, if you like."

"Thanks! It's a good idea: not yet though."

George had much to think about and prepared a number of ways in which he could talk to his father. It would be a difficult conversation, even if he could find his father at leisure and prepared to talk. He needed to present a sensible plan to present, probably after Christmas, and in the meantime, find out more about the navy and qualifications. Was there a Naval Matriculation? Who would know?

* * *

That Christmas, matters came to a head. His father, having questioned the Regent regarding George's progress, remonstrated with him about lack of interest in Latin and said he expected greater efforts next term. George said he would do his best but saw little point in the subject. His father said that he would understand when he took up his place at university: Latin was the basis for a sound education.

George found it increasingly difficult to fulfil his promise and this led to moments of frustration, bad temper and angry words with his parents. No solution emerged from discussion with his father for whom the decision was as good as made. He spent more time at the Manor as a means of avoiding further confrontation. His uncle only suggested that he should follow his father's wishes since, once he was qualified, he would have complete freedom to follow his own inclinations about a choice of a career. He found that sailing his boat distracted him completely the problem and, one day, launched his skiff and set out from St Aubin sailing up the coast. He retained vivid memories of the many occasions when he had watched the fishing fleet set out or return to port, as his mood improved. Bringing his boat ashore several hours later, he dragged it up the beach at Greve de Lecq and set off for the Manor where he was sure of a welcome from two-year-old Philippe, and his baby sister.

His Aunt noticed that he was not happy and suggested he should come with the children to collect nuts. To lighten his mood, she asked whether he was ever worried when sailing alone: she had never learned to sail, and neither had her brothers. George was astonished and spoke so enthusiastically about the joys of sailing that his aunt asked him if he was ambitious to be a sailor. George poured out his ambitions, his realisation that it would never be achieved, and his utter dislike of abstract learning, though he said, "pointless knowledge!". Somewhat to his surprise, Anne Carteret proved to be a patient listener. While George helped a lively small nephew collect conkers and hazelnuts, they strolled through the grounds.

She enquired whether Sir Philippe's advice had been helpful. George said that he had advised he obeyed his father's wishes but told her of his intention to become a navigator, and to visit new lands. He was carrying Hakluyt's publication, "Divers Voyages" with him and, when they returned to the Manor, read her short extracts from it, hoping to convey his enthusiasm. She understood the way in which a combination of several accounts could create an impression of a world full of wonders and places waiting to be fully explored with the aid of careful sailing and navigation. She told him that years ago she had been impressed by stories of Drake and Raleigh and could see that others might also gain similar fame and fortune, and that those opportunities still existed.

To his surprise she asked if he would accept her help and advice. He expressed thanks but could not understand how she would go about it. His father was a very determined man, he told her, and his uncle would support his brother. His aunt seemed undeterred but asked if she could give it some thought. She suggested he tried to forget it as a problem, since time was on his side, and he should leave her to think about it. He returned home feeling a little happier and worked at Latin with renewed vigour, for which his father commended him.

Anne was not quite as confident as she appeared but had a plan in mind. She would begin by seeking careers advice from an expert. Her father, Sir Francis Dowse, had two sons, both of whom had found well rewarded employment in the City. He himself was a lawyer and had safeguarded the lives of a number of Wards of Court, young boys and girls without living parents, who had inherited considerable wealth, and might fall into the clutches of greedy relatives or lawyers. By chance he would be visiting the Manor next week to see his new grand-daughter, and Anne would ask his advice. He was very much a man of the world, and his work brought him into contact with men in many professions.

* * *

Sir Francis was a little confused when Anne raised the subject of careers at sea, thinking she might be planning the life of her two-year-old.

"I have someone else in mind," she said with a smile. "Elie's son George has a burning ambition to go to sea with the English Navy. He's a perfectly normal, healthy young man, and big for his age, except he spends hours in our library reading and pouring over old maps and charts. Hakluyt's Voyages is always in his pocket. I've said I will try to find a way for him to persuade his father. He knows nothing about the way to join, for example."

"If you are seriously planning to advise young George, you must be careful. It is a difficult matter at present. English life is in a process of change and nothing is as clear and obvious as it was when I was a lad, and there were big changes made then! When I was a boy, even the laziest, greedy lad could become a vicar and, with a little bribery, there were deaneries and Bishoprics available. He might become Lord Chancellor, like Cardinal Wolsey. That promotion route, however, had become outdated and Queen Elizabeth had sold off the remaining Abbey lands, reduced the Church to a department of government under her control and expected landowners to appoint vicars or rectors and pay them himself. University students no longer became Priests, and many were turning to the sciences of mechanics and optics, and rational experiments with metals and chemicals.

"There was, of course, the Law. That is the career I chose, and it was the right one for me, despite family doubts, and I made money for us, and obtained a baronetcy. Nowadays it's becoming a somewhat overcrowded profession, with international trade creating so many new possibilities."

Many lawyers became Members of Parliament, as he had done, and that was becoming quite rewarding as a profession, even Buckingham entered the Middle Temple. Lastly there was the Navy and Army to consider. The Navy, he knew, was due for a complete overhaul, and though King James was firmly against wars, Prince Charles was sure that Britain needed a powerful navy, and might keep concealed a desire to conquer France, and make it British once more.

"What do you suggest I should do, Father? George is very unhappy about an academic life and I would like to help him. I would need to be able to convince George's father that it would be a good career, even though no-one in the family has gone into it before. I shall probably speak to his mother first. If I can persuade her, she should be able to talk her husband round!"

"Anne, my dear, I see you have learned all your mother's persuasive skills."

"In fact, there is a further discussion which must be had. He is determined to go with the cod fishing fleet to Newfoundland next spring, when his father expects he will be at school preparing for matriculation. I am not sure my powers of persuasion are strong enough."

"How old is the boy? I suppose he must be rising fourteen if he is to matriculate. Many boys of his age are contributing to the family income by that time. Surely Elie employs some on his trading vessels. Is George big and strong enough for the work?"

"He is older looking than some of his friends, and very reliable. He does all the things my brothers used to do, and more besides. I think he could stand up for himself and explain what he wants to do.

"If George is really keen on a life at sea, it could well become the next profession to gain greater significance in English life, but he would have to be qualified if he wanted his own ship. He could not become an officer until he was eighteen."

"So, can I hope for your advice, father. I shall need all the information you can provide, if I am to succeed."

"I will do my best, Anne. Money should not be a problem; Elie is not a poor man, I know... and his family is quite well known, which may be an advantage. I will put your uncle Amyas on to it: he knows everybody!"

Sir Francis made a return visit a few weeks later, remarking that he was spending time at Moor Court while he worked in Southampton where he was a Magistrate. The weather was predicted to remain calm for some time, but he had some information and thought a meeting might be preferable to a letter.

On a warm evening, seated on the terrace, they discussed George's situation, her father hoping that he would have a chance to meet George and sound him out.

"He knows he is always welcome, father, and I expect him tomorrow. He is spending more time here than ever; I think he is afraid he may lose his temper with his father, or his brother may let the cat out of the bag. How did you find information?"

"By chance, I met your husband and Amyas and, remembering that Philippe recommended George to go to University, as his father expected, I took him into my confidence. I'm sure they can be trusted, and you will find your husband supportive."

"Thank you. I hoped I would be able to persuade him, but I'm grateful that you were successful. What did he suggest?"

"He thinks well of George and believes that with increased trade and the danger to ships and coastal ports, a larger Navy will be a necessity before long. He has been sailing with George and has seen him bringing back baskets of fish, helped by a group of friends. George was clearly in charge, by the way."

"I didn't know that, but it's good news."

"Wait, there is more. A young man wanting a career must qualify first as a Lieutenant which means that he must pass a written test and an interview at the Admiralty. In addition, he must have the recommendation of experienced Officers, that he can thrive on board a

Naval vessel, and that he has gained experience as servant to a competent captain."

"That may be a problem, I think."

"Yes, but not insolvable. If he goes to the Banks with his father, Elie can speak for him. He cannot qualify until he is eighteen, so he would need to find a berth after his sixteenth birthday. Amyas tells me that the best Captain is a Hampshire man named Pennington; he may be from the little port, west of Lymington. I will meet him in London soon and, if we can begin to persuade Elie, he may be given a berth."

"Father, this is wonderful. You make it sound so easy! However, I can see a problem. If he must spend time in London, he will need a lodging, and we know no-one there."

"Philippe rents a house in London where he and Amyas live, as you know. There are also my sons who share a house which I own, and I would tell them they were to have a lodger. It would save Elie from a lot of expense, in case George fails."

* * *

Already they had the beginnings of a sound case to support George in his ambition. Anne asked questions until she felt confident she could put together a course of action for her nephew to adopt, and place before his father after Christmas, when everyone was in a relaxed frame of mind. In the meantime, George would be able to placate the Regent and his father. Her next step was finding an opportunity to discuss George's discontent, with his mother, Elizabeth.

Fortunately, the first opportunity arose in a matter of days. Anne and she were good friends and close allies over controversial family issues, including the running of a complex farm, and the shipping and trading business, where a woman's intervention seemed the most effective way of finding a solution to trying situations.

Elizabeth had told her about George's moods, and her concern that he and his father rarely spoke together, even at mealtimes. She sought Anne's opinion, eager to heal the breach.

"Elie wants him to be an academic and go to University", she said.

He should matriculate next year, but she knew that George wanted a physically active life which would challenge him in a different way. She knew how popular he was with his friends in the harbours, and all the small children loved him.

Anne agreed absolutely and broached George's dilemma and reluctance to challenge his father's authority. With great care she explained carefully to Elizabeth how they might solve the difficulty. Elizabeth was convinced that George was far too young to leave home and go to sea. Anne pointed out that next April, he would matriculate and go to live alone in Oxford, England! She reminded her how difficult her brothers had found it to live away from home and care for themselves. Yet they had survived the experience. If George joined the fleet, he would be among people he knew and liked, and his father would be near at hand.

Since George was not yet fourteen and wanted adventure, Elie should be persuaded to allow George to join the fishing fleet that spring and learn new skills and meet fresh challenges. He would be well looked after on the trip and, if he took to the life, after a second trip, perhaps he might try for a Lieutenancy in the Royal Navy. If he decided it was not what he wanted, he would still be able to matriculate and become a graduate and work with those developing new sciences.

"But Anne!" wailed Elizabeth. "He's only a child. He would be cold and lonely. I would be worried about him all the time."

"Yes, Lizzy, but that is what mothers do. My mother died worrying about the three of us and look at us now. We have all survived and have done quite well, I think."

"But Anne, I can't lose him so soon, and they will be speaking different languages!"

"I'm sure he will manage. We generally speak English, when he is here, and he is big for his age. Of course, you must remember he reads books in English, and I've heard him speaking French with some of his father's friends. Why don't you talk to Elie about the way Universities are teaching the new learning and experimenting with new ideas and practical skills and navigational instruments. He has time to try a fishing trip, or even two, and if it doesn't work, he will only need a little more effort for University."

Lizzy eventually talked to George, telling him that she would help his father to realise that their plan was good and suggesting that his father might be open to conversation about his future opportunities and mentioned some of Anne's ideas. George was delighted that he had gathered so much support for the fishing trip and suggested he might ask his father to sail with him to Sark to see his aunts and cousins, who lived there. It might provide time to talk about his future.

"What a good idea, Lizzy", Anne remarked. "Philippe, apparently, thinks very highly of George, now he has spoken to him and believes he has the temperament to make a success of whatever he takes on. He shows such determination. When George visits us on Friday, he will try to talk to him about life outside Jersey, where so many opportunities exist. I think he might raise the matter with Elie, if the opportunity arises."

"I think, Anne, that Elie might be persuaded to approve of George joining the Navy, and he would be gaining experience on the trip. George might find his father helpful if he asks him how he could go about qualifying as a lieutenant. We haven't told George what you have discovered, but George can say that he thinks his brother knows all about it."

＊ ＊ ＊

It was April 1623 when, tall for his age, and smart in his hempen breeches and coat, George strode on, his dark hair with a touch of ginger, tied back with twine. On his back was slung a canvas bag containing a few essentials, and he wore a linen undershirt, with an oiled wool jersey, knitted for him by his favourite Aunt Collette on Sark. Hessian breeches and jacket completed his outfit and, in his pack, was a tarred, canvas hat with strong ties to keep it in place when the sea blinded him with sand and stinging saltwater. It also contained the end of yesterday's fresh loaf and a hunk of hard cheese to tide him over until his next meal. It was the 16 April 1623, a fortnight after the start of the New Year.

In his pack, wrapped in oiled silk for protection, was his most precious possession, a well-read copy of Hakluyt's "Divers Voyages," with the descriptions of the Cabots and their voyages and exploration of Newfoundland; this was his favourite reading. Newfoundland was the place he was longing to visit. Also, carefully wrapped, he carried cartridge paper, on which to sketch striking scenes to aid his memory. He had left at home, tucked carefully into an unused drawer, the copy of the Book of Common Prayer, containing loving sentiments written by his mother, which she had pressed into his hand in a sad farewell. He had promised her that he would always keep it safe, and the safety of home seemed the right place. Most of its contents he knew by rote having heard them read every Sunday morning at Matins for more years than he could remember. Its contents seemed to him either too obvious to be worth writing down, or extremely improbable. He felt that it could be saved until his adulthood when he supposed the meaning would become clearer.

He began to make out the shapes of small groups of cottages where farm labourers and fishermen lived with their families. They were small, having only one room and little by way of furniture. The heavy roof timbers gave little headroom but made useful storage space for meat or fish to smoke. The smoke from the hearthstones in the centre, rose up and found its way out through the thick layer of thatch. Those who lived in these hovels were workers on the farms, orchards, fishing vessels and at the manor houses of the Seigneurs of the twelve fiefdoms, inherited down the ages by the principal families of Jersey.

George's father, Elie, was the younger brother of Sir Philippe de Carteret, Seigneur of St Ouen and its extensive acreage in the North West of the island. He lived at la Mont des Vignes, one of the farms of the Manor. Both he and his brother were Jurats in the Estates Royale, which administered justice on the island with a Council of twelve Jurats. Jurats were chosen from prosperous farmers, merchants, or traders when a vacancy occurred. Their homes were generally of stone construction and with two floors. The ground floor was for the livestock and the floor above, divided into two or more rooms, was accommodation for the family and visitors. Round about were stone barns, granaries, dairies and some simple accommodation for those permanently employed in caring for the needs of the family. Jurats and the wealthy, were remitted to build and maintain a dovecote. Doves fly only short distances and will only take seeds in a small area.

* * *

"Oh, My Goodness me! You always drink your milk as though it is your last... you little minx! Philippe- be a good boy for Mummy, who's in a little mess. Our Bessie has brought up her milk all over my neckerchief. It's cold and smelly and I've got a clean one all ready for once. Will you hold your little sister, while I change? I hope it will not confuse him when he finds that everyone speaks Jersiaise, except some family members. I'm so grateful to Elizabeth for teaching me so well.

"Now, Miss, your big brother is going to hold you, very carefully, please! - for a minute. There's a good girl! Go to Philippe now. Well done, Philippe! Here it is! (I must put another one ready for next time.) Don't jiggle her around too much, will you? You know what will happen. There's a good boy! She likes to be held. I'm ready to take her now! My Goodness, you are heavy! Yes, you're a big, heavy girl, aren't you? I think she's trying to wear me out. That's right!"

"Ma, Ma, Ma…."

"Yes, Mama-MA!"

"G.. g.. g.. og!"

"Philippe, listen! I think she's trying to say "George". What a clever girl. Oh, Look, she's looking for him! Yes, he'll come back to see you soon."

"And when he comes, he'll be able to give me lots of piggy backs, won't he, and take me fishing. Won't he mother?"

"Yes, my darling, of course he will. You're nearly tall enough to ride a pony. Would you like George to help you to ride one day?"

Having satisfied the hunger of Lisa, her baby, Lady Anne de Carteret laid the child in her cradle and turned her attention to her son who was engrossed in a complex game with square bricks, which were soldiers, and rectangular pieces, which were "horses". She turned, moving her long, dark hair away from her oval face, her Florentine beauty made individual by the straight Roman nose, frequent in members of the Dowse family, and arched eyebrows. When at rest, it seemed to some to indicate arrogance, but in fact she possessed a warm nature and great

18

kindness. This was a game he often played, but on this occasion she was expected take part and complied willingly to neigh from time to time, or shout "Charge!" While following these orders, her mind wandered to her nephew, George, pleased that he had taken the food she had left ready for him.

Now the boy was striding firmly across high undulating land, broken by strange circular mounds and groups of standing stones having some long-forgotten purpose. This was a favourite hunting ground for George and his young followers. It was a perfect place to launch an ambush, and beyond it were cliffs, a challenge to climb but a worthwhile risk for the eggs of seabirds there for the taking. Slightly to the west, was the marsh of St Peter's parish with its great pond, and the dunes lining the long, curving, coastline. There, westerly winds drove twenty-foot-high surf to break on the dunes which formed a natural barrier to invasion, despite its inviting appearance.

Crossing southward, he passed La Chaumiere de Tchene, the Parish mill, one of the largest in the Island and improved by his father recently. As the land slopped away, he glimpsed the water of St Aubyn's Bay where, hidden by the trees crowding the steep coastline, a fleet of fishing boats was probably assembling. When the full fleet assembled, there were usually about a hundred, forty of them crewed by Jersey men, and others from ports anywhere from Portugal to the low countries, who chose to start the Atlantic crossing in good company. Not all had arrived yet, and many of the crew and their friends and families were going between St Breadless church where, as always, the vicar was bestowing generous blessings on their enterprise. Their prayer was that the trip would bring financial reward to all, and see them through the long winter, but the popular Saint had a long reputation for protecting honest fishermen from attack by pirates.

19

Down the slope he walked, through the gathering crowd, toward four figures standing in earnest conversation. He had walked past Robert and Gaiches, his closest friends, who shouted encouragement but knew better than to distract a boy aged fourteen years, give or take a few months, and almost a man, who was about the meet his Commander. Childish things, they realised, were now behind him. When he returned, he would be changed.

He stopped a few feet away, almost the height of his Uncle's shoulder: his dark-haired father was much taller, but less tall than his brother, Philippe, though that was perhaps caused by a slight rounding of the shoulders. Philippe, distinguished by his head of auburn hair, was the most good-humoured of men, a feature he shared with Elie's young son, Amyas, a great favourite of George. Waiting until these important men chose to speak to him, he suddenly flinched as a sharp pinch on his left elbow almost caused him to drop his bag. Turning defensively, he found his Uncle Gideon, who was grinning about him with a wide-eyed look of total innocence, only his clenched fist revealed him as the attacker.

"Gideon, I know that was you!" said the boy, pretending indignation and rubbing his elbow. "Pick on someone your own size!"

"Remember who's in charge, George. Once we are afloat, I am Captain and you obey orders. How are you feeling? Don't worry! You'll be fine once you get on board. I'll keep an eye on you and train you up ready to join the King's Navy."

"There Gideon, I told you he'd be here early," exclaimed his father. "George knows that I am not leading our men on this trip, and that you will be in charge. By the look of him he is fully equipped to face the perils of the wild ocean, and even wilder fishermen!" He added, joking aside: "Listen to what your Uncle says, and see how he organises the men. A few trips with the fishing fleet will be the best training you can get for a life in the King's Navy. There will always be a place for a well-trained officer."

"Not trying to scare him into changing his mind are you, Tiny?"

Philippe, who could never take his brother quite as seriously as he took himself, referred to him by his nickname. His good humour often defused awkward situations, and he and Amyas made a good team.

"Brother, I've been trying to do that for the past month and failed completely. I know when I'm beaten, Reynard," he said affectionately, with reference to the tints of red in his hair, "Don't I, boy?"

"So, I place him in your charge, Gideon, and we both know he works hard at any job in hand and knows a few useful things about seamanship. I know he won't let you down; he's got the examples of Drake, Grenville and Raleigh to emulate, not to mention his blessed Cabots, and Claude Personne, our doctor, filling his head with dreams of adventure. He'll be on the lookout for Spanish doubloons - once he gets over seasickness. Don't forget, if you've nothing else to be sick in, boy, use your hat. Don't look so horrified! It was just a joke. It'll be fine again after a good wash."

"If that is your best piece of advice, Elie, you'd better leave the rest to me."

"I think I've said all I need to say to George. He knows he goes with the love of his mother and me, and our best wishes. I'd appreciate it, Gideon, if you'd bring him back with the right number of arms and legs and so on, and I've told him to look sharp, keep his ears open and expect no favours from you, because you are a cruel man with a foul temper when crossed."

"Thanks for your kind words, brother; I'm sure he feels much happier now." This was Philippe again.

"I hope so too! George! You know that you go with my blessing, and I am sure that what you will learn at sea will stand you in good stead

21

for life. Now, salute your Uncle, your Commander, and then go and report yourself to his Ship's Master.

"The boat is the Fair Haven and the Master is Mr. Tull - and you must call him Sir!"

George saluted and went down to find his uncle's ship.

* * *

"Oh, For Heaven's sake, girls! Every time I move, there's one of you under my feet. The first warm day we've had for weeks, and a fine day for drying, and we're only half-way into the laundry."

"Now, listen Anne, Rachel… Anne!! Stop playing with the kittens and listen! Please! I want you to help Louise carry out the laundry and spread it out on the hedges."

Using both hands she grasped her wind-tangled, blonde hair firmly, and looked around her for the length of ribbon which had fallen to the floor.

"Yes, Rachel, I know it's heavy— so, try one thing at a time. Perhaps Reginald will help you - He's walking about like a wet week… Now where's he gone? Never mind — Philippe, just do your best — I need some clear space…" Breathing hard, she grasped her errant curls again, and retied the ribbon, challenging it to fall out…

"Mother, you told him to take the leather jerkins over to the stable hands and tell them to soap them when they've finished the harness."

"Off you both go - no arguing! And try not to trail that sheet in the mud…

"Now Margery, where were we? I want you to get one of the other girls to collect up all the woollen coats and breeches they can find and lay them out in the sun to air. Try to bang the mud off with a stick

22

or use a brush and water. But don't get them too wet or it will take days to dry."

"Mother! That boy Gaiches is standing outside scratching. I think he might have a message, but he won't speak. Shall I tell him to go away?"

"Gaiches, aren't you? If you want to say something, come in and say it, Oh! Now listen… and Robert as well, is it? Trying to hide behind you. You're not usually shy. Speak, do! We're very busy today."

"Please, Mistress Carteret, George asked us to come and say he has sailed. You were with the little ones when he left, and he slipped out not to upset them."

"Oh, Bless the boy! How we will miss him. Philippe, you'll have to step into his shoes. Has his boat sailed already? Perhaps if I ran down there, he could see me waving my apron."

"They were just underway when we ran back here. He was working hard reefing lines."

"Too late then! Ah-here's Reginald, still looking like a wet week. Come on, tell me what you're so miserable about."

She gave him a sympathetic hug, running her fingers through his hair, unruly like hers. "George has only gone away for a long fishing trip. He's done that before, hasn't he? You mustn't worry. Are those lazy stable lads working hard? Good! What's that you're holding."

"It's the boat George was helping him to build," Anne explained.

"So, what are you crying for? Have you broken it?"

"No, mother. Look! George has finished it."

"That's nothing to cry about, is it?" With tears running freely, her youngest son sobbed, "Perhaps he'll never come back".

"Oh, Reggie, come here to me. Of course, he will come back and you'll be able to show him how well it sails, won't you?" Now, off you go and find a wide, high shelf to stand it where it won't be damaged or

23

trodden on. Perhaps a window ledge. Oh! Thank goodness, Philippe. Please take Robert and Gaiches and help Reggie sail his old boat on the pond. Take the ball with you: it's just behind the door. Then you can have a good kick around on the meadow. And try not to break your necks! Boys!!"

Chapter 2

A few days earlier, two other members of the family had been taking an early breakfast in that popular coaching inn, The King's Arms, in the business centre of London, The Strand. It was early April 1623, and a new financial year was beginning. Sir Philippe de Carteret, and his nephew, Amyas, were in London for yet another session of the Privy Council concerning the rights and privileges permitted to islanders of Jersey.

"Perhaps while you finish off this dish of bacon, liver and kidney, I can have a few words with you, Amyas. I think my discussions concerning the preservation of Jersey's Ancient Privileges and Duties, may reach a successful conclusion quite soon, thank Heaven! They are the ones we call "The Coutume de Normandie". I have to meet Lord Chief Justice Coke today and I had feared our requests might have been rejected, but I am more confident now that Sir John Peyton, our Governor, has pointed out that, if they are withdrawn, the French may lay claim to the Channel Islands, which have, as you know, never been an English possession, belonging entirely to His Majesty, our Duke of Normandy."

He checked the wide lace collar at his neck, as though preparing to face the King.

"I woke this morning thinking about Jersey, Uncle. I think I shall get use to the London way of life, though it might take some time. I don't think as quickly in English as in Jersiais: I'm impressed by your fluency: I hope I improve! I had no idea that English property laws were so different from the Coutume. I must re-read them both!"

"I will have a copy for you when mine returns from the man making a fresh one for the King. They seem to have mislaid the one I gave him six years ago. You must be watchful whenever Jersey is mentioned, Amyas. The King may be persuaded that a favourite subject deserves a parcel of land and it would result in War in Jersey if the unlucky fellow turned up to claim it. He would need to bring an army. We would be blamed by the whole population for allowing it to happen. I hope no problems arise from our new agreement: we can't have the King settling problems which are not his business!

Amyas was, by a year or two, the younger brother of Philippe, the Seigneur, He had made a late decision to try the law, and was living in London, and gaining valuable experience as his uncle's assistant. Though Sir Philippe had doubted at first whether Amyas was cut out for this career, he had been surprised by his ready mind, and he could remain to keep an eye on the interests of Jersey, while Philippe was in London doing his other duties. Amyas, in his mid-twenties, was dark-haired and had the ability to charm elder statesmen and endear himself to beautiful young women.

"I was wondering about young George, uncle. When we sailed for England, my brother had accepted the reality that George would leave school and sail with the fishing fleet to gain experience. I hope he has not come to regret his decision. Is it difficult to gain a Lieutenancy in the Navy?"

"It's certainly not easy, Amyas. There is money needed to pay for training and when you are certificated, you have to buy your berth on a ship and pay for all your equipment. It probably costs as much as graduating from Oxford; even then you have to buy yourself a legal pupillage. Fortunately, we can give him a roof over his head, and spending money. Pity those, Amyas, who lack our privileges."

"I'm very grateful to you, brother, for paying me for work experience with you and Sir Francis and allowing me the use of the London house. I appreciate your kindness and will do my best to assist you."

"That's the way the world works, Amyas. One day you may be able to do the same for some deserving fellow. We all think you're worth it, Amyas. I expect George will use the house if he goes ahead with his Naval career. He will have to stay close to Admiralty. Of course, we are talking about what may happen in two years' time. Many things may change before then. George may come to loath the sea."

"Have you any indication how long it will be for the King to reach a decision?"

"I don't want to be in London any longer than necessary, whatever His Majesty's decision. I know you are enjoying London life, but we must prepare to leave with a few days' notice. I want you to ride down to Southampton and hire a suitable boat and crew to sail us home. It may take days to find one, and we probably will not need it for another fortnight, but I'd like to have one standing by. Take one lackey with you to do the necessary chores and running about and attending to the horses. When you find the right Captain, give him a handsome retainer to persuade him to wait until we are ready."

"Should I set off at once, uncle? In that case, can I assume that an agreement has been reached to satisfy our disputatious islanders?"

"You know as well as I that no agreement is final until all parties are signed up. I am hopeful that we will have something to resolve most of their problems, if only in the short term."

"Did you see Fanshaw or the King before you left Royston, and explain that our laws are not always the same as English laws?"

"He took me through to His Majesty's Cabinet Chamber and delivered a surprisingly clear outline of the facts to the King himself, which was a very great favour to me, personally, Amyas."

"So, what happens next?"

"The King has had time to consider it and someone will tell me the result at the Council Chamber at Whitehall this very morning. I have been given an assurance, unofficially, that he has agreed with us. Of course, he may decide to go hunting and sign it when he returns. You never know what the King will do next."

"Well, at least it has reached the King's notice. How did you find His Majesty? I've never been close to him, except riding. He's out riding every day whatever the weather is like."

"Exhausted! His cheeks are drawn, and he is a constant fidget, itching and twitching, and suffering with bad leg pains. When he eats, those close to him are scattered with fragments of food, and he splutters as he speaks. He is quite frail, and looks elderly, but insists on hunting three days a week. It is too much for him, but his mind drives him on, though he is a sick man and tormented by anxiety for his daughter and her family. He is not the same man as he was when he came to London fifteen years ago and gave me an English knighthood. He is fifty-six years of age, and often looks much older."

"Do you think he is seriously ill, father? Are there fears he may die?"

"Nothing would surprise me. It is beginning to be seen that his plans for a lasting peace between the princes of Europe are falling apart, and the Queen of Bohemia, his daughter, has lost her country, and her throne. They are hostages in Heidelberg and Rupert and Maurice, her sons, are here at court. I am informed by Sir John that the King believes it is essential that Charles should marry a Spanish Princess. He thinks it will secure peace with Spain to the advantage of both countries. No-one

28

likes the idea. There's too much ill-feeling against Spain I think, going back to the Armada, and they probably haven't forgotten Drake's raids on their treasure fleet in Cadiz, either!"

"But I hear that he has been losing interest in State affairs for several years and seems only to be interested in hunting and Masques. I wonder whether he was distracted by the deaths of the Queen and Prince Arthur within one year?"

"I suppose it might be that; it's nine years since Prince Arthur died, and the Queen soon after: they both loved masques and hunting. The Queen had chosen George Villiers to be his right-hand man before she died, and he may rely on him too heavily. As Duke of Buckingham, James thinks highly of his abilities, and he attempts to keep the King's mind active. I remember how your grandmother's kind nature changed after the death of my father. I used to think she blamed me for not being more like him, though I've always worked hard at my duties, having no alternative. We must remember he is fifty-six years old. He was very intelligent when he was younger. I see occasional flashes of it still during our heated discussions."

There was a spontaneous pause while both considered the implications of having Royal obligations.

* * *

"My brother tells me the legal business in London took even longer than he expected. The last time we stood here we watched the last pair of masts vanishing over the horizon. I reckon there must have been nigh on fifty vessels all told. Well! God Speed them!" Elie remarked.

"It was an amazing sight. Surely that is the largest fleet we've ever sent, I suppose that about thirty of the ships had crews from Europe; I heard French, Normandy men, Portuguese and Spanish and possibly Norwegian from the old Hanse ports."

"I'm sure you are right, Amyas. I would think that half our boats' crews are volunteers from many countries. Some of them don't know they are supposed to be at war with each other. I think they don't mind about that since they earn good money if they work hard."

"Doesn't it seem strange not to be out there leading the trip?"

"It does, after so many years, but it's time Gideon took over to grow the enterprise. You know I've taken on the role of Attorney General and, as though that is not enough, I've decided that Mont Orgueil is in need of improved fortifications, and Elizabeth Fort, and I intend to see it done. I'm looking forward to being in Jersey for the summer, instead of Newfoundland, to see the hay harvest, and perhaps the corn brought in. And Liz will have to learn to tolerate my presence here, also, and being about the farm quite often. She might even allow me to see if I can still milk cows!"

"Gideon was so pleased to be leading the fleet he could hardly restrain his impatience to be on board and away. I know he will make a good job of it. I was a little surprised you were not going to keep an eye on George making his first long trip, Elie."

"Bring us another jug of ale, please, boy!"

"Umm! You see, Amyas, I saw it this way. Gideon is good with the men and a fine seaman - better than me, I suspect. He'll treat George like any other young member of the crew, but he will always keep one eye on him. If I were there, they might be expecting me to show him special favours, even if I didn't. In that case they would think less of me and less of George. The boy has a great regard for fairness and sharing and I would be a distraction from his work."

30

"I am impressed by George's self-sufficiency and bravery. I glad no-one in the family ever insisted that I take a trip to the Newfoundland Banks."

"I think you would survive, though your interests lie elsewhere in the work you are doing for your brother, Philippe. George would hate office work and being trapped by paperwork. Besides, you can sail a boat as well as any of us and our people like having you in charge. There are many valuable skills people can acquire and they give us the space to shape our lives. History tells us that the Black Prince won the Battle of Poitiers while his father was enjoying relaxation in England, and he was only sixteen, two years older than George."

"But, Elie. Five months! If he doesn't like it, it will seem like a lifetime. Time is strange, I think. I've been here for only about two weeks, just time to discover whether there were any fresh concerns for Philippe to deal with. I think this spot, just above the launch cove, is my favourite place on the island! When we came near the land, I had that homecoming experience the sailors speak of. They know the island is near because of the smell of apple blossom which carries far out to sea."

"It will be too late in the year for George to smell it: it is more likely to be the smell of rotten seaweed when he returns. But he won't regret it! He is absolutely set on spending his life at sea and our men are a good crowd to be with."

"I'm aware that I haven't eaten anything since breakfast. I might go into St Aubyn to the Jolly Sailor, which has good food. If you've no other plans perhaps you could join me. I've business to do in the town tomorrow and I'll sleep over in Broad Street. I'd enjoy your company and sharing a few thoughts, and if we get too squiffy for you to ride home, there's room for you to sleep. With all the men gone, the town will be like a tomb tonight. When we have dined, I expect I can ride the horse to St Helier along the beach. She seems to enjoy a good gallop."

31

"In a few days' time, Amyas, you will have to leave to assist Sir Philippe in London. You are lucky to have the opportunity to see the law in action, and our brother needs your help until young Philippe grows up."

* * *

A line of dishevelled and sweaty boys trailed through the water of St, Peter's Pond in an attempt to cool off. Gaiches and Robert had been joined by Will, Michel, and one or two others, including Reggie.

"I'm so hot!" declared Gaiches.

"Let's go down to Queen's Bay and swim," suggested Philippe. "Better leave your old boat by the bush here, Reggie: it might be carried away by the current, you can try it in the pond when we come back."

The idea gaining general acceptance, they set off at once to one of their favourite beaches. Robert suddenly caused consternation by running at full speed from the sand into the waves before launching himself forward into the sea, swamping his friends with a miniature tidal wave before rising, spluttering and dashing water in all directions and shouting; "Why can't I dive!"

"You need to jump from somewhere higher, fathead!" Gaiches asserted. "My big brother can really dive!"

"We all know your big brother," someone remarked scornfully.

"Well, he can," the boy asserted. "He could jump off Greve de Lecq if he wanted to. He's the egg- gathering champion and climbs all the cliffs…"

"…and will kill himself," said Philippe. "Look- let's have a war game! Pretend! Just over there is Providence Island, and in the distance that way is the port of Pernambuco and we all know what a couple of miles is away from it in the deep tropical jungle, *don't we*?"

32

His companions appeared uncertain and waited to be informed.

"Why, *El Dorado*, of course! Where all the palaces and farms are solid gold! Gold for the taking lads, waiting for us to seize it and take it back to King James, who will make us Lords. And the King will come on board our ship and say, "Rise, Sir Robert!" or Sir Reggie, or whoever."

"First off, we must get our hands on the gold, and the Spanish soldiers will be bringing it down to the sea in wagon loads to take back to Spain so they can build another Armada to attack us, and we are going to stop them."

They waited in anticipation to be stirred into action.

"We are the fearsome Jersey Privateers, the Terror of the five oceans, and we are going to ambush them, and kill them and make them run away in panic, because that is what we do. Now our ambush is going to be deep, deep in the forest back there. Let's go now, find the right place, and build our ambush."

* * *

"Right, you lads, come over here with me and we'll make ourselves comfortable and have a chat. Your Uncle has asked Mr. Tull to find a good seaman to teach you the things you'll need to know, on the long trip over the Atlantic Ocean.

"My name is Mr. Hawkins, and that is how you must address me. I've been asked to teach you and see that you learn useful skills. We're making smooth progress down the Channel and you've been on board one night. No problems so far? Oh, you enjoyed a good breakfast, did you? I'm pleased to hear it!

"In the next day or so, you're to try to make yourselves helpful; coiling up lines, helping in the galley, washing the platters and mugs, and

33

keeping the deck clear and clean. I'll be watching you Carteret and Le Seuel- and those are the names you will answer to. Don't expect them all to remember but be polite whatever they say.

"We're bound for Falmouth first where we'll pick up water and fresh supplies, and probably one or two more hands. When we get there Mr. Tull will allow you on shore and tell you when to return. Never leave without his permission! You will both need a good knife and a hat and possibly other things you'll be told about.

"Next time we'll learn about knotting and sewing. If you need a question answered, come to me. Now off you go, and collect, and wash those platters, then it's time to wash the deck."

* * *

"You look tired, uncle. Was it a difficult meeting?"

"Amyas! - I thought you would be on your way to Southampton by this time. Is there a problem?"

"Several small ones. Beauty had cast a shoe and needs another, and Pierre, my man, got a bellyache while we were clearing up; but I think we'll be ready for an early start. I've said goodbye to everyone."

"Including Annabelle- and Susie- and that other one with long curly hair, whatever her name is? I expect they all needed new shoes or something more personal, didn't they? In my experience Beauty always needs new shoes."

"You are avoiding the issue, brother, with your dubious reminiscences. Try to tell me, briefly, about the meeting, after you've ordered your breakfast. I'll pour you some beer."

"Thank you. Just what I need. I think the business is all settled, and we can count on leaving in the coming week. His Majesty is in a distressed state, though, with a constant stream of messengers.

34

Buckingham is not there to fend them off from bringing more bad news from abroad. The Catholic armies are sweeping the reformers and their leaders before them, and every tree in the Protestant lands is hung with the corpses of peasants, many of them not even Protestants. The Medici woman is trying to start another persecution of Huguenots in France, the name they give to Protestants, and if so, I expect we will have members of our families seeking refuge in Jersey. Personally, I don't think Richelieu wants this to happen. He wants the Dutch and Huguenots on the side of France for protection against the Pope and Austrians, who want the whole of Europe under Imperial rule. Richelieu wants to make France safe and united. Some of the best men in France are Protestant, including their Chief Treasury officer."

"Please get to the point. Your food is on the way!"

"Well, Fanshaw, Conway, and the Cabinet seem to have prevailed and shown his Majesty that our islands are independent from France and England, and His Majesty will sign our requests in the near future. However, he has a new anxiety concerning Prince Charles, which I hope will not distract him."

"I appreciate that you have only been in London for a few weeks: I wonder whether you have noticed that Buckingham has not been seen recently?"

"No. I assumed that he was visiting those who might be persuaded to vote for increasing the Royal allowance for the Navy or had remained at Newmarket for the racing."

"Wrong, my boy! It seems that the truth is not out in the open yet as the Court fears. I will tell you, in complete confidence, that he and Prince Charles have arrived safely in Spain!"

"In Spain! Good Heavens, what is going on? Why have they gone over to the enemy?

"Not the enemy any more, it seems. The King is convinced that only Spain has the strength to oppose the Emperor and stop his persecution of the Reformers. Prince Charles has been sent to marry King Philip's sister, the Infanta, and thus ensure that this Alliance will force the Emperor to withdraw."

"How would that help England? I thought you were trying to make this story short!"

"The King is desperate to help his son-in-law, the King of Bohemia, and prevent the French massacring Protestants. Charles is twenty-three years old and unmarried. The King has decided that if Charles marries the Spanish Infanta, King Philip, her brother, might be able to dissuade King Louis from his murderous intentions."

"I have not heard of a Fleet of ships laden with Ambassadors leaving London. You say the Prince has already arrived. How is this possible? Are you sure you are not making it up? It sounds like Shakespeare's Prospero amusing Miranda!"

"It seems to be very much a cloak-and-dagger business, I agree with you, Amyas. Apparently, Charles, and Buckingham, with false papers and pretending to be John and Tom Smith, sailed for France in February with that brainless artist Endymion Porter to arrange coaches. Their pretence was revealed, as soon as they landed in France, unable to account for their presence, and they were sent to Paris under escort to stay with the English Ambassador, who had to pretend not to know them. He had them escorted to the Spanish border and sent them on their way. What a dilemma to be placed in! It looks like total irresponsibility! They would be an obvious target for any gang of murderers!"

"It sounds to me like one of Buckingham's hare-brained schemes. Meanwhile His Majesty is terrified at the thought that he has sent his heir into the hands of his greatest enemy, and that he might never see his only son again, or the Duke, for that matter! The King wants to believe that if the plan works, Frederick's throne will be saved, and Britain spared from conquest by the unstoppable armies of the Emperor."

"Amyas, you must have heard bursts of applause and cheering while we have been eating. I think I have seen a sweaty young fellow run past the windows several times. I think some villagers are playing a village game they call crack it. I've never seen it played. Shall we order another jug and watch them outside: it's a fine afternoon?"

"A very good idea, Uncle. We are in no hurry and while we try to understand the rules of the game, if there are any, we can go on with our conversation."

"How will he manage to marry the King's sister, I wonder? Do you think he is likely to sweep her off her feet, and carry her back to England like a trophy won in battle? This is fantasy surely, and she is a Catholic, which will be a very unpopular choice."

"You may well laugh, Amyas. We shall have to wait and see. I simply hope that he returns to us alive: I suspect that the last thing Parliament wants is an alliance with Spain."

"I know the Prince is fond of acting, but I'm not sure he'll play the role of ardent lover for long! He lacks the height and charm which his elder brother had. His brother looked and sounded like a Prince among men.

"I have seen Charles recently and he has made great efforts to overcome his weakness. He is barely five feet in height, but he stands and walks with dignity, and is a fine horseman like his mother, who was often at Newmarket. He is also the best tennis player at court and a determined opponent who contests every point.

"However, despite everything, I've always found James easy enough to talk to. We used to laugh often when we were younger about our different ways of speaking English. You know how at Court they all try to speak like Shakespeare, and I don't understand some of the new words, our first language being old Norman French, and our English is the dialect of Hampshire, where your mother was brought up. There were times of great confusion. We both fell about laughing and drank another toast.

"Well, James speaks Paris French as a first language, and Latin, Greek and Old Scottish as well as English. You can imagine the wealth of misunderstanding it created. It used to reduce him to giggles of delight until we settled on a language to use that day. But you know how it is, you start in one language and God knows where you end."

"So, he has a sense of humour, unlike Charles. It's sad. isn't it?"

"His humour is not like his father's, who enjoys filthy jokes; a pleasure he shared with Queen Elizabeth. When we got down to business he got me to read the old Statutes in six hundred year old Norman, repeating phrases as though trying them on his palate: I explained again that, though he was King with power to take his subjects" land at will and award it to another, he could not do that with land in Jersey, where land could only be owned or inherited by Jersey men or women. Of course, the wording can't be conveyed in English, which has no equivalent terms. He asked why "the Conqueror" would have given his land away to mere subjects. I said I thought it was a safeguard in law. Any foreign ruler trying to seize the Islands for himself would be faced with an uprising by angry owners out to defend their property; leaseholders might be more willing to surrender."

"What did he say to that?"

"He was fascinated. When he came to the Scottish throne he was crowned as King of the Scots not King of Scotland. As King by public acclamation, he could be deposed and replaced by another if he lost favour. Several of his ancestors had faced that end. The Union of England and Scotland as a new nation named "Great Britain" made him King of both with total ownership of all his lands. He chuckled at the idea that I had more power in Jersey than he had."

"So, all we wanted has been achieved. Is that what all this amounts to?"

"I believe so, and the King has accepted that in Jersey, our Statutes must always take precedence over British law when disputes arise. A strange man, His Majesty. Of course, his father was killed by a bomb, his mother a prisoner in England, whom he never met, and Scotland a land of warring Lords snatching him from each other so that they would control him when one of them made him King. You may not know that one of your mother's Paulet ancestors was present at the execution of James' mother. Be careful what you say if the subject comes up!"

"I'm beginning to fear I'm on dangerous ground!"

"Such is life, Amyas! Then, like magic, he gained freedom as King of England with all the liberty to rule which his ancestor Henry VIII had seized; freedom from the Calvinists: and the throne of England, too. So, he made them obedient to England: one in the eye for them! Was it revenge? What must he feel, sitting on the throne of the woman who killed his mother? What does he dream about? It makes me grateful for my own family and sorry for him. One shouldn't feel sorry for a King, but how can you do anything else. Sorry. my boy. I'm rambling on again. Forget it all."

"I think we should get back to Jersey before they change their minds. Finish your dinner uncle, before it congeals."

Chapter 3

They learned where food and water were stored, and weapons and anchors. Where the crew rested and were shown the depth of the holds where the dried, salted bacalao would be stored for the journey home. At present they were carrying supplies for the small boats which, when they reached the banks, would catch the fish and, when filled, go to the factory on shore for gutting, salting and drying. Fair Haven was one of two mother ships owned by the Carterets and when loaded each would carry 1,000 quintals of stockfish ready for sale to keep landsmen fed in winter.

Each of the larger boats had a crew of 25/30 men and weighed about 60 tons, loaded. The best name for their design was "Ketch," a Dutch word. Many of them were built in the Netherlands, but Fair Haven was built in St Malo, where most of the Carteret boats were built. The smaller boats were all shapes and sizes and built for catching fish, not for passenger comfort. The factory settlement was a mile or so from St Johns and consisted of big, dry sheds where the men could sleep in hammocks, a bed, if they built one. Mainly beds were for officers. The small boats were called "Doggers" originally built in England for fish the Dogger Bank. They had only a three-foot draught at most, to prevent running aground. Crossing the Atlantic they would gather like chicks round the mother ships in case supplies ran out or they were attacked at sea, but they were remarkably stable.

"Each big boat fully loaded carries 1,000 quintals as that is worth 5,000 pure gold doubloons and that is better than pirates earn lying in wait for bullion carriers. Every man and boy onboard these ships gets his share of the profits! You will each carry home a bag of gold coins.! That's why we all work hard!"

Hawkins mentioned this for the sake of Le Seuel a farming boy, new to the sea and ships.

All this was taken in pretty well and Hawkins then quizzed them on their knowledge of knots. Both boys knew some, but Hawkins taught them three more and gave them cord to practice. Calling them back later, he examined their proficiency and taught them about other articles and their uses. Each did well and was awarded a pat on the back and promised an extra scoop of dinner. Their new life had begun.

＊ ＊ ＊

"I can't remember enjoying a braised leg of lamb so much for a long time- and fine leeks too, I feel absolutely replete, Philippe! A very good idea to eat here... We were talking about the raiders who pillage the channel coasts and take the villagers away as slaves. I hope our fleet won't run into them though they should be able to scare them off. Your father told me that in 1607, the king ordered a list of all the ships captured from English ports in that year. The total was over four hundred. Six years ago, the Spanish King ordered the expulsion of all Moslems. The only ones remaining had been converted to Christianity in the reign of "Their Most Catholic Majesties", Ferdinand and Isabella. Those who refused had all their possessions confiscated and were transported forcibly to Morocco where they knew no-one and spoke only Spanish. As

Christians they were far from welcome in a Moslem country and employment was denied to them, so many became smugglers raiding the Spanish ports. which had banished them. Many were men of education and skills but had no money and could neither write nor speak Arabic. They become Pirates, preying on those who had persecuted them, over a constantly increasing coastline, including Britain. My contacts in France say only a few pirates have been seen this early in the season, but it seems likely they may be trying to raise raiding fleets. I gather that they have a tyrannical King who has set up a huge city named Sallee where they auction slaves by the hundred. Perhaps it is false news. I hope so."

"And yet Elie is prepared to send George, his eldest son, to sea in such a time of peril? Surely this is very unwise?"

"Amyas, life itself, and the sea, are always perilous. It would be perfectly possible for them to snatch him from his skiff in St Helier Bay. I'm absolutely serious!" We lost a dozen men last year to pirates."

"I will tell you a story about Elie and George learning to sail. When he was about seven, I took him to Sark to visit his grandmother who thinks the world of him. George can charm the birds from the trees if he wants to. I told him that on the way back I might let him steer or hold the sheet to go about. I showed him how to do it and he understood at once. I asked him to do the same and he got it at once. I was astonished. Until then it had been "chatter, chatter," nonstop. On the way back I asked him if he would like to take over the steering. He took his place and brought us back to Jersey. At the point where we rounded the headland, I began to offer advice and he said. "Shhh! Father. I'm listening to the wind!"

"We all grow up with boats and I've never met a better natural sailor. That's why Gideon has taken him."

"You speak very highly of him, Philippe."

"I say no more than he deserves. Philippe and I are very fortunate in our sons and he has heaped equal praise upon you, Amyas, - although I don't think I've ever heard him praise your sailing skills. Now I really must get my head down or I'll not get through tomorrow. Sleep well, my boy. I suppose George must be arriving in Newfoundland shortly, if he's not already there."

* * *

"Now there's some peace and quiet on board I want to tell you what is to happen next. You know about knots and understand pulleys and cleats, can help lower a boom and furl a sail. You must pick up and stow anything sliding about deck and do lots of useful things. Before you are real sailors you've got to have a good knife, for freeing a jammed pulley perhaps, or cutting your food, trimming branches when we get to build shelters, and making drying racks. So here you are, boys; one knife each. This is where you keep it, in your belt, so you don't hurt yourself and one day you can use it for target practice for they won't be giving you a dag. Know what that is? It's sailor talk for a handgun. Look after your knife: it may save your life- and never threaten anyone with it just because you are angry. Walk away. Never run, especially on board!

"This is Falmouth. We are here to pick up supplies and we'll be joined by a number of small ships, then we'll set off to cross the Atlantic. We'll be watching out for our ships on the way, so get a good look at them so you can recognise them in case you see one in trouble. If you see anything wrong, you shout out as loud as you can!

"The same thing will happen in Plymouth, Saltram, Plympton and other fishing ports. This has all been arranged by Mr. 'elier and we'll be here for a day or two so that everyone can be ready to face the

Atlantic, which can be very nasty, though I myself think the Pacific is worse.

"The trip from here to the Atlantic is often the worst part and you'll probably be sick: in fact, most of us will. Lie flat as much as possible and if you are going to throw up, keep your hat handy. You'll find many uses for it and it will come clean with a good wash. I'll try to get you hammocks because they hold you steady. When you come around feeling bright and hungry, get on your feet and do something useful for all of us. Once we have passed the Scillies and the Fastnet Rock, things should settle down, but we never count on it.

"If you want to go on shore, you can, but you must tell the watch you're going. The crew will tell you what's what, and remember to tell them when you return, so we know you're safe. The Shipmaster, Mr. Tull, is giving you a few pence and you, young fellow, should buy yourself a hat like George's."

* * *

"I am getting to like Alton, Amyas, you should always try to get a room here in The Cricketers. Food and service here is are excellent. Next stop, Southampton, I hope! Then we sit in the Admiral's Arms and wait for the wind and tide to be favourable for the return to Jersey."

"A lot of good heathland round here: good for riding. Her Majesty spent some of her time here. She loved riding and was a good selector of horses; ran her own stud and bred from Arab stock. Delicate small heads they have, very elegant and fiery apparently. She placed bets too, and often beat the touts."

"I came up from the port today, to tell you that the boat is ready and the Captain looking forward to being paid in full. I expect you are

44

anticipating a triumphant session in the States when we tell them what you have achieved."

"Yes, Good! Of course! But modesty must be my touchstone. You know that I am only one of the landowners who are all of equal importance. I have to convey that it was pure luck, that any one of them could have achieved as much or more. Otherwise they'll be thinking, "Here's another Carteret getting above himself and too big for his boots." I can't have that.

"I think I might say we now have a means for putting any interfering Governor in his place- though, in the main, Governors never come near us, provided that they get their salary. Anthony Paulet was generally helpful, as a father-in-law should be. I have a feeling that Sir John will be supportive."

"Since we are alone and there are no eavesdroppers, Uncle, I would like to tell you my latest impression of Prince Charles."

"I hope this is not going to be scurrilous hearsay."

"No. It is an incident which I witnessed myself. It seemed to cast light on his character- and I have reservations about telling you."

"I'm glad to hear it, Amyas. Please continue. Perhaps I can refill your glass. Talking makes me thirsty."

"I'll try to be brief. The incident took place, when I was in London, last November. There were about a dozen of us at the Prince's Leveé that morning: now that he is heir to the throne, he has twice the number of attendants. Some work closely about the Prince's person, others wash and dress him for his duties of the day. He was quite relaxed and accommodating to his assistants and had clearly enjoyed taking part in the previous evening's entertainment.

"We got to talking about the play he had acted in. I think it was by Shakespeare. I understand that the prince is a fine actor and stands confidently, speaking his lines clearly from memory. People were

45

praising the content of the play and praising the various ladies of the Court. No-one mentioned the Prince, and he began to look around quizzically, until Lord March said, "Not wishing to deny praise of the Ladies, but I felt that the moral sentiments expressed in the lines given to the character whose name, Hamlet, graced the title page, were tellingly delivered by His Highness: so well, in fact, that they might have come from the mouth of Burbage himself.

"After a long pause and a long gaze at him, the Prince said, "You flatter me I think…", and we all breathed a smile of relief, then the Prince continued. "However, I think you are well suited to the role of Rosenkranz." He then indicated that the young fellow should leave his presence. Gossip says that he will stay on the Prince's blacklist for some time."

"Thank you, Amyas. Such fulsome praise perhaps deserved a put-down but seems somewhat brutal. James, I suspect, would have brushed it aside with a laugh and given him a crown for his effort.

"I suggest that we should remember, that, when addressing the powerful, one should consider every word carefully."

"We may find difficulty in striking the right note, for the future of Jersey may depend on it. Of course, you will have many years ahead to refine your style, but I shall have to make an effort to weigh my words with care. I am told that the Prince is offended by offers of advice, preferring to make his own judgements."

* * *

Two smart young "tars" in the making, aged thirteen and a few more months, smart, and one with hair like the bristles of a brush and the other with hair tied in a queue with a black cord, issued forth onto the streets of their first unfamiliar port. Men in similar dress were standing about gossiping, or seeking a welcoming pub, though it was early in the day and the market stallholders were just beginning to drag in their carts of produce.

Pausing to gaze at the Marine glasses and other instruments displayed in a window, they discussed the possible uses of unfamiliar ones and the price.

"What's that?" asked le Seuel.

"It's a sextant", was the reply. "It's like a quadrant but gives steadier readings: it's useful when you have to use dead reckoning." His companion sought further information. "I've never used one, but they are used for fine bearings: our great Naval Captains would never find the Bermudas without they used one."

"Jawge?", said his companion.

"Why you saying that? I'm Jarge not Jawge: that's London talk!"

"Jarge, these people talk a bit quick, don't they? Are we in foreign parts? I wish more people spoke Jersiais."

"Well we're in Kernow or Cornouaille like the French say it, Pierre. Some of them speak Breton, which is different."

"I can understand sailors from here. They come to St Helier."

"This place is called Falmouth and that's the River Fal— Morning, Mr. Higgins! Can we help you carry them?"

"Yes, thank you, boys. It's some new tin platters and mugs. We seem to be running short. I know I'm always putting them down while I'm working and forget to pick them up. Go to that workshop there and they'll give you the rest. While we are here-you see that warehouse over there - no, not that one! the one with the tree in front… Go in there and you'll find hats! You must have one! Make sure it's a close fit before you buy it. When they ask you for money have those three coins ready in your hand, hand them over and tell them you haven't been paid yet. If they say it costs more, tell them the purser says you must have one. When you've got it, go and look round. They sell little compasses, pencils and note pads so you could keep your own log."

"That's for afterwards!! - you must fetch those mugs first!"

Purchases stowed, the two boys found a grassy patch where some lads about their age were kicking a ball about. George and Pierre joined in, and several others, released from their workplaces to let off steam, and a fine time was had by all. One of them, Petroc Tremaine, revealed that he had persuaded his family to let him go on a Falmouth boat. His father fished the inshore waters nowadays but had fished on the Banks before his son was born. The boys were enthusiastic, and he took them to see his ship before taking them to meet his family.

Gideon had left the Fair Haven within an hour of their arrival. Falmouth was a town where he knew many of the people. Some of them were friends of long standing, with others he knew he would need to establish a fresh understanding. Others yet, who had recently come to play a significant role in the community, would need to know he could be trusted. He had come there first with his grandfather, who had brought his own son there, when he was young. Now he was representing his brother and had brought his nephew to introduce him to old and trusted tradesmen. It was all about showing that the long-standing trust between Cornishmen and Jersiaise was to continue.

He had no intention of thrusting the lad forward but hoped that they would receive a good impression of him, as the boy walked at his side across the street or came into a clothing shop whose owner he was intended to meet. Informal first impressions created less stress and were more effective. The news would soon spread:

"Carteret's brought his nephew this time! No, it's Gideon, Elie's younger brother.... My son got him to buy a pasty yesterday, you should have seen him. My boy said, "I reckons they don't feed them on your ship, Gideon..."

48

"Likes a fierce game of camp-ball, I'm told!"

Chapter 4

Granvilles were Cornish and long established in and around Bridport where ships carried tin to Normandy and up the Severn Sea. The Carterets and Granvilles were related, to many other families, including the Paulets, Raleighs, Duces, who will feature significantly in George's life. They came with the Norman conquest of Britain.

Henry VIII declared his intention to reconquer the land in France lost by the Plantagenet kings. The money was eventually secured by the confiscation of all monasteries and lands. These were sold to rich supporters. An embargo on trade with Europe was imposed, and Customs Officers instructed to prevent exports to France. The Cornish tin trade halved in value as a result, and miners were laid off and starving. Tin was their main product. When hunger marchers set out for London, Henry sent an army which defeated the rebellion, then executed their leaders. Sir John Paulet was their Judge.

Now an absolute ruler, Henry's new Church of England set out a Christianity based on "reason" and freed from all superstition. He would now be the only source of Law and Truth and Justice would be his decision. His subjects were forced to swear an oath of obedience to him. Statues, vestments, incense and coloured windows in churches were smashed, burned or melted down for their gold. A new account of British history was to be taught in new Grammar schools- a new history, more suitable to embody the new England, was invented by Raphael Holinshed. Henry claimed descent from Troilus, Prince of Troy, and King Arthur. Britain was promised a glorious future.

The effect of these policies on the Channel Islanders was considerable. They depended on a steady demand for fish in Britain and France and the transportation of tin, wool, wines, and spirits freely among their usual customers. These trading bans threatened ruin in the Islands and West Country. In the Islands, some landowners owned more land than others, but the combined wealth of Jersey was fairly evenly distributed and very low. They were not the Subjects of the English King however, since their constitution made them leaseholders of the Dukedom of Normandy. Each Island paid an annual Tax, in exchange for which they were promised protection from attack and respect for their traditional rights and the privilege of governing their own affairs.

As a guarantee of their liberty, a Guarantor, entitled Governor, was appointed to ensure the observation of these freedoms and obligations. His role was that of a mediator and supporter, and not that of a Controller. Until recently the Governor was Sir Anthony Paulet, who resided in Elizabeth Castle, an island in St Helier Bay. He was, by and large, a benevolent presence and related by marriage to Sir Phillippe de Carteret, who was Knighted by Henry VIII. When Sir Anthony died and Sir John became Governor, there was concern that foreigners might be awarded land in the islands contrary to the Statutes. Sir John gave them his full support on this issue, however, but It was for this reason that Sir Philippe and his nephew were in London seeking confirmation of these and a number of other legal matters from King James, hereditary Duke of Normandy, and to ensure that he understood the extent of his authority.

The ban on the eating of fish on Friday, had, under Henry, brought the fishing industry of Jersey to its knees, throwing fishermen out of work, where there was no other means of a living. Their French customers continued to demand fish, but there was embargo on exports. Eating fish on Friday became a potentially treasonable offence if repeated, for which the death penalty was recommended. The Cornish, Channel Islanders, and Manxmen complied outwardly, but the Carterets were among many who continued to trade under cover of darkness, using little known harbours, to avoid starvation. The outlying parts of the British Isles were learning to help each other in times of need. A lesson which George would learn in his infancy and turn to good account in the future. Sir Philippe would need to avoid bringing their necessary, though illegal, trading activities to the King's notice. His acknowledgement of their "special status" made their actions legal!

George's father and uncle, and several of their friends were Jurats and Ministers of the Jersey Parliament, named The States. He may have heard discussion of these issues at the age of fourteen; be this as it may, he would become aware of the situation as he grew up and take his place among those who protected the island and its proud independence.

Gideon's purpose was keeping these trading connections open and in the course of time, to teach these traditions to the next generation. His grandfather probably inherited this Cornish connection, and he and Elie had been accepted as Honorary Members of the Stannary Court. This organisation of Mine Owners, and Mineworkers, settled disputes, when mining rights were infringed, or when poor quality ore was mixed with better to sell at a high price. There were no hereditary officers, and all members had one vote. Voting was by show of hands at a meeting in a public place. The Tudors failed to gain control by imposing a Royal Governor, though their known Stannary Court members support of the rebellion was never forgiven. Strangely, this was to influence George's life in the near future.

Meanwhile, Gideon booked a large meeting room, and a quiet sitting room, where he could entertain local dignitaries. The fair wind which had brought them thus far had died down, though ships were still creeping into harbour. The captains of the other ships had agreed that when the right wind blew, they would make a start. Local experts advised Gideon to expect another three days delay before the wind was favourable; time to renew friendships for him and for George. He had received reports that George was having a wonderful time with boys of his own age and had eaten all that their mothers offered him. The cook at the inn said that George had asked him if there was any chance of pasties for dinner. Gideon drank a silent toast to the next generation.

* * *

They enjoyed fine weather for some time after leaving Land's End behind them. They sailed past St Mawes and Penzance though the old hands remarked that, if they had a good catch, they would visit those towns on their return. The sun, which had made the hosing of decks a welcome task, continued to shine from a clear sky but the sea seemed, slowly, to wake up from a deep sleep, A sudden yaw to port quite unexpectedly, would see the helmsman throwing all his weight on the wheel, and crewmen staggering to remain upright as the deck swung away below them. George, who had been noting that day's speed in knots, was caught unaware as his head came into painful contact with a bulkhead. Pierre, snoozing over his sketch pad, woke saying, "Where are we?" under the impression that they were entering a harbour.

The behaviour of the ocean grew ever stranger as the days wore on. The best they could do was keep the bow pointed close to the wind and trust that some progress was being made, though for much of the time it was the force of the current moving them forward. The effect of the constant four metre rise and fall of the tide on the narrowing channels of the Severn and Irish Sea, created a massive funnel effect, through which the deep waters of the ocean were constricted from all sides while being raised from below by the narrowing of the surrounding rocky coastlines.

As though this was not enough to deter ships from attempting to cross the seas, when all these effects failed to foil their intention, destruction was handed out by the Atlantic itself with the power to confer life or death. As they neared the Fastnet rock, a great storm blew in from the Atlantic. The boom shattered and had to be replaced in driving wind and rain, and the sun no longer shone, so that they were constantly soaked despite their storm-proof gear, and their hats proved their value while on deck, and also when they were prostrated with seasickness. The suffering was general, though Gideon was pleased to rediscover that he was one of the lucky ones, and only slightly affected. It was a constantly changing skeleton crew which preserved a semblance of order and had little appetite for the cold food available.

As the ship was carried up on the crest of a wave as high as a tall building, they could see in the distance some others of their ships and shout to them. Then their ship would be flung down and down at sickening speed, new waves towering above them, as though intent on crushing them. The timbers of the ship creaked and groaned as though in agony. At last they became inured to it all and learned to do essential tasks while hanging on with one hand and braced legs. They fell into a sleep of exhaustion to wake up and do it all again.

In a sort of lull, which usually meant that the storm was gathering strength for a fresh assault, Hawkins found them trailing a weighted rope overboard.

"You're shaping up to be real sailors, boys. I'm proud of the way you helped get the sail under control when it was trying to make a getaway."

They gazed in wonder at this sallow faced, bearded personage, recognisable by his voice.

"Look a bit different, do I? Well, I have to say, I hardly recognise you. You're all skin and bone!"

"When's the storm going to finish, Mr. Hawkins? I'm really hungry!

"You must be over the sickness then: next time it might not get you so bad. I'm hoping we'll all be getting some hot food inside us if it stays calm for a few hours."

"Where are we, Mr. Hawkins?"

"Somewhere in the Atlantic, my old lad, as near as I can tell. We're past Fastnet and this might be the end of the storm if we're lucky. Mr. Tull says he thinks most of our boats have come through, and we'll be picking up the North Atlantic current soon to speed us on our way at a steady four knots an hour, faster if the wind is favourable. So, did you enjoy the little blow of wind we had?"

"I never knew waves could be so high and come at you from all directions. The ship made a lot of noise, creaking and groaning! I thought she was going to break up! Is she all right?"

"Right as rain young fellow, that noise was her happy song! She was built for foul weather."

"How long is it since we left Falmouth? Is it a week?"

"No, it's a couple of days short of three weeks. We're doing quite well and with this strong westerly, we should make good progress and be in plenty of time to catch the best of the harvest."

* * *

"Did Mr. Jones put all that bandage on your arm, Pierre? I thought it was getting better"

"He saw me struggling with a bow hitch, and he felt it, and I yelled blue murder. I told him I done it when I lost my balance and slid the length of the deck on my backside. Crashed into a hatch cover, I did, and it got folded under me."

"I heard you yell: it's well wrapped up. Does it hurt badly?"

"Not as much as it did. It's good to smell hot food cooking again: I'm really hungry."

"Me, too! Did he say it was broken?"

"He didn't. He said it was a green-stick fracture."

"What's that then?"

"He said it was like planting a young tree, if it snaps in a strong wind, you straighten it and tie it to a splint, and it will join up like new. He said it mainly happens when you're young so he wouldn't need to cut my arm off."

"Was he serious?"

"I thought he was, but he was laughing, so I knew he wasn't really. He said a missing arm was better than a missing head, "cos you only have one of those: everything else you've got two of, so there always a spare to get by with. Then he said I'd got some good teeth coming up to fill the gaps: perhaps next time God gives it some thought, he'll fix it so we could grow a new leg if we mislaid one. He says some funny things. I told him you were keeping a log and you would write about my green stick in it."

"What did he say?"

"He'd like to see it. Was that all right?"

"I expect so. Come on! Let's go and wash some dishes and get a second helping of dough-boys and stew."

56

* * *

"Good morning, Mr. Lawrence, I'm sorry I kept you waiting. One of the girls fell in a blackthorn hedge and there were thorns. You must have wondered if I was killing her from the fuss she made."

Elizabeth Carteret, faced with an angry tenant farmer, concealed her anxiety by comforting her child, while taking a deep breath to steady her nerves.

"Let me pour you a little more cider, and you must try to relax and tell me what is troubling you."

"Well, Madam, it's like this…"

Elizabeth spent the next ten minutes paying apparently close attention to the circumstantial narrative of a dispute between Lawrence and his neighbour, Mr. Turner, over the question of who was entitled to the use of the lower meadow in May. Lawrence wanted to fence his eight young bullocks there to graze on sweet grass. Turner insisted that the meadow grass was his to cut for winter feed and Lawrence had pulled up his fencing, allowing the beasts to run about freely. Other neighbours ware complaining to Lawrence about the damage his beasts had caused.

What would Elie do?? While pouring a little more cider for them both, her thoughts returned to Sark and the complex grazing rights which required unquestioned conformity, with such restricted acreage. She came to a decision, but before speaking took a deep breath to quiet her thumping heart.

"How long will it be before you take your beasts to market? Two weeks?"

"I was thinking three, Madam, to get the benefit of the good feed."

"Good! Three weeks then. That will give you two days to get the animals out and ready for the Friday sales. I know several farmers are crossing over from Normandy for the sales, so you can count on good prices. Don't speak about it to Mr. Turner, please. I shall take my little ones over to his farm this afternoon, I promised him two or three pullets, and I'll tell him he can have the grass for himself until market day. Just make sure you take down those fences without delay or replace them when needed. Now, you must forgive me- I have so many things to do…. Good Day to you!"

"Well done, Elizabeth, but go on. What happened afterwards? Did they come to blows? You can't stop there. Did they follow your suggestions? When was this? I haven't spoken to you for weeks. What happened?"

"I suppose it worked. The sale was on Friday last and Lawrence got better prices than he expected. Nobody has mentioned it, but Turner was boasting about the fine quality of his meadow grass after the young bulls had been on it."

"That's the way to settle problems; show men the common-sense solution, and they usually accept it after a lot of bluster."

"Thanks to you, Anne, I'm taking your advice. You said, "While your husband is away, and you are left in charge, if there's a problem don't panic." Think how you deal with squabbling children; tell them how it can be resolved and promise a sweetmeat if they follow your advice. That's what I will always try in future."

"It's a trick my mother taught me, for dealing with my brothers. Of course, it doesn't always work. You can't order an angry farmer to go to the next room and come back when he is ready to apologise. Personally, I prefer to appeal to them for assistance, rather than resort to tears, or to refer it to my husband when he comes home. My husband

and yours are not very good with problems, they get flustered. I always try to help them make decisions. I'm sure you can do it as well as I can."

"They will all be concentrating on digging in the craic and planting potatoes, I can't see that leading to arguments-but I suppose anything is possible with some of these men."

"I will have to go to St Ouen tomorrow. I hope Rachel, Philippe's mother, hasn't upset too many of our servants. She is more difficult to deal with than any truculent farmer!"

* * *

"Good Day, Mr. Spalling and Mr. Ramsey. It's a pleasure to speak to you, after all the activity of the past few weeks. I see you have come through our storms in good health with no broken limbs. I cannot hold myself responsible for the foul weather we experienced, but, believe me, it could have been much worse. I expect you are finding sea travel tedious with nothing to observe but the sea, which is pretending that it cannot ever surprise us, and never change from one day to the next, and that the sun shines every day."

"Good morning, Commander. We have found the past day or two a joy after the terrifying weather earlier on. I know we are both enjoying the ensuing tedium! May we thank you for your attention to our clocks while we were both indisposed? I believe you and Mr. Tull kept them wound and one, or the other, was always kept working. From time to time neither Mr. Ramsey nor myself was able to take charge of our regular readings and I thank you for the care which has saved our project from failure."

"Having offered to take you on board in the interests of science, and because it was worthwhile research, I decided to see it through, or the whole project would have failed."

59

"You are too modest, Sir. You seem to me to have the same spirit of inquiry which inspires men like Napier and Descartes."

"That seems excessive praise, Mr. Spalling, though a kind thought; but tell me, what is the condition of the other clocks?"

"Michael Ramsey is the true scientist; I am merely a facilitator. I will sit back and he can explain all. I shall listen spellbound. Please wake me if I fall asleep, I can't imagine how I can be so tired after two weeks lying down."

Mr. Ramsey, who seemed in need of rest rather than conversation, replied, with a sigh: "I will try to be brief, Commander. As you know, we started the experiment at twelve noon by the sun on the day we sailed from Falmouth. I hope to find definite evidence of the variations of time in distant lands. For that I must have a reliable clock set to a known time, such as London time, so that when we reach Newfoundland and discover the time from the Sun we may calculate the exact time difference between those two places. Of course, we also have to know the distance travelled, to discover an average speed. Similar tests have failed because the clocks have stopped and had to be restarted, or they have rusted, or their wooden cases have shrunk, damaging the mechanics."

At this point he paused for breath and swallowed a small glass of a strong cordial which Gideon offered him, before continuing with renewed enthusiasm.

"I can hardly believe our success thus far, that with your remarkable help the clock we started almost a month ago is still going. However, my recovery from sickness was timely for, while I sat sipping water, I heard it stop! Imagine my horror! Fortunately, I had been looking at our reserve clocks and set one going. I had only to set it at once to the time on the stopped clock, and so the experiment continues. May I beg that when you enter the cabin at any time and hear it stop you bring another into action to take its place. The first clock is working again, though I oiled it, for the first oil had dried up completely. It seems however to be losing time. Personally, I shall be astonished if we have an accurate "Time" when we reach Newfoundland. It is very unlikely that it will be told by the same clock, for their mechanics are so fragile, and I lack the facilities of my workshop, and a fairly constant temperature. As you know, clocks seem to dislike draughts. Here they have constant wind so we cannot expect too much."

"We will all do our best to see the experiment through, for even if all the clocks fail, which, Heaven forbid, the time difference is established, it will encourage the government to pay for the building of a weather resistant clock as reliable as a compass resting in its binnacle. With accurate English time available on board, we will be able to calculate our exact position on the featureless ocean, and not be hopelessly lost if blown off course in a gale. The advantage this will give our merchant ships is inestimable and I am sure that the Royal Navy will turn it to good use also. At the moment, Gentlemen, we are reliant on sextant and dead reckoning, but I am confident we are on course to create a totally reliable navigation instrument, to the benefit of our country."

* * *

Time passes in Jersey and elsewhere, and it is now the third week of May, and two Sisters-in-Law are at the Manor House while their husbands are engaged in administrative affairs. Apart from Anne Carteret and her two young children, there is Lizzy Carteret and her brood of five. As always, she is in a constant state of unease and worry about their safety. George is constantly present in her mind. "Is he well? Is he missing us? Is he regretting his decision?"

There is no-one to answer her constant questioning, and they are, at present, house guests at the home of her sister-in-law, Anne de Carteret,

Lady Anne - née Dowse- who, with her well known empathy with troubled souls, tries to calm their fears with reassurance and tactful distractions. St. Ouen's Manor is the largest of the island's twelve Manor Houses and quite large enough for the whole Carteret family to gather, as they always do at Christmas. Those never to be forgotten Feasts! They would linger in the memory of those present for long years after. There were also leisurely summer meals, on the lawns with friends and their children visiting in the knowledge that they would be welcome. Sir Philippe is the perfect host and Lady Anne known for her sympathy and hospitality. At present Philippe's mother, Rachel, the Dowager Lady de Carteret, (née Paulet), is thought to be on her way to her home at Basing House, or she may still be with her brother, the Earl of Winchester, at Netley Abbey, his Hampshire home. Her brother, Sir Anthony, was among those who tried Robert Carr, the King's disgraced favourite, and his murdering wife. Her death sentence, if announced, may be regarded as long overdue, and the Paulets are loyal administrators of Royal Justice, having presided at the Fotheringay execution of the King's mother, Mary, Queen of Scots.

Liz is pleased that Rachel is elsewhere, and on arriving, felt a cloud lifted when she found Lady Rachel had gone to Basing. Anne also, seems more relaxed in her absence.

Their children are at present somewhere around the gardens and have been warned not to roam into the park: their laughter bursts forth at frequent intervals and they can be traced from place to place by the distance of their voices as they roam freely. They know the old, almost dry, moat is not to be crossed and the farm staff always enjoy these events and guard them, giving them small tasks to occupy them and reward them with sweetmeats. Her children love to be there with their cousins, and gradually the sadness, created by George's absence, grows smaller. Young Philippe has come out of the shadow cast by George, and is becoming a reliable elder brother, and a favourite of the younger ones. Reginald will be enjoying adventures, with his cousin Frank, and the girls are playing house with Bessie and her brother, aged nearly two. Pony rides and picnics are promised. When Philippe and Anne married, their armorials were carved and placed over the gatehouse arch to announce their happy union.

Elie, Elizabeth's husband, after two weeks of boredom at Mont des Vignes, has taken his skiff and a team of workmen to Mont Orgueil Castle, which is receiving long-overdue repairs. He is happiest when engaged on a demanding project. Will George be like him? She believes Elie may be regretting his decision not to lead the boats to Newfoundland. His last-minute decision came as a considerable surprise, because she was sure it was a task for a younger man. She had not expected he would hand over command to his younger brother.

At this point the sound of eager voices made her aware that hungry children were approaching.

Chapter 5

George emerged one morning, rubbing the sleep from his eyes, and gazed about in search of the group due to set out tree-felling in the forest. It was still early in the day and, though the sun shone brightly, the wind from the sea was keen. He was glad of his knitted jersey, though he might cast it aside later as the sun rose. A small group of men, gathering outside a nearby sleeping hut, spotted him and Hion Storace beckoned him over. A member of his ship's crew, he was a popular man: George murmured a greeting and responded with a grin to a question about his hunger.

"Always hungry this one, aren't you George? And he's not had any fish since yesterday, have you? I reckon you're getting to like it, eh?"

Smoke rising from the chimney of the canteen was an indication that food was being prepared. As more men appeared from other huts, general movement in the direction of the canteen began, as a large man in a sleeveless shirt emerged to stand beating a large copper pan with a wooden mallet.

Inside, tables and benches, well-constructed and designed, were occupied by groups of large and cheerful fishermen, each of whom held a sizeable bowl of stew in one hand and a large hunk of bread in the other. George joined the queue and received a man-sized bowl of fish stew which he polished off with an appetite for food which seemed to grow each day. At a suitable interval, the ships' captains called them to order and divided them into two large parties, one to go tree-felling, and the other to continue work on the drying racks.

This was a routine George knew well. This was his fourth full day; having begun on simple wood shaping tasks, he would be tree-felling today. His part in this work was cutting off useless twigs from useful branches and sawing them to be taken to a bonfire for burning. The branches were heaped together and needed holding firmly while he attacked them with knife and pruning saw. Other wood was already cut to length for various uses including platform slats, support brackets, or to repair leaky roofs. Some way off was the saw pit and trestles with metal clamps, where large sections were trimmed to size or cut lengthways into planks, some for flooring the huts, others reserved for deck timbers. Some pine trunks were being set aside as potential spare masts; replacements were often necessary on a long voyage. Young crew members, such as George, could not take on this work, which required great strength and stamina, but they went about their work with the usual energy he saw in his father's shipyard workers. Whatever work the teams undertook, there was plenty of work a boy could do, such as sharpening chisels and saws, and George enjoyed it, especially when he was told he had done a good job.

He was less keen on working around the forge as the days grew warmer and the finishing work needed to file a good point on dozens of nails was tedious in the extreme. Sawing up the rejected branches into useful lengths and burning the unusable stuff was more to his taste. From time to time his thoughts turned to home, Philippe, and young Reggie, and the hope that he might try to build a boat himself. The forest was another fascination. The men had no idea of its size, and explorers were discouraged by sightings of bears, wolves and wolverine. They were seen

65

less often than buffalo, who moved in herds and were prepared to attack to protect their young. George knew that, despite these dangers, there were settlers who had made a home in the region and hoped that he might meet them.

That evening, as he ate pork and vegetables in the canteen, he heard the men describing the daily arrival of cod and other great fish in increasing numbers. He had read in Hakluyt's Discoveries of the huge quantities arriving on the Great Banks of Newfoundland and had seen with his own eyes more fish swimming together than he had ever seen before: and Cabot had reported that the waters were so thick with fish that you might think of walking on their backs! This he must see! Any day now, everything on shore would be ready and all the damage done to the ships in the Atlantic crossing repaired. Then the crew would be lining the ships' sides with baited rods and lines reeling in fish after fish and he would be with them he was determined: he knew he was a good fisherman: he had always fished off Jersey as far south as Biscay.

He wondered idly where this fresh food originated but he was soon to be enlightened, for as the repair-work was completed, other trips to the boats became more frequent. Each fishing boat had consumed its stock of victuals during the crossing. The supply ships, like the Fair Haven, would need restocking eventually. Basically, all goods had to be unloaded and space made in the holds for the great tonnage of dried fish which must be brought on board, preferably shortly before the return journey commenced. Water casks were taken ashore, cleaned and stored under cover and refilled to prevent shrinkage and leaks. Each ship held some beer and spirits, of which many preferred calvados to the regulation rum, used as an additional source of calories for energy. Salt pork and beef as well as cod were reallocated to each ship. These and bacon could be supplied by chandlers on shore and root vegetables supplied for the voyage.

St. John was the main source of any other needs and the fishing fleet's annual arrival was its main economic activity. Its total population was about 200 families, though others made their way to St John to pick up work or sell fruit and vegetables. Bearing in mind that the crews of a hundred fishing boats would add about 2,500 newcomers to the population, it is remarkable that supplies were always, by some means, provided. The inhabitants in 1623, were largely of English origin, and of farming stock, so there was every encouragement for the promotion of agricultural crops and beasts.

Winters were severe, but spring arrived with sunny days and gentle showers to add to the snow melt. The soil was of good quality, the growing season long enough for grain to be harvested and for stocks to be built up for the incomers. The first settlers had been mainly Dutch, with a scattering of other races, but the English had ousted them and made St John an English town. Other settlements existed, mainly in the North, and were largely French, who also controlled the fishing grounds near St Pierre and Miquelon.

It was to St. John that George was sent, alone, with a cart, several times for fresh foodstuffs for the ships' crews. When not fetching and loading, and on a fishing boat, he found the opportunity to steer and trim the sails when necessary, and his ability to control a heavily laden boat in a choppy sea was noted favourably. Seaman Storace was often around, offering advice and encouragement when necessary, and a number of those who often worked together, also chose each other's company in leisure time, generally after the evening meal, when some produced acorn-shell pipes and smoked tobacco. Among them were Le Clerk and Bristowe, a joiner from his uncle's ship, whose younger brother he knew, and Napper, who kept them laughing from the moment he told them he had escaped to sea rather than scaring rooks in Norfolk. He met one day Tremaine, whom he had got to know well in Falmouth. Their paths often crossed in future. George's mother had warned him of the dangers of drink, but she need not have worried. Island people had long been associated with people of the French coast, their closest neighbours, and they were mainly "Huguenot" in faith and almost Puritanical in regard to alcohol and tobacco. Fishing was acknowledged to be thirsty work, however, and a few tankards did you a power of good! Their common purpose, to earn money, brought these disparate men together and arguments rarely led to blows, and most slept the sleep of exhaustion as soon as they lay down.

* * *

On one of these mornings, shortly before the serious work of fishing began, his Uncle came on board, carrying a portfolio. He selected George and his usual team of associates to go with him to one of the boats, and they sailed directly into the port of St John. On shore he walked with them to the market stalls on the quay, putting Bristowe in charge of gathering fruit and vegetables, Gideon asked George to go with him to meet an old friend of his father. They walked to a squat stone house near the Quay, where a stout and cheerful man, welcomed them warmly. He learned that Mr. Smith, who leaned heavily on a stick, was a successful farmer who was grateful to the Carterets for building up the trade in fish, which the English King, some years before, had attempted to prevent people eating, on the grounds, that fishing was of benefit to the French, as a result the English were forbidden to eat dried fish.

Mrs. Smith hurried in, flushed from her exertions in a hot kitchen, and greeted Gideon with hugs and kisses, remarking that he was a fine figure of a man since she had seen him last. News was exchanged concerning Elie and the family and Bessie gave the news that their elder son, Edward, was doing well in Boston, while Lawrence was running the farm for his father. John Smith himself had been appointed Chairman of the local Traders' company and was attempting to ensure that fair trading regulations were observed.

"I'll leave you two to your money talk," she declared. "I think my cookies are about to burn. George, would you join me in the kitchen and telling me what you think of them? I'd value your opinion, and I've made some strawberry buttermilk which you might like to try."

The boy was on his feet at once, gesturing Mrs. Smith to lead the way. The house was a smaller version of those at home, with workshops and stables nearby. Mrs. Smith was eager to make him feel at home. Her cookies were excellent, and the buttermilk, mixed with blueberries. George relaxed and forgetting his initial home sickness, began to talk about his brothers and sisters. Distracted for a moment by a soft sound of a slipper, he caught sight of the slight figure of a girl in the doorway. She must have been listening for several minutes, he realised and, perhaps annoyed with herself for being seen staring, was startled, reaching into her pocket, as though looking for something mislaid, and moved back out of sight. George heard his Uncle call his name and rose at once to join him in the office, where his Uncle brushed crumbs from his coat and remarked that they should soon be on their way. George hoped he might see the girl again and hoped no-one would notice he was blushing, and his heart was beating quickly too. Their business concluded, Smith and Carteret moved on to the exchange of news.

"I must thank all your fishermen for what you have done for us. No, Gideon, don't look modest! You and your father have put us "on the map," as they say; in fact you have probably rescued the colony, and now, with so many English ships sailing up the coast looking for possible places to make settlements, I hope more will realise, that if they put in here, they can find good quality supplies- and our small ship-yards are feeling the benefit too!"

"I believe you are among the earliest settlers, John. How many years is it since then?"

"I was hoping to sail with Frobisher in 1577, but he decided I was too young. I was disappointed at the time, but in fact it turned out to be for the good since he didn't settle here then. He was on the search of black pyrites which can be refined into gold. I gather he found reasonable quantities, but investors turned it down as too expensive, and involving long term investment and slow returns.

"So, then I went away and learned farming, in case I had another chance: and, of course I did. I married Bessie in 1581 and, we sailed over with Sir Humphrey Gilbert who had a License from Her Majesty, to found a colony. Here we are now, enjoying our success, with a fine family and good friends. We've never looked back!"

"No trouble with the Indians?"

"They were a bit puzzled at first- didn't know what to make of us, I suppose! But they saw we wanted to stay in the cove here and not steal their lands. There were only a couple of dozen of us, so they knew we were no threat. In fact, the Beothuk are decent, helpful folk and like river fish but not fishing from boats. So we get on well. Now! What does young George make of it all, eh?"

"George? Oh, he's as happy as a dog with a fresh bone. Loves ships and sailing and has been on fishing trips with me in coastal waters since he was ten. He came through a ten-day Atlantic gale a month back without a word of complaint. Whenever he wasn't sick, or on deck helping, he had his head stuck in a book. He's a great reader; sleeps with Hakluyt's Traffiques under his pillow, I'm told. Knows all about the North West Passage! — Here he is, full of biscuits! I hope you said thank you, George."

"So, you've read Hakluyt, have you? I've just been telling your father, that Bessie and I came over with Sir Gilbert- Humphrey Gilbert, though you are related, I believe. I think you and I need to talk seriously about his voyages, and living in Indian territory"

"Do you know the Beothuk Indians?"

"I certainly do. They live all around the town. Very good neighbours, too."

"Do you speak Algonquin, Mr. Smith?"

"I suppose you have read the name of their tongue in one of your books, eh? Not as well as I should, young Sir. But I'm still learning."

George's silence spoke a great deal of admiration.

"I have a suggestion to make, Gideon. It seems as though George has an enquiring mind. Personally, I have no time for lads who show no curiosity and are afraid to ask questions. My son, Lawrence, will be coming here for a meal shortly. He runs the farms for me now. His son, Mark, usually invites himself too on these occasions, not because he loves his grandparents, you understand, but because he likes Bessie's cooking! Mark is about your age, George, and knows all the Indians round here and everyone else too. If you have no objection, Gideon, I suggest Lawrence's boy and George both eat with us. Later on, the boys can decide whether they want to spend time getting familiar with the place? It's a fine place for young people. They can't spend all their time gutting fish and George is eager to learn new things, and we have so much to share with him."

Over lunch there was animated conversation which led to a broad agreement that George would spend a few days with the younger Smith family, to see the Humber River and perhaps climb the Cabox Mountain. Smith commented that increased shipping indicated that the Virginia Company founded in 1606, was at last beginning to succeed and also The

Plymouth Company, only three years old, but growing quickly. It was to be hoped that others would follow to please His Majesty.

"For all we know, Gideon," laughed Smith, "young George may found a Colony of his own if he likes what he sees in the next few weeks."

"Shall we drink to that?"

* * *

At the other end of the town, money was changing hands. The man receiving it was Parson Vincent Houchin, a gentle man and a Minister, and the man bestowing it, with ponderous condescension, was Mr. Gregory Spalding.

"I am assuming that the house is likely to remain vacant for some time, therefore I am giving you three month's rent, Houchin. I will probably be returning with the fleet to civilisation but may as well travel round the island while we are here. Mr. Ramsey will probably wish to make assessments and measurements in a variety of locations- you know what scientists are? Never still - always active!

"That will be him, and the boy, arriving with even more gear. Thank heaven you have four spare rooms."

"Leave that case for me, Pierre! It's heavy and rather delicate. Put it there for the time! While you are here, would you help me move this trestle? I need a clear work surface under the window and then I'll place these clocks on this shelf. You and George have done your best to help me, although carrying valuable things down a rocking gang plank, caused me considerable anxiety. You are both clumsy"

"Is there anything else to do, Mr. Ramsey?"

"Not until I've unpacked these boxes and tripods. Why don't you take this and buy us two of those meat pies I smelled in the bakery. Then we will have new strength for the next task."

Later, brushing crumbs from his waistcoat, Ramsey asked Pierre:

"How did George get such accurate figures for reckoning the knots before I gave him the clock? The early ones are the same as they were earlier. How did he count time?"

"Carteret!" said Pierre, inserting the last piece of crust.

"Please explain, I have no idea what you mean."

"He says "Carteret" over and over and counts them in his head."

"?"

"Each time you say it, is a second." he says, "If you keep steady. Like a heartbeat."

"That's strange! Who taught him to do it?"

Pierre le Seuel shrugged. "I don't know. I think he did it himself. He makes things seem easy. He knows lots of things and he's made a list of six different fish he's never seen before, except in books. He reads a lot: he's making me read while he darns his shirt. If he's not reading, he's sketching the boats or the harbour. I like drawing people. I"m a bit slow at reading, but I"m getting better. I'm teaching him to draw."

"If you've finished putting away your toys, Ramsey, I think it's time we went for dinner. Did the boy break much? You should have asked me to help, I would have engaged one of those layabout sailors. I have completed all the really important business, by the way, so there's nothing more for you to bother with!"

Chapter 6

The start of the fishing season came as a surprise to George who had been expecting a ceremony of some kind. There was no announcement, but one day, those awake early returned to camp, where heated discussion resulted. Gideon came on the scene, making his way as usual, to inspect the sea and survey the horizon with his telescope, returned to join the captains in earnest conversation. Agreement being reached, Captains gathered their crews and a small number of boats loaded with baskets, crates, rods, and lines, and casks of drinking water were launched. Those remaining behind cheered them on their way with shouts of good luck, and turned with new energy, to make the necessary preparations for the return of the boats which might be within an hour or so, or late in the afternoon if the fish were plentiful.

Launch and loading was an amazingly speedy process since those involved were mainly of considerable experience, and it was watched and commented on by those whose turn would be next or who sought clarification of procedures they did not know. George, Pierre and the other servants were kept busy fetching and carrying and gaining information about matters of greater or lesser importance. Extraneous articles were unloaded first and available space created for the storage of the huge fish. Each man was prepared to serve as an angler, or as a dispatcher of the fish hauled on board. It would take strength and skill to master and subdue a healthy adult eight-foot cod without damaging the fish or injuring himself. It was a matter of preventing the creature from taking advantage of its own slippery skin and agile strength. Those fishermen who had learned sheep shearing seemed to have an inborn skill with a full-grown cod.

George and the others had much to learn, but after the initial rush were gathered together by seaman Hawkins who brought them into the dining hut, where he asked them to discuss what they had learned and decide what matters were most important. Later he turned to the actions they should be prepared for when the ships returned. Many from fishing families, knew about the unloading of fish and its transportation to market to be auctioned after division into lots. They had helped to carry skeps of slippery fish and unload them for rapid processing. What they would be expected to deal with today was somewhat more difficult.

They were reminded of the varied sizes and weight of the individual fish which they would be handling, some of which would be alive, since not all could be killed on board. All had to be unloaded as quickly and carefully as possible and brought to the sheds, where the men would be helping to gut and fillet some fish for salting and hanging the majority on the racks to dry in the sun and wind. These processes were messy and bloody, and speed was essential since a rotting fish was not only nauseating but was also a good fish wasted. Some of the fish would be carried to St John at once for eating or drying for later consumption. They should all remember that, though it might be unpleasant, they were working for the good of their families.

The Commander himself had arrived by this time, with Mr. Jones, the Surgeon on board Fair Haven. The young servants were reminded that their knives had many practical uses during the fishing trips, which they would be taught by example of expert fishermen and that great care was essential. Cuts were almost inevitable, but most could be avoided. Mr. Rogers reminded them that fingers and thumbs were easily lost and that they would be using larger and sharper knives than were usual and sometimes saws, though most of that work needed the strength of strong men. They would be taught how to fillet a fish but, in the main, they would be helping to arrange them on the racks. They would be fetching and carrying and getting knives sharpened much of the time and cutting many lengths of twine.

De Carteret himself reminded them that most of them would not be involved in the fishing but only those who were older and stronger would be taken on board when their colleagues knew that they were reliable. They had many skills to learn before they used the rods themselves which were within their capacity. They must remember that the profit from future sales was divided fairly among all those engaged so that the more effort they made, the greater the reward for everyone.

Before they dispersed to make preparations for the return of the crews, Mr. Jones reminded them that all cuts needed to be washed and covered because inflammation could grow in a cut and lead perhaps to the loss of a finger. They were to come to him, or their ship's surgeon to have it cleaned and covered.

The day was spent preparing crates and tarpaulins for the evening's work, in sharpening knives, washing benches for the filleting, and buckets for the reject material which would need to be disposed of, or used as manure. Much of it must be buried, and trenches dug for the purpose. After that a nourishing meal must be prepared for the exhausted fishermen on their return.

By mid-afternoon the first of the boats came in, carried by its momentum up the sloping, pebbly shore and hauled higher by those waiting to catch the flung lines tied securely to firmly fixed moorings. Other ropes were wound round windlasses attached to sledges, onto which crates containing the smaller cod, weighing 20 lbs. or less, were placed before being dragged up to the higher ground, by means of the windlass. This work was made easier, when men from the township arrived bringing dogs with them. George and the younger men had never before seen such huge and magnificent creatures. Their origins were European where many were bred to survive the cold and wet of mountainous climates. They had long and apparently waterproof coats, and loved to be in water, however cold. George was surprised to find one standing quietly beside him, its head level with his chest. Its tail was wagging gently so, hoping this was a sign of friendliness, George placed his hand on its back and received a firm face nuzzling his ribs. Jersey dogs were either short and quick rat catchers, excavators of rabbit warrens, or sheep dogs. The Labradors and Newfoundlands could seize ropes in their jaws and pull boats on to the hard, or haul loaded sledges with gigantic cod, to the filleting benches. Though he had always liked dogs, he had never before felt that a dog might be a good companion.

Dragged from the benches, the fish were tied in pairs, head to head, and hoisted by the gills onto the cross bars fixed across the series of A frames, each above the height of an average man. The hanging must be carefully managed so as to balance the weight of the dead fish, which would remain there until the following spring, or later, if the local experts in assessing the quality of the Stock fish were not fully satisfied with its state of maturity.

The largest cod, weighing between 70 and 80 lbs. each, were hauled from the hold on ropes attached to pulley wheels bolted to the mast and then swung overboard where their landing, on one of the sledges, was achieved with skill and force by the men on shore. Then, two or three monsters of the ocean, sometimes six or seven years old, were hauled to the racks and hung from the top bars so that their weight strengthened the downward thrust of the angled struts.

George and the other boys were kept busy unloading the lighter fish, some of which were taken at once to the filleting tables where they were dressed for food in the next few days, or laid on trays of sea salt, covered by it, and wrapped in fine cloth to be place on level rocks until the salt was absorbed and the liquid drained from the fish, which could then be kept in a cool place for several weeks. The stockfish, so named for being dried on sticks, was very popular in France and the Low Countries in winter, when fresh fish were scarce. George had a knife with a seven-inch blade, though he had never had to fillet such large fish at home. He had acquired the basic skills of gutting fish and butchery from childhood, where he learned from watching his mother and aunts, who had all the essential culinary skills. Large cod were a challenge, but they all became faster with practice.

Initially they had been a little disappointed not to be sent fishing. They could now understand that it would be several years before they were strong enough to get a cod the size of their younger brothers, or larger, on board the ship and kill it with a well-aimed club. That day's harvest was greeted with quiet satisfaction and the next trip took place two days later. The fish were eager to be caught it seemed, and as input increased, proper treatment of the produce required time and care. The men required rest after their labours and there was still construction work needed, and hunting parties to arrange. Many of the men enjoyed hunting game and venison and the challenge of making a good kill and eating the meat. Jersey offered little opportunity for such activity and fish was all too common as a basic diet. Varied meats were a great pleasure.

Several days later saw most of the boats out fishing, bringing their catch to the gravel beach every ten minutes or so to where dogs and men were standing ready to unload and turn the boats round. There seemed no respite and the harvest seemed likely to be one of the most plentiful they had ever gleaned. The men seemed to get stronger each day and work developed a rhythm so that the turn round became faster. George and the others on the filleting benches became correspondingly faster at the work, since the framers seemed constantly standing impatiently for the next pair to be hooked and slid to the A frame. More racks for salting were in demand and more A frames; George and his friends worked with a will, but at the end of the day were almost too tired to eat, and the nights seemed to get shorter as spring moved on.

Some of the older boys joined the crews to bait the hooks and cudgel the fish, and some fishermen with pulled muscles or leg injuries went to assist at the tables. There were other injuries, of course, but nothing out of the ordinary in such a dangerous pursuit, until one evening, while he stood by with the dog, he became aware of a group of three men attempting, with some urgency, to lift and carry a shipmate to shore. Someone in the meantime, running to bring the surgeon. The man, now unconscious, was carried to a raised table and tarred cloth wrapped tightly round the stump which was all that remained of his right arm. The accident was unexpected and occurred when a fisherman or two were dragging on board a large and struggling cod. As it arrived on board, it was seen that the body of the fish was held in the vice-like grip of a conger eel at least six foot in length. It suddenly released its grip, perhaps realising that it had a rival, and slithered away across the deck.

Those on deck shouted warnings while moving swiftly aside. The monstrous creature crashed into the scuppers and lashed about aggressively, seeking to impose its destructive force upon another object. Several of the crew, knowing that it must be killed to forestall its intention, grabbed axes and mallets and, with great bravery, surrounded it while it glared about, searching for prey. It was capable of living for hours out of water and must be killed, since it had no means of escape. At last, two or three men attacked it, by cornering it, and succeeded in

79

chopping off its head; the tail flailing about the deck and the head rolling away. The danger was not averted, however, as all were aware and discussion about possible action was interrupted by a sudden surge of the ship.

Several of the crew were taken unaware and lost their footing for a moment, one man fell and slid across the deck arriving close to the eel's head, which opened its huge jaws and clamped his arm with its teeth. There was no escape, and after several minutes the man's arm was severed and remained in its grip. Both sections of the eel remained, twitching vindictively while the man was dragged to safety and attempts made to stem the loss of blood. Fortunately, the shore was close and the man lived.

A shift system developed so the boys could take an occasional hour off. For several days, George had been surreptitiously slipping morsels of meat to a fat and friendly Newfoundland dog who seemed to have adopted him. The fishermen looked on tolerantly and warned him to watch out for the dog's master who might not approve. His uncle found him one morning and told him to find Pierre, Bristowe and Napper; they were invited to spend a few days in St. John where Mr. Smith and his family would like their help on the farm and warehouses. Their mates wished them luck with the ladies and told them to mind their manners, with much good-natured laughter, as they climbed aboard a farm wagon, George taking a choice morsel from breakfast to his dog before they left.

* * *

"Thank you for joining me, Gentlemen. I saw you walking across; the causeway can be very slippery when the tide is out. I always think the Castle looks its best when the tide makes it seem a real island. It is a formidable bastion from the sea, to anyone who has never seen it from the land. We know you could march an army across at low tide. We should think about building a strong defensive gate: though I hope we never need to use it."

Governor Peyton had invited Elie and Sir Philippe to meet him at his residence. This was not unusual but neither knew a reason to meet on this occasion.

"Yes, Sir John, and I expect you have come to realise, that the air is less noxious when the tide is full. Raleigh was sensible to build his residence close to the open sea for the fresh breezes"

"In a storm, it is almost like being at sea: Raleigh would have felt at home here I expect. But, please sit, gentlemen. I have brought in ale and water and I want to make this meeting "off the record" since what I have to say will need careful handling. You appreciate, I hope, I always try not to interfere in Island affairs, as you know. I follow the advice of Sir Anthony, my predecessor."

"I was only informed just before I took up the post, that His Majesty had confirmed you the Hereditary Bailiff of the island so that, in effect, you Carterets have control of the Militias, as well as most roles in the legislature. My Governorship is really only an Honorary post. I suppose, Philippe, that your successor will be your brother, Elie."

Philippe nodded his agreement, and added:

"You understand my lord, that the situation we are in is not of our choosing. The Honours I have received were a compliment from His Majesty. I could not refuse them. Carterets are occupying too many posts already, I know that, and some people won't like it. They don't realise that honours cannot be refused. The King knows we have been supporting the island defences, at our own expense, for years, and it was a gesture of thanks, which cost him nothing, but will damage our reputation. A concentration of roles in a small coterie, is contrary to the spirit of our constitution, which aims to preserve a spirit of equality. I

81

have been Sieur de St. Ouen for many years and a knight of the realm of England for the past six years. I should not have more powers! Unfortunately, no-one is willing to take them on!"

"Well, Sir Philippe, it would seem that you may have a lighter burden in future. I have in fact, only my own small personal staff to pay. The full-time Militia regiments set to protect my safety are your responsibility by Royal command. All the militias will now fall under your control, which you have been financing for some years. When I am absent on the mainland, you will have only the cost of two guards at the Town Gate and a few fusiliers whose duty is to patrol and check the defences in times of danger. I will try to stay away!" He laughed briefly at his own joke.

"Please accept my thanks," was the ironic response. "At least control is not in two hands. I am not trained in military skills, and it would not be my choice. Now we are speaking in confidence, I assume that there are significant matters we need to discuss."

"I think, Philippe, that if they were of great significance, Sir John would have informed the States this morning."

"Very perceptive, Elie! I will reach that point shortly. The fact is that the lack of reliable Parliamentary intelligence makes me cautious. You know that His Majesty rarely consults parliament on matters of government, He is King, and that is his Royal prerogative. Parliament, on the few occasions when it meets, must not discuss matters of State: ministers of state and their servants, carry out the instructions they are given, which they may not understand.

"I am informed that the King may be seeking a bride for his son: she might be Spanish, though I hope not! "

The faces of his companions registered shock as the implications of the statement sank in.

"We know nothing of this," protested Elie. "If it is true, it is an outrage that he should think of such a project after the Armada and Gunpowder plot. The English will be outraged and so will our people!"

"I see that you have no knowledge of this business and there has been no intelligence, only rumour, to show the truth of the matter."

"So, would it be true to say that you have some additional tales passed around at court by unknown informants, Sir John, who would deny it if questioned?" Philippe suggested with caution.

"Exactly so," said Sir. John. "I prefer not to listen to rumour, but I heard mention of a possible alliance. I will listen for new information and will inform you confident in your discretion."

"I think I can say that my brother and I accept that you would tell us only of matters which might help us to deal with future events!

"Indeed, Sir Philippe. What I have to say may lead to a greater understanding of those who will govern us in future. I assume you know that His Majesty is a sick man, though extremely perceptive when his health improves. Do not show agreement: we should not know this, whether or not it is true."

"You may know that I was for some years one of several secretaries to Sir Francis Bacon, for whom Prince Charles spoke so eloquently at his impeachment for accepting bribes to favoured applicants. Those who knew him innocent., They knew he enjoyed receiving gifts, but in the two charges of which he was found guilty, although the givers hoped for favourable verdicts, he decided against them! Everyone knew that they had set entrapments, and the King decided to spare him humiliation, permitting him to retire to the country. Bacon's problem was that he had a degree of tolerance for our human weaknesses. Coke, the next Lord Chief Justice, was an implacable pursuer of law breakers, among whom were many of the King's favourites whom he had rewarded with Trade Monopolies, Knighthoods and other Honours. Bacon is a complex man with interests in the heretical sciences and a degree of tolerance of the licentious indulgences at Court. Coke would have been shocked at the choice of Bacon as his successor.

"Coke loathed Buckingham and his power over the King and feared for his influence on Prince Charles. Charles will have done well to study Buckingham's methods provided he is not contaminated by them. The man is reckless and inexperienced: he should be stopped!"

Chapter 7

His Uncle sat on the driving seat next to the warehouseman who was in charge of the horses and told them the names of the many new sights which they encountered. Trees were rare in Jersey and Napper had never seen anything as tall as the conifers at the trackside. There were trees near St Aubin and George's farm, Mont des Vignes, but they were mainly birch and aspen: only at St. Ouen was there an attempt at regular planting for visual pleasure. The scent of pine and acacia was almost intoxicating and in the marshy areas close to the coast mallards, potshards and dabchicks abounded.

St. John itself was less of a surprise, having only one real street roughly levelled by frequent footfall and pitted by wagon wheels. There were buildings set further back accessible by pathways and a small, plain church sat awkwardly on a low eminence at one end. With its strongly constructed stone houses generally without stairs, the boys might have been gazing upon Orgueil, St Aubin or Rozel.

Here they climbed down so that the horses could be stabled and de Carteret and the boys, carrying a change of linen rolled in their hammocks, walked with him along the street to the Smith house. On the way, George's uncle greeted a number of residents going about their business, including Robert Litherland, a tall, somewhat severe person, who, with a partner, was the main provider of general merchandise, and Vincent Houchin, the Minister, and father of six healthy children. At the Smith house they arrived at the same time as John Gyon, clerk, and business manager to John Smith who welcomed them all inside. A meal had been prepared for their arrival and Gyon took them to a warm and solidly built annex to the stables where they could sling their hammocks in comfort. Returning, washed, to the house, Gyon pointed out to them the stables, styes and walled yards for fowls and ducks, and yards for goats. The family had more of the same on their farm managed by their elder son, whom George had met on his earlier visit. They were rounded up by Gideon, who informed them that table manners were to be remembered, and that they would not be the only young people. It was to be a family meal, but everyone would want to be home by eight pm before it was quite dark, since the moon had waned only yesterday.

While they were there, he informed them that they were not in St John for a rest, now the voyage was over. He went on to explain that he knew they would not be able to perform all the processes of preparing the fish: the work demanded all their strength, and their tasks would be allocated so as not to injure them or their colleagues. Much of the work was repetitive and boring so he was placing them with the craftsmen of the village so that they could gain insight to work which they had never tried before in Jersey so they could learn new skills which they might use later in life. He would draw up lists and move them about, so they met many of the people. Some of them might decide to emigrate: it was good to have more than one skill in life.

* * *

There were seventeen at table; their hosts, John and Elizabeth Smith; Morag Menzies and her daughters, Mairi and Innis, and son, Lyall; also,

86

Vincent and Elizabeth Houchin and Sarah, Jane, Vincent and Thomas, their children, of whom their eldest, Rachel, was sharing kitchen duties with Morag and Mrs. Smith. Then there was the schoolmaster, George Hovel and his wife Emma and their two sons, Nicholas and Paul. Gideon was very much the guest of honour and the four young fishermen, tanned and energetic, George, Pierre Le Seuel, Jim Bristowe and Kit Napper were very much the centre of attention, since visitors were a rarity and the object of enthusiastic welcome. All the young guests were sizing each other up and attempting to detect kindred spirits, or allies to existing friendships and discover mutual interests. All shared a farming background and a life in the open air, which drew them together, and, at the end of the meal, the family dogs were fed outside by the whole party before they were taken to their roomy kennel.

In their bunks that night they talked of farm work, helping the blacksmith or leather tanning, or better still, hunting. Perhaps there really were bears and buffaloes; probably there were rabbits. They knew how to catch them! Sleepy discussion of which of the girls was prettiest and who had been flirting or touching hands, and of previous attempts at familiarity with such incomprehensible creatures, and their reactions. Jim said that his foot had been tapped by someone opposite, so he had tapped thinking it was Jane. Unfortunately, it was her father, who had kicked him back. Amid laughter, he told everyone that he had seen George holding Sarah's hand twice and hoped to meet her again. They drifted off to sleep telling bedtime stories about what might be. George thought of Louise, a dairy girl he had walked home before dark, and decided holding Sarah's hand was permissible, since no promise had been broken.

* * *

Porridge, bacon and eggs, cheese, buttermilk and fresh bread made a welcome breakfast and heralded a three-hour Presbyterian service of Thanksgiving, for the plentiful harvest of fish. Mr. Houchin in his lengthy address made many references to an English preacher, John Owen who was able to inspire 2000 people at open air meetings while remaining a vicar and a Presbyterian Minister. Thus, he said, the frivolous practices of Bishop Laud and the Arminians were being refuted and the gospel would soon enfold the whole Church. As new pilgrims arrived, they would bear witness to the wonder of his words. George soon found his attention wandering from this earnest fervour to the profiles features of girls in the congregation. Sitting in a side pew, facing inward, he caught a glimpse of Sarah's face and caught her looking at him. He chatted to her briefly after the service.

This was followed by a communal meal served in the Chapel field in the bright sunlight before they went back for communal discussion on issues of public and private conduct in relation to received Truth! This pattern of activity was familiar to the boys from Jersey which, like all the islands and Cornwall was used to selecting their own preachers and Ministers of religion. Bishops appeared to have no purpose or role in community life and were never seen in Jersey. The younger people were always present and encouraged to ask about any difficult matter. On the whole they yawned and fidgeted, but nevertheless some things were of personal interest to them, especially friendship with the opposite sex which roused further thoughts, sometimes discussed with friends.

Mr. Houchin was an interesting and amusing speaker and, when the women left for home to prepare the evening meal, the men stayed on the discussion became animated with the thoughts raised by Mr. Hovel, who was an excellent debater, and a good example of the way in which heated discussion could lead to conclusions as well as fisticuffs! George had begun earlier to feel that talk could solve most problems. The unexpected

88

arrival of Mr. Jones, the ship's surgeon, and Will Love, the Apothecary Surgeon of St. John, scarcely broke the flow of words, and both of them contributed thoughtful and lively ideas drawn from their own experience. Afterwards, in conversation with Gideon, Gareth Jones explained that he had come over to refresh supplies of bandages and surgical spirit, which were running short. Some of the men were suffering from disjointed thumbs, torn ligaments in back or legs and shoulders; some personnel were being lent to understaffed ships to help them fill their holds.

"I shall be going back to the boats tomorrow, George. Seaman Hawkins would want to know whether You are learning new things."

George, somewhat embarrassed, said that he hoped he was.

"Just as well," Jones stated with mock severity. "Hawkins promises that he will test your new knowledge when he sees you next!"

* * *

"I wish I could remember the name of the tallest one. He's all arms and legs, and the tallest of them. The short one's cheerful: I can hear him laughing, but what was he called?"

"Mairi, don't stand there daydreaming! Those carrots won't scrape themselves. Are you keeping an eye on Lyall? He's gone down to the shore for samphire. Oh! Now I see! It's those boys from the ship you're mooning over. The tall one is Kit, and the jolly one is Pierre. Nice lads all of them, I think. I hope your brother will be all right: he saw them arrive and was a bit scared of them. I told him he need not be, if he kept well away. When you've finished those, you can start on the leeks.

"What did you make of them, Mairi? When I was your age, I would have favoured Kit; he reminds me of your father when I first met him. Those other carrots need scraping too! So, what do you think?"

"Noisy, clumsy and they stink of fish."

"So— apart from that, you like them! Elizabeth will have their linen in the boiler this morning. They don't have hot water on the boats. They're just over-excited, being on dry land again. Look, there go the Hovel boys, and Nick has a ball so they will be having a kick-about. If you and Ennis get dressed for school, you can go and chat to them. Of with you, now!"

"Oh, Mother!"

Morag smiled to herself hearing her daughter stamp along the passage.

* * *

Down on the shoreline a growing number of boys were arriving and taking up a position on the "field" and jostling and kicking for the ball. Already teams had formed, locals and ship boys together. Younger children ran and girls passed by them with much giggling. The players kept forgetting, their attention should be on the ball, resulting in cries of, "You missed it, Mate! You've let them score!"

When summoned by the bell, only the ship boys remained and the lads of working age: John, the butcher's son, Ed, whose father was the tailor, Vincent Houchin, and Tom, the blacksmith's assistant. They huddled, watching the tide fall, talking about the fishing, and the best local boats and bouncing flat pebbles on the waves before collapsing on the pebbles to gossip. Just before 9.00, Tom roused them, and led them to the forge where they would wait until a village tradesman arrived to take them to their place of work. They had been selected on the basis of some previous knowledge. The Smithy was, as always, the place where the men met to talk. There was beer available of low alcohol content, but

Presbyterian to a man, they were not drinkers. In the next few minutes their employers for the day collected them.

George returned to the Smith's house where his Uncle and John Smith had devised a programme for him, beginning with an introduction to the Algonkian people and their language and way of life.

"Good Day, Sir!"

"Ah, a well-timed arrival! Good day to you, young man. Your Uncle Gideon left in the cart earlier with Mr. Jones and his medical supplies. Let me find my walking stick and I'll introduce you to some old friends among the market ladies. They only speak Algonkian, but they will be pleased that you have come specially to learn their language. They always arrive early, with fresh produce, duck eggs, partridges drawn and threaded on a spit, and of course, cloth and necklaces they have woven themselves. Just bow politely and offer your name and a hand and they will tell you their names. After that try to keep up and remember the things they name and repeat them. They will be delighted. I will stand by; I may be able to help if you lose the thread— but don't count on it; I'm not very good."

Morning greeting and welcome words followed and one of the women adopted George, who was soon showing himself to be a ready learner. "You must thank her, before we go home, so say goodbye and call her *wawatseka*!"

George followed the order and the woman glowed with pleasure and gripped his hand.

"What did that word mean, Mr. Smith?"

"It means something like "beautiful woman" I think. I believe you have made a friend for life. Your good reputation will spread widely, and I hope many people will want to know you. Now, let us go home and write down some of the words which will be most useful. After some bread and cheese, we will set out for the farm. You remember meeting

91

Matthew? His parents are going to entertain you for a day or two. I gather you asked him whether there was hunting, and it seems they have scores of hares running about. Matthew has an Indian friend who is a hunter and hopes you will go out with them."

* * *

"Oh! There he is, with Mr. Smith. He's putting some beads in his pocket… George? … I've never known anyone with that name before… I think it suits him. I was so confused yesterday with everyone speaking at once and that gangling boy dropping peas everywhere, and I think he was saying something naughty, and George made them change the subject.

"Sarah was saying how much they ate this morning. The tall one had the last of the food Elizabeth had cooked— she thought there would be some left over— I asked her, was he the one called Jim? I said I couldn't remember their names, or which was which. I turned away to sweep the floor, and I know I was blushing, and she said all their names, and what they looked like. I know I was really blushing! He is George! I wonder when I shall see him again. I don't think I will be able to answer, if he speaks to me. I can hardly breathe. I hope he doesn't sail away, yet."

* * *

Smith and George set out on the slow journey to the farmhouse. They went by a small four seat wagonette, drawn by a sturdy horse. The farm had of a number of areas of cultivated land, surrounded by trees which grew in belts giving shelter from the most destructive winds. There were quite a number set out like smallholdings, planted with vegetables, though others grew crops of oats and barley. Plank bridges crossed several streams and, though they were moving inland, there were sizeable stretches of water where mallard and teal abounded. A strong bank of branches holding back a stream drew his attention, and he learned that this was constructed by beavers as their home, where fish swam to them; which seemed a convenient arrangement.

Canada geese were beginning to arrive from England where they had spent the warm winter and were arriving to enjoy a warm summer in Labrador. There were at least eight different breeds of geese and smaller ducks including gadwall, wigeon, goldeneyes and chickadee. Gannets and gulls abounded and overhead it was possible to see Golden Eagles and Osprey. Of course, he learned, they would try to trap hares and grouse or quail.

"What do you hunt at home?" Smith asked. George mentioned duck, geese and rabbits and explained that they only had a few trees because of the storms but the land was covered with small farms like theirs. "I think Jersey is a county in the west of England, am I right?"

George said it was more of an island near France, like England, but smaller. Smith was astonished, since he thought Portsmouth was at the top of England. George decided not to correct him, because he had never been in England, though he had spent long days in French and Spanish ports, waiting for the right wind to blow them home.

* * *

The sound of their approaching trap stopped Edward Smith on his progress from the stables toward the house, and he turned and stood, awaiting the arrival of his father. An affectionate greeting was extended to George, who unloaded his pack and followed the adults into the house.

"I'd welcome a bite to eat, Edward. — I would like to stay over, but I don't want to drive on a moonless night. —Ann is well, I hope. And the children?"

"We have all recovered from your hospitality, Pa. I hope Gideon finds the fishing satisfactory. Ah! Here's Matthew now. He's rigged up a bed for you in his room, George. You'd better show him the lie of the land Matt, as they say at sea. I've found a passenger for you to take back to St John— a friend of Jane's came over yesterday to admire Jane's new horse, she's grown again. They are in the stables, grooming. It will not take long so there is time for a sandwich!"

Matthew's room, at the back, had a door to the outside where he kicked off muddy boots before showing where George could hang his spare shirt.

"You will need some warmer clothing for hunting— there will be a lot of standing about — and I'll find you a pair of strong boots too. I'm taller than you, so my old things should fit you. Here —have a look at these. You may as well wear them now, then we can go out and decide where we will go tomorrow. I'll show you our animals. What kind of cows do they have in Jersey?"

A short walk round the farm buildings, where Matthew explained that the strength of the buildings was, in part, protection against bad weather but also, against wolves and wolverines. George asked whether they often attacked and was told not often: the sound of a musket was generally enough.

"We don't even have snakes in Jersey," said George. "Are bears the most dangerous beasts here?"

"The black bears are very dangerous! Best not to get in their way! They come down to the farm or the town in very cold weather when food is scarce. They have a good sense of smell and can pick up the smell of our food cooking from miles away! The worst, I think, are wolverines; they hunt in packs and never give up, and they cannot be scared off!"

As they walked to the back door, they heard the sound of girls laughing and shouting their farewells to their horses.

"That's Jane and her new best friend" remarked Matthew, with brotherly condescension. "With any luck they won't notice us. Indoors, Quickly!"

George wrenched at his boots and was staggering on one foot when Edward said, "Too late, she's seen us. Horses tucked up in bed, Jane? What have you done with your friend? She's not staying overnight, is she?"

"No. She's going to the front door. Pleased to meet you again, George. Look, if you step outside you can see her before you meet in the parlour."

Obeying her imperious instruction, George experienced a feeling of emptiness in the vicinity of his heart as he saw clearly, for a moment, the face he had glimpsed earlier.

"Come on, George," said Edward impatiently. "We are wasting good eating time. Don't just stand there. You've missed her! The trap's going."

George felt very strange as he moved across the room and changed his shirt. There was a tightness in his chest and knew he was being spoken to but could not understand. "What is wrong with me? It had felt strange enough when he had first seen her. What was this all about? What was happening to him?"

"George! I asked you if you were prepared to make an early start. What do you think? You've not heard a word I have said. What's wrong? The cat got your tongue?"

"I'm sorry," said George, making an effort to respond. "I was thinking about those guns and whether, I would be able to hit anything."

"George, I said that we would not be using them tomorrow. Remember? — We are going out at dawn to see what the traps I set have caught and check the nets for partridge. I like to put them out of their misery as soon as I can."

"Yes, of course, I remember now."

"If you are sure you are feeling well, let's go to the dining room. I want to make sure they've brought a jug of cider; I'm not allowed to drink beer yet. My father won't allow it. Do you drink beer?"

"No, it's water for me, but I'm going to be given cider this Christmas to drink the King's health."

"I'll go down to the kitchen and bring a jug of cider. We'll have some before the family come in. Wait here, this is a secret mission!"

George's eye was caught as he gazed round, by a bright picture hanging on the wall opposite the fireplace. Crossing to examine it, he found it was a tapestry of a hunt in a forest with hounds, hunters, horses and all in pursuit of a terrified hind. One of the riders looked like the girl. "I'm mad!" he thought, but was interrupted by a peremptory voice demanding:

"What was that my brother was saying about "a mission"? What cunning little plan is he devising? Don't get involved with it, George. His plots always cause problems."

"Did he say mission? I'm sorry I didn't hear it. I was looking at this picture: my uncle has one like it in his hall. It's called an Arras because that's where it was made." His words tailed off as he saw the scorn on her face.

"I suppose that's a place in England. It was given to my mother by an old English lady who used to live here. I think it looks creepy. Where do you live in England?"

"Well — I don't. I've never been there."

"Of course you have! You speak English. Ask my father to explain the countries to you. He's very clever."

Fortunately, they were interrupted by Edward Smith and his wife, Jane, who came over to greet George. As they talked, George noticed Matthew enter the room surreptitiously and place the jug on the table.

"Father tell George he lives in England, please. He says he's never been there, though he's English!"

"Jane, you do not need to shout. I hope you will believe our guest, for his home is Jersey, an English island, you see."

"So, that is what I said: he is English!" In the silence that followed, her father avoided pointless discussion, with a smile.

"Now let us sit, while your mother brings in the food, then I shall say a grace. Tomorrow I'll show you a map of Great Britain, Jane, and you will see where Jersey is. No- not now, Jane! Tell me all about your horse. Is she co-operating? Make sure you write a letter thanking your grandfather, and George will give it to him."

Chapter 8

"That was a good result, George, I may have to name you "Quick Hands"; you had the first two conies out of the snares, killed and gutted, before I'd untangled the first one."

"The first one was only a bunny and I wanted to put him out of his pain quickly."

"It was good thinking to bring gloves for wringing the necks of the pheasants— they hardly had time to start flapping. Neat work, George! You've clearly had some practice."

"It's much easier than catching and stunning a full-grown cod- or even a young one. There's nothing to get a hold on. I haven't managed to twist them into the boat yet. I think Kit will get the hang of it before we leave."

"Father will be pleased we've trapped enough for the next week and we'll hang the pheasants for you to take to my Grandmother. They rely on us to supply food for visiting traders. They will have three brace hanging in their pantry. I enjoy your company; it's always better for two to go hunting in case of accidents. Wild animals fight for their lives!"

"Will there be a chance to go hunting something wild?"

"I've been thinking about that, George. Let's go home a different way. I only go hunting with an Algonquin lad who has taught me a little about hunting. He is very good but is not allowed to attempt anything he cannot manage. His father and uncle are still training him. He often practices with his arrows in a clear place down this way. We could discuss it with him."

In the next minutes George heard a repeated "tock" sound. that he knew was the sound of an arrow striking a target.

"Don't worry. He won't shoot us: he will have heard us already!"

"Kwey, Samoset!" called Matthew and "Kwey, Matthew!" came the answer. The speaker walked across to a distant pile of logs and pulled out a long arrow before walking back to them. Slightly taller than Matthew, he thrust out a hand which Matthew grasped while they exchanged stares of friendly greeting. Matthew introduced him briefly and George seized and grasped the proffered hand and said "Kwey, Samoset", Matthew offered George's name, which was repeated with a nod of acknowledgement, before they both fell into conversation.

George realised Matthew was talking about the possibility of hunting game, and Samoset seemed inclined to dismiss the idea. After further talk, Matthew pointed to that morning's catch and described George's contribution.

"He is not happy," Matthew explained. "He may want to test your skill: can you fire a bow?"

George shrugged, knowing that he, like every boy, was expected to use a bow effectively, but wondered if it would be enough.

Samoset strode away a considerable distance and set up a log before turning back. Matthew asked him whether he had used a bow of the length he was being offered. George said his was just that size. Selecting an arrow from the quiver, he flexed the bow a few times to try the tension, then put arrow to bow and released it. He felt his finger slip, but though the arrow had fallen short, it was only a little to the left. He shrugged and taking the second arrow rubbed his fingers on his breeches, before taking aim. Again, the arrow fell short, but it was on target.

George collected the arrows and returned them to their owner. A decision had been made. Samoset would bring a shorter bow and tomorrow they would go with him to empty his nets before trying to shoot a muskrat or two, possibly a beaver. These were valued because their fur was waterproof. An early start would be essential, and silence. Before they parted, Samoset was persuaded to show his skill, and set up various targets at great distances. Each one was pierced at the first attempt. On their way home, Matthew and George agreed on signs which could be exchanged to avoid speech. They agreed that they would be safe from animal attack if Samoset was close by.

* * *

Later, while Matthew was gutting and hanging the game, George was commandeered by Jane who insisted that he should admire her new pony. At first it seemed a little nervous but with the offer of a few words and a fresh carrot, Sammy soon consented to be touched, and to seek a pocket containing treats. Jane showed him the section of field she used and demonstrated her riding skills. Asked whether he would like to try, he accepted the challenge. Picking up another carrot for Sammy he took him round. Jane seemed satisfied and suggested that they should go for a ride together on his next visit. As casually as he could manage, allowing for his increased heart rate, George asked whether her friend was a good rider.

"She didn't have anything suitable for riding", she had informed him. "Her family only settled in Plymouth a year ago and she hasn't bought a pony yet."

"She liked Sammy and helped me groom him. Her father brought her when he came to meet my grandfather. I think he is an Attorney — he came to talk business."

George concluded that she left to visit the farm before the family dinner. "What is her father's name, in case I meet him?"

100

"His name is Arblaster, my mother says it is a Norfolk name but it's very strange. Norfolk is the name of an English village. I'm glad I'm called Smith. Her first name is odd too, It's Celia. That's a poetry name!"

"Celia...", thought George, knowing he was blushing.

"Come on!" ordered Jane, "It's time for dinner!"

As dawn rose next day, they left the house eating slices of pork pie from the larder. Matthew was less than pleased to see that his sister was also awake and making her way to the stable. True to form she demanded that they should speak to her horse. As they opened the half door, Sammy's head emerged, ears pricked and looking pleased to see visitors. Jane was nudged affectionately, and George was offered a lowered head, which he stroked vigorously. Sammy nudged his side as the door was opened as an indication that a carrot would be acceptable.

Leaving Jane to muck out and groom, they made their way to the prearranged meeting place where Samoset met them, accompanied by a beautiful black Labrador. He presented George with a bow and sheaf of arrows: Matthew had his own and since no traps had been set previously, they moved off in silence to a discreet hide. A short time later George saw his first musquash and was surprised by its size when it emerged from a burrow in the bank of the stream, and plunged into the deeper water, propelling itself with its long, flat tail. It was about the size of a large cat, though half of its length was tail. Urging patience, Samoset waited, indicating that several openings which he had previously stuffed with "doors" made of plants, were really traps. Indicating that they should be ready to take aim as they emerged, He made a kill. The boys each achieved success and when a half dozen had been dispatched, sent the labrador to collect them.

Once all had been carried to a suitable place, Samoset explained that they had killed only young males not essential to the survival of the local stock. Their fur was in prime condition at that time of year and he would take them to his village where his brother would butcher them for their meat, which made fine eating despite their rank odour. The fur would be processed over the coming weeks and used to make hats, muffs and mittens. Once they were delivered to the house, and because the weather was excellent, they set out to explore the forest surroundings. Already they had heard the dawn chorus and had identified the calls of particular species, some of which they had identified by name. After some time, their guide called a halt and, facing the sun, lowered his hand into the water and shortly after they had three fine trout. George exercised his filleting skills, while Matthew lit a fire and found three large leaves. Samoset returned with a handful of nuts, fruit and leaves which he shredded. Scattering the fish with these he rolled them in the leaves and covered them in the hot ash. They enjoyed a satisfying snack before setting off on further exploration.

* * *

George was astonished by the variety of birds and animals which he saw, and their numbers. Jersey was a popular resting place for migratory birds, but the otters, caribou, muskrats and countless varieties of duck and geese amazed him. He had never seen mountains and Matthew hoped that if he returned, he might be able to see golden eagles and ospreys in flight. Over dinner, he asked Edward about the severity of winter: Matthew was surprised that Jersey rarely had snow or even frost and had remarkable amounts of warm winter weather. Winter brought heavy snow to Newfoundland, but they were near the ocean and so it rarely lasted for more than a few days. Sometimes they were briefly snowbound. However, they always laid up supplies for themselves and their vegetables were stored in clamps. Their houses had dry attics where apples could be stored, and green vegetables were bottled in vinegar.

George had expected that he and his companion working in the town, would be returning to the fish factory. Edward Smith took George on a quick tour of the farm buildings to see that they had already begun to store hay for winter feed and bedding, Apples would be picked in a few weeks and spring vegetables were being bottled that day. All house owners made the same preparations. This also happened in Jersey on a smaller scale. At worse, they could eat stock fish, which was always available. While waiting for his Uncle to arrive, George decided to go to the quay where the Indian women set up their stalls.

"Kwey, Wawatseka!" he greeted them, grinning at his own memory. His greeting was enthusiastically returned and the discussion which followed revealed that Samoset was her nephew and had spoken well of him. By gesture and repetition, George established that he had understood them. He had a small amount of cash in a pocket, and when they offered vegetables, he asked to see their beadwork. He was offered a large amount of embroidered material decorated with tasselled hems, and lengths of multicoloured beadwork. He indicated that he wanted a small amount. One of the women came to a sudden conclusion and hung a small string round her neck. George nodded an affirmative and was shown how bracelets, earrings could also be made to measure. George decided that small gifts for his mother and sister might be within his means and made a selection. They would only accept a few small coins, and, on impulse, he bought a simple but pretty necklace for his little cousin Elizabeth, after which he chose several bracelets thinking he might offer one to Celia, if they ever met again.

As he was making his fond farewells, Kit appeared at his side and, glancing at the beadwork he was storing in a coat pocket, asked with a grin whether they were for his girl in St Helier. Concealing his other intentions, he accepted the suggestion and received a slap on the back and a congratulatory, "Young rascal, ain't you, George!" Not entirely sure about that, George decided his remark was complimentary. George thought of Louise and claimed he was finding it difficult to decide which girl to choose. Kit expressed sympathy with a knowing wink and they walked round to see the others and tell them he had, "Come to catch them out idling." He pretended to be serious in his accusation before they realised that he was pretending.

"You really worried them, George. Just at first they thought you were serious!"

George was surprised. He had tried to be severe, like Gideon when he was giving his orders at the camp but decided it might be of use one day.

* * *

A few hundred yards away, new torment was being experienced.

"Oh, it's George. Please stay there talking until I get there. No- slow down! You're not to run to him like a little girl! Be dignified! It's no good, he's walking away. I mustn't run after him."

"Mother- don't shout my name like that. I don't want him to look at me now!"

* * *

Gideon found all four of them at the forge where a number of locals ate and drank during a midday "waygooze". Kit explained that this was Essex talk and meant, "a break taken during work hours with the master's permission". He interrupted their animated chatter about their new work, to say that they could continue for at least another day or two because he had business in St Johns. George would not be returning either, and they would be taking rooms with Ellen Scarlett who ran a

104

small boarding house and was an excellent cook. In due course, they made their way to the Ordinary and on the way Gideon took him to meet John Larke, the lawyer. He had a backlog of letters to write and accounts to check. His uncle thought George might seem, in the eyes of shipmates, to be leading a life of leisure and excitement, while they had demanding physical tasks. It seemed wise to let it be known that he was applying himself to boring office tasks.

He knew at once when he heard the boys talking that there was no animosity and, in fact other lads would be taking their places, in the coming weeks. In the back of his mind he was constantly aware that it would soon be mid-July. Another month and they should be loading and preparing to be ready for the strengthening south-westerlies, taking them to the Channel ports by mid-September. The harvest had been excellent and the quality second to none. Towards the end of July matters would come to a conclusion when declining numbers of fish and decreasing capacity of the ships' holds would coincide. The men would be thinking similar thoughts, he knew. Captains were even now remarking that some men would not be returning. Among the many ships which had come together, there were some who had undertaken the trip in the hope of settling in the new world, prompted by the lack of work in England, or France, or whatever their country: others wanted new opportunities and planned to bring wives and children over. Some who found the tyrannical control the Church burdensome wished for freedom to exercise their own minds and convictions.

George had no previous knowledge or experience to inform him that these problems existed and that the lives of men and women were being ruined by ideas and policies of Government beyond their control. He raised these matters one evening when he and Gideon were sitting on a timber stack by the hard, when the workers had left for home, Gideon chose to answer him. by saying that Mr. Arblaster had lost his post at the

105

church he had served for several years, because he had refused to use the new orders of service provided.

"I can't believe he could be dismissed for speaking his mind, Uncle. You wouldn't be his friend if he was a traitor, would you?"

"He wanted to stay in England for his daughter's sake, because her mother died, and his sister was willing to help to bring her up. He was instructed to leave the country, or he would be imprisoned, so he knew he must join friends in Plymouth for their own safety."

"Poor Celia- to be forced to leave her family and friends. That would never happen in Jersey, would it? Something like that happened to witches in Guernsey, when Amice was Governor, did they go to the wrong church?"

Gideon smiled sadly, shaking his head and placed his hand on George's shoulder in a sympathetic gesture. George waited, wondering whether he should not have asked.

"I will try to answer, George, though I know little more than you do. You know that there are crews from France, Spain, Portugal here as well as men from Jersey, and we all rub along together to earn a decent living- and that includes the Carterets."

George nodded an affirmative.

"You have realised that some joined us as one-way crew and will be remaining here because there is no work for them in their homelands, and there are others who like the life here so much that they have found work which is not permitted for them in England because they go to the wrong church."

"Uncle, what is the wrong church? The one here is like ours in Jersey, is that the wrong church?

"Heaven Forbid! George, you see, whatever we think, it is the Government in England that decides which is the right church and stops paying you if you attend the wrong church. Uncle Amice thought

Catholics might capture Guernsey so he thought the Witches might be Catholic and traitors, so he executed them."

"Were they like Celia's father and the people in Plymouth?"

Gideon nodded. "I will remind you of something you know but may not understand. You remember our cousins who came over from Normandy last year? Some of them went home, but most of them settled in Jersey. Before we sailed, back in February, a lot more families came over to settle and Jersey and your Uncle Philippe helped them to buy houses?"

"Yes," said George in reply to the unasked question. "Did the King make them come because they went to the wrong church?"

"Yes, George, but not our King, it was King Louis of France."

"I thought kings were to protect all their people and not let them starve. Why is this happening? Will it happen in Jersey one day?"

Gideon shrugged and suggested that George's father or Uncle Philippe were people who might know the answer to that question, because they were in charge.

George was not sure that he understood what he had heard but thought he might be punished for a wrong action, but not for what he thought, surely.

This was a time of changes happening everywhere it seemed, and although Jersey remained unchanged and unchanging, even Gideon felt that stability would end sooner or later. Their visits to French ports revealed that the Catholics were gaining political strength and locally appointed ministers of religion were being ousted by black robed Jesuit priests, imposing new forms of worship, and insisting on conformity at the risk of a prosecution. He had met and spoken to Arblaster- a thoroughly good man, who had been forced to resign by the new Bishop of Norwich, a confirmed Arminian. He had been told that he could not retain his public office and maintain views contrary to those of the

107

Bishops in Parliament. Britain was already infected. If any evidence was needed there was the sudden crop of new settlements in the new world. Plymouth, he had believed was the most recent, but only yesterday he had learned that four new settlements had been successfully established in Virginia, and, in the past three years, five others in Fort Nassau, Massachusetts, Maine and New Hampshire. Common sense told him that thousands of sensible people do not risk their lives while crossing three thousand miles of ocean on a sudden whim or for entertainment. Only fear for their lives could be the cause of such panic.

Gideon found it very difficult to explain this to someone of George's age. Indeed, he found he himself was confused. He would soon know which fishermen would be remaining behind. The return journey did not demand so many crewmen and in fact fish would occupy their place so he was already gathering impressions of how many would be leaving. He wondered what George's reaction would be at losing the companionship of men he had worked and lived with. He must try to discover what the boy liked about life in Newfoundland since it was obvious that he did.

The following day was Saturday, and the boy's work would not begin until Monday. In the meantime, John Larke met George, his new employee, and introduced his orphaned nephew, Thomas, who lived with Larke and Amy his wife, and had just become his uncle's apprentice.

* * *

George began working for the lawyer. Mostly it was simple repetitive work but there were always wrong ways to express thoughts in writing and he began to play with the many stock phrases and verbal tropes of legal English. He and the lawyer's clerk, Tom, who took on his training, got on well. It was he who mentioned that some of the older lads used to meet in the next cove to lark about there, and swim and dive when the water warmed up. As the days passed, George realised how warm the summers were, and on his next visit, swimming in lakes and rivers was possible, and families often got together for picnics on the beaches. On one of these occasions George was offering a basket of fresh rolls to friends, when he found he was speaking to Celia. His reaction was genuine surprise since he had not seen her for weeks. She said that she could remember seeing him briefly at the Smiths' house just before she left with her father to visit Canso. He asked where Canso was, and learned it was in the next bay, and founded by settlers twenty years earlier. In the meantime, there was time for trout and salmon fishing: fish of remarkable size and a finer flavour than any he had tried before, and wondrous scallops, lobsters and crabs, and so easy to catch.

Her father was now a visiting magistrate invited to adjudicate on matters on which no agreement could be found locally. Celia said that she went to be company for her father, and to satisfy her own curiosity. Her family had only emigrated to Plymouth two years before, in 1621, but a ship named Mayflower had arrived in 1620, commissioned by Essex migrants who feared dispossession for not conforming to the laws of the Church of England. Her own father had had his License to Practise removed and had crossed earlier. She was already fond of the Smiths and hoped that when they had settled in, she would be able to have a horse of her own. She thought Jane's horse, Samuel, had a fine disposition for an eleven-year-old. Since both were strangers in a foreign land, they found a common bond in sharing their new experiences of settler living.

Absorbed in conversation, they wandered far along the waterside, exploring rock pools and helping each other to scramble over the rocks. George showed her the abandoned nests of seabirds, their young having flown, and others where chicks were strongly defended by their parents. Some were birds she had seen on the Norfolk marshes, but many were new to her, and George told her of the many birds and animals he had seen with Edward on their trips in the forest. Celia was enchanted and decided that they should imagine themselves to be settlers trying to make a new home. Talk of settlement led George to speak of Samoset and the tented encampment where he and his family lived together all year round and their hunting skills and well-trained horses.

Hand in hand they shared their enthusiasm for the simple life and animals. George told her of his love for dogs and how he often wondered how Rosie, the camp Newfoundland, was in his absence. Celia told him about Princess Pocahontas, who had come to England to meet the King and some of her people in 1617 when she was a small girl. The princess had saved the life of a Captain Smith but married a man named Thomas Rolfe. They had planned to return to Virginia where there was another colony, but she said with great sadness, the princess had died before reaching home. For the last three days working on the fish, he had not seen her. George, seeing the sadness in her expression, pulled her close where they were sitting, and gave her a warm and reassuring hug. With his arm round her waist, they walked and talked, in this way on their future meetings, and the rock where they had first sat and talked, became holy as their regular meeting place.

These became more frequent as the days passed and their friendship grew. George grew to love to feel her head on his shoulder, and his arm round her waist. The scent of her hair was intoxicating and the touch of her fingers, made time pass so rapidly, though there was never enough time. Their ardour grew with the wonderful discoveries each was making about the other and knowing that there was so much more left undiscovered. They each seemed to be in a new country, filled with unexpected wonders while striving constantly for new discoveries. In their exploratory travels each seemed to take a turn. George felt that he was living in a wonderful dream in which only Celia had any important

110

contribution, Gideon noticed very soon and knew he should mention the Arblasters would soon be leaving, having completed their work.

Walking to their rock one morning, while the last of the young children made their way to the schoolhouse, George exchanged greetings with working men opening their workshops. He often went to see progress on one of the first boats being built on the nearby hard: shipbuilding being a recent enterprise sponsored by John Smith. His curiosity was roused by something different displayed on the colourful mats where the women displayed their wares. They expressed their satisfaction that they had found new things for him to admire made by their husbands for their children. He handled and examined these small but life-like replicas of seals, beaver, shell duck, quail and puffin. All made with love and understanding and each, by some magic, an individual creature. There must be space for some in his pack.

The women had their attention distracted for a moment to register another customer approaching. They nodded their approval at Celia who had come to join him. These were models of creatures she had not seen in real life, and he identified them for her, describing their actions and making their sounds. Celia was captivated and the women found others, explaining that Samoset and his friends made them "real" to improve their recognition even at a slight glimpse. George selected several as gifts for his brothers and a puffin which Celia accepted, offering a kiss in return, to the slight embarrassment of the receiver when he saw the smiling faces of the women.

Absorbed as they were, they eventually found themselves sitting on a convenient rock with no wish other than to gaze at the sea and talk. So absorbed in each other's company that it was not until Nicholas Hovel shouted their names that they realised that the party was already dispersing. On the walk back to St John, George mentioned that he would be returning to the Fair Haven on the following day. Celia was

111

unsure when they were returning to Plymouth. As they parted, Celia said how much she enjoyed his company, and planted a generous kiss on his cheek, which George returned generously, with some enthusiasm. He found himself later in the Smith house having no memory of walking there but with a feeling of great happiness.

Chapter 9

Days passed, and at the camp the hard work was decreasing, and turning fish drying in the sun, was easier than fishing. The morning meetings, with Gideon and his captains had less business to discuss. Most time was spent checking on the "ripeness" of the fish harvest for transfer to the ships. All seemed to be proceeding well, but the time was not yet: maturity and wind direction would be the decider and when it was ready, they would depart at once. Each captain recited his losses in terms of non-returners. A crew needed a balance of skills and some retainers were more ready than others to fill an unfortunate skill gap. Proposals were made but question marks were left suspended in air for the final leaving day. George and some of the younger ones hung about knowing that they would be allocated where needed.

※ ※ ※

One morning, while kicking pebbles into the sea, George was stopped by his uncle, who asked, "George, how much do you like it, here in St. John?"

"If I was here, I could go hunting any day and learn the skills of trapping and perhaps I'd be a farmer or a fur trader and sell my goods to ports down the coast. I like the people, especially the Smiths. Everyone is so kind and shares with everyone else: it's like being in Jersey but with better weather!"

"Do you like it enough to stay here forever?"

"Only if it was impossible for me to live any longer in Jersey, or perhaps England. I don't want to be told I cannot think what I want to or be criticised because of the people I go to church with."

"I don't think you like going to church; am I right, George? Do you believe that God controls our lives and everything we do?"

"I know that I cannot know another person's deepest thoughts, and that no-one can say he knows mine, Uncle. Not even you or my parents."

"What do you believe, George?"

"I know that I cannot stay here always. If I remained, I would see as little as if I spent my life in Jersey. I want to know France and Spain and even go to England. I would like to make another visit to Guernsey. I want to go to Africa and India and the lands in Hakluyt's Papers. I don't want people to ask me what I believe before I go ashore."

"I believe that is why you refused to go to University as your father wished. Do you think your father knows?"

"I think he knew that I want new places and people and that is why he allowed me to come with you. Whether he understands why, I cannot say."

"I wonder whether he knew that we might have this conversation? He used to hope that you would go to Oxford, as he and Philippe both did, but I believe you have made the right choice. I shall tell your father that is what I think, George."

* * *

The days passed, the weather remained sunny, and the temperature rose to levels hotter than any George had experienced. Farm work was over, and the harvests in. Hard work would be finished when the fall came, bringing rain to the parched earth. The Smith farm contained only those delegated to serve the daily needs of the livestock and Matthew and his sister came to stay with their grandparents. With the long summer recess, the town's waterfront became the playground of the young by day, and an area for exercise and loud conversation after the working day. Those who usually met to gossip at the forge, now took up residence in the shade of the sail lofts.

The young romped about noisily in the shallows, floating toys and dolls and needing frequent rescues or swimming lessons which were quite similar. One afternoon, Tom, the lawyer's clerk, suggested that, if George could swim, he would take him along the shore to a sheltered bay which was popular with older lads, being protected from great waves and with good rocks for diving. George was enthusiastic, and a meeting time agreed. Older ones, boys wearing cast off drawers, and girls dressed in flimsy cotton loose garments which clung to the figure when climbing, or, while in motion, formed a dangerous impediment to stability, and a threat of strangulation when wrapped round the head by a passing wave. Will, George and his increasing circle of friends played an energetic part in the eternal game of showing their skills; splashing, diving, rising from underwater to the astonishment of a screaming girl, and laughing at their angry threats with laughter and scooping handfuls of water at them before repeating the whole exercise. Like the rest of them, he abandoned the combat sometimes having chased a girl from the hazards of the water to the grassy bank, where they both lay gasping, lolling about and tickling newly exposed bodies until the teasing ceased to be pleasant.

Most of the young seemed to be there often. Members of the crews relaxed, lay in the sun and ate food served to them by the Indian ladies of the tribe or kindly housewives. Relaxing one afternoon in the shade following a water battle with Susan, George was surprised to hear Seaman Parry's voice call out:

"Ev'nin', young George. Just goin' with my young lady here, for a short walk in the woods. No harm intended, eh, my love?"

To judge by the happy giggles of the girl, no harm was taken. Again, that wink! It made him wonder what the hidden meaning was. Though, in fact he did understand when the following afternoon, meeting Celia with planned coincidence and setting out for their favourite walk, said he wanted to walk in the woods with her. The very words roused anticipation, and the answer to the question almost choked him with joy. Her serious agreement left him with scarcely enough energy to run after her among the trees.

When the younger children had been sent protesting and exhausted to bed the older ones continued, moving away from the houses where the young might be woken. The next cove had an inclined beach created for the setting up of a length of old fishing nets suspended between two poles hammered into the seabed. The boys and young men divided into teams of about ten about equal in size, the largest at the back, the lightest and quickest in front. An inflated pig bladder was the ball which each team must prevent landing on their side, or a point was scored against them. For speed and agility, most discarded the old drawers they usually wore.

There were enough to form extra teams when those playing declared a game finished when one team had scored five points more than the other. Each game over, the players retired to sprawl exhausted on the sand until their time for the next game. There was general agreement among the community that this was a boys' game played in that cove. Spectators were not encouraged, but parents, brothers and sisters and friends were often present to offer encouragement.

116

In winter, they told him, after snow had confined people to their house for many days, the first response to a calm day of warm sunshine was a community snowball battle, fought with similar rules. George knew that he would enjoy that very much though realising that it was something he would never take part in.

* * *

"Are you the lad I used to see slipping away to feed that Newfoundland that used to hang around looking for food?"

George with some caution admitted that it might have been him.

"Thought so! I'm Stubbs. Got a dog myself in England. You want to see her?"

George nodded acquiescence and Stubbs led the way to introduce him to Angus. They found him at work on a beaver skin. It was smelly work and following introductory stuff, Angus suggested that they might sit to windward for a few minutes while he finished his tidying work.

"Stubby told me you and my Beauty had hit it off while I was away hunting with my Indian pals. I gather we have friends in common, so I'll say "Kwey, George!"

"Kwey, Angus!"

"Good lad! Samoset tells me you're a neat little bowman. Plan to be a hunter, do you?"

"No, though I'd like the dogs."

"Just as well, I'd say. Sometimes I wish I had done what my dad had in mind for me, but only on bad days! Samoset says you will be in charge of the fishing fleet before long. He's been watching the way you behave with people. Now do you want to see Beauty or not?"

Angus led the way to a lean-to hut behind the sleeping quarters.

117

"Quiet here and sheltered," he said. "Surprising how delicate they are when young. Right, leave the door on the jar and come in quietly." Angus lowered his voice to say in warm tones "Hello Beauty, my favourite girl, how are we all this evening? All fit and healthy, are they? Squat you down and have look at what Beauty has given us - six lovely little pups. I think she knows your scent, come and stroke her gently, George. While you get on with that, I'll sort out some tasty morsels for her."

"Told you she took to this boy, didn't I, Angus?"

"Here you are girl, a tasty snack for a lucky lady. Now we'll slip away and let her rest."

Closing the door, they returned to their former seats. Angus explained that Stubbs had been present when she gave birth, because he had been delayed on a futile trek in the jungle which was a complete waste of everybody's time. He had heard that George had spent time with her and taken her for walks as well as feeding her. Would George like to come back and see her again when she was up on her feet and the puppies were safe? George was determined to accept the invitation. He could not imagine a Newfoundland dog on Jersey, but on second thoughts perhaps he would think about it more.

As he left, Angus asked whether he knew Mrs. Morag Menzies. George remembered the kindly woman who had plied them with food at their first meal.

"When you get back to St John, go and meet her husband, Alexander, my elder brother. His tale will be common knowledge by the time you get there, you'll see why I'm so angry to have missed the puppies."

* * *

118

With an assumed confidence, he walked slowly toward their agreed meeting place, his heart beating a little faster than usual in tune of the new assurance which typified their first moments after meeting, almost as though, in their absence, each had in their heart made a new assessment, taken new soundings of words and motions, and had reached a new set of conclusions. In their minds each reached a mutual understanding of personal morality and had taken several steps forward in understanding their relationship. Words saved in reserve could wait for the next meeting. It was as if they had somehow moved on during the past hours and time was standing still, the centuries poised, waiting for the new unplanned events.

Celia, appearing unexpectedly at his side, took his hand with a smile, saying,

"Shall we go this way and along the cliff top? We could walk back along the beach if you like."

He agreed that anywhere would be good; simply to be together again was all he could wish for, and she seized him and gave him an affectionate hug.

"Why did you come from that direction?" He asked, hoping, as he said it, that he had not sounded aggressive.

"I thought it would be a nice surprise and confuse any spies. Are you cross?"

"No," he said, "just surprised." He added; "I was looking forward to seeing you walk towards me; it gives me such pleasure to see you move."

"Perhaps we can run time backward and I will go back and start from the house."

They laughed at the thought, and she explained that she had unexpectedly changed her house, her father being delayed once more by something unexpected.

The light glinting among the late summer leaves, created blinding flashes of sunlight illuminating the unexpectedly beautiful and iridescent tail feathers of a bird perching on the branch of a tree neither could identify. A colourful feather floated down, and George offered to twine it in her hair, as an excuse for stroking it.

Later he decided to tell her about the puppies: a story surely designed for them to share, which he thought she would like to hear.

Wrapped in each other's arms, George began to tell tale of the reunion with this wonderful creature who had made his life of the camp so agreeable. He had only begun to mention his meeting with Angus, when she moved her finger to his lips and murmured, "And he showed you a dog and six wonderful little puppies," and laughed, as though she was humouring a baby. A chill entered his heart, and he stopped, started, and drew back. Her tone of voice seemed wrong: almost dismissive, as though she was bored. He felt diminished by her tone and was silent.

"What is wrong? Is it pins and needles?" George tried to recapture the moment, since he no longer felt aroused, as he often did when they were together. It was over: the moment was spoiled.

"I'm sorry if I spoiled your story, but I heard it last night when Angus came to his brother's house, where I am living for the time. You won't be able to take a puppy with you; it won't be old enough to feed itself. Poor you! I expect you will see her again, so there's something for you to look forward to, if you come here again."

Once more her tone of voice was patronising. He feared she was about to add, "But you won't see me again, if you return!"

Walking on, he knew they were both making an effort to talk as usual, until Celia drew back slightly before remarking, "I saw you last night." George was about to say he saw her every night, when she said;

"Don't look so puzzled. I mean that I saw you playing ball in the cove. You are a good player- and you are so very beautiful. I haven't any

120

brothers of course, but I thought you were more beautiful than the other boys." She paused and noticed his expression.

"I'm so sorry! I shouldn't have said that, I suppose. I'm so embarrassed. I must run! They'll be wondering where I am. Oh! Why can't men see what is important and are only excited by such silly trivial matters?"

George walked slowly after her toward the town. He remembered having heard someone saying, "Oh! It's only a lovers' quarrel" Could that be what had happened to them? Were they lovers? So many questions which he could not answer?"

* * *

Someone unexpectedly flopped down on the grass beside him and, thinking it might be Celia, he turned, but It was Kit, lying back turned toward him... He heard him sniff loudly and moistly before he decided to ask the accustomed question when a friend was distressed, "Are you all right?"

With another loud sniff, Kit dashed a hand over his face, as he shook his head, finally regaining enough breath to speak.

"George, I need your help. I don't know what to do. I'm in such a mess. I feel as though I'm falling into a deep pit. Help me sort it out."

"I'm not the right person to ask, Kit. I've got problems of my own! I'm afraid you've chosen the wrong man."

Regretting his abruptness, immediately, George began again.

"No, I'm sorry, Kit. Tell me what's wrong."

"I don't want to go back to England, George. I came over on the Welkin and it's leaving in a few days."

"Why don't you want to go; it's your country, isn't it?"

"No! Not anymore! I ran away from it, George!"

121

George heard him inhale a deep breath end in a sob and asked him why.

"Girls!" exclaimed Kit. "I'm having trouble with my Suzy. I reckon we are in the same boat, George; I saw your Celia shouting at you before she ran off. A pity to lose her: she's a real beauty. What did you do? I saw you were fixing your lace."

George saw his look of sympathy and decided not to respond. While George lay recovering, as though from a painful punch, he was trying to adjust to this new state of being. He was not sure whether it was fatal or only temporary. Rejection, he found, could cause physical discomfort.

Kit had neither home nor family, he explained. His widowed mother had remarried when he was ten, and Kit was a superfluous elder brother. Several half brothers and sisters were born, and money became tight. Kit was stable boy to a city merchant, and when he became bankrupt, Kit had no chance of work following years of poor harvests. His stepfather suggested that, for the sake of his family, he should go to seek work in the Channel ports.

Dejected and angry, he set off declaring he would not return, ever. His mother and siblings were sad to see him go, which caused him greater grief. Unsuccessful in one port after another, he walked one morning down towards Deal, where he was set on and captured by Barbary pirates, who were raiding the coast unhindered. He woke to find himself bound hand and foot in the hold of an Arab dhow with a half dozen others. Their captors fed them and told them they would live good lives in Morocco, where European boys were popular servants. They made clear by word and gesture the reason for their popularity and value. They were certain to make their owners happy!

Two nights later, their ship was surrounded, under cover of darkness, by three other pirate vessels. After a fierce and bloody attack, their captors were put to the sword and flung overboard, and the hull stove

122

in. The boys were taken aboard a new ship and two days later were landed in Dunkirk, a Spanish port, controlled by English privateers. Taken under duress to the market cross, they were lined up with the out of work, and offered employment in exchange for a small down payment. Kit pleaded a pressing need for a necessary house and, while his escort lit his pipe, sneaked out and ran for freedom.

By this time, Kit was more cheerful, and sat up for the first time. A look of consternation on his face, he enquired about George's problem. He had sat up too, to change his position,

"Terrible things these nice girls do to a man, ain't it George. When they turn on you that way and you're feeling your luck is in, it's like a knee in the belly, ain't it. I'm lucky with my Suzy, though."

George, though, ignored this and told him to make a rapid end to his story.

"Luck was on my side," Kit continued. Hiding among the stalls, Kit was greeted by an attractive kitchen maid who asked him what he was looking for. Kit bluntly said it was food he needed and was handed a hot roll and a warm smile. He ate it ravenously and stepped forward to bow and kiss her hand. Marie blushed at the courtesy, then burst into laughter as he fell down a step, lost his balance, and sat in a heap of vegetable refuse.

At this point he had to warn George that he could stop sniggering at once, or he would punch his nose. Kit completed his story while they both picked up stones to chuck at the waves, which became a competition.

"So, did you and Marie…?"

"Whose story is this? It's none of your business!"

Marie took him to the accountant's house, where she cleaned and cooked three days a week. There he was cleaned up and fed by the housekeeper, while the master left his office to pay his two employees.

He showed much sympathy with Kit's story and asked whether he was good with figures- for he was in need of an apprentice. At first Kit was inclined to accept the offer, but the housekeeper shook her head as she caught his eye and said, unfortunately her husband had found Kit work at the sawmill. The accountant expressed disappointment and returned to his desk.

Kit was informed that her employer was trying to find a young man to satisfy his particular requirements. Kit did not need to be told what was implied.

There was a pause while Kit offered to explain what she meant. George said it was unnecessary. Finally, Kit reached the end of his tale and seemed to have calmed down. The tale was reaching its end.

There was no place at the Mill where he worked, and the Welkin needed nimble servants. He was taken on and received a small advance, enough for food until the ships sailed for St. Aubyn. This was how he had come to Jersey and become a fisherman.

"Kit! What is the point of this? Why can you not return to England. What have you done to annoy Suzy?"

"Don't you see, George? I'll look a fool if I go home and, it will break my heart if I have to leave Suzy and her parents, who are very kind. I can't work in the carpenter's shop: I can't even plane a plank properly. Everything else I try, I either break or fall over! I'm useless and clumsy and stupid, and Suzy loves me, and I love her, but I've got to earn a living. I'm at my wits' end, George. You are really clever; you amaze me! Help me! What shall I do?"

More stones were thrown; both of them now at the water's edge. "He must be two years older than me." George reflected. "What can I say? It's all about money, people and a place to work." He began talking to fill the silence.

"When I was about seven, we lived in St Helier and there were older boys leaving school to go to work. Of course, they were missed at first, but we eventually filled their places. My family moved a few miles inland to live on a farm and I made new friends at a different school. I sometimes went back to the town with my father and met old friends and I was surprised we had all grown taller! Last year I went back again after four years and met some of them. I didn't recognise my best friend, Ned, until my father pointed him out. He said, "Have you fallen out with your old friend?"

"I gazed around, the only person I could see was a big lad, about six-foot tall with broad shoulders and heaving a huge plank of wood like it was a feather. He sawed it down the middle and made two perfect planks.

"Yes," said my father, "that's old Ned. Come and have a word with him. He's going to run his own team in a month or so!"

Kit stood open mouthed. "Are you talking about me, George?"

"I'm saying we are all of us growing still and learning new things most days. We all grow, don't we? Why not wait and see what you change into? People like you and me are given lots of chances in life."

"I hope Suzy will still love me if I get that big!"

"Another point, Kit. When this trip ends, we all get paid. How much, depends on what we earn, but we'll all be weighed down with coin. Our fishermen live on their earnings on the Banks during the winter months, and we don't starve on Jersey. I think you should return with us to get full pay, then go to see your mother and brothers and say a proper goodbye, otherwise they will be anxious. Then you can pay for lodging while you work."

"My ship is going back to Dunkirk. I want to go to England."

"You should go to your Captain and tell him you want a transfer-lots of men are doing it. You could speak to Captain Carteret: there

125

might be a place on a Jersey ship and there is work in our shipyards because we are building more ships."

"What about my Suzy?"

"Well! she's only thirteen. She'll wait for you till next year and you'll be bigger and stronger then and then maybe you'll find work here."

Kit flung an arm round George's shoulder saying, with a cheerful grin, "Well, it's worth a try. Come on, mate! I'll treat you to a cider."

Chapter 10

Home at last, tired, confused and restless, George concluded that since rest was impossible, he would distract and centre his mind by opening his journal. It ran already to some length for, though he had been engaged in so many activities, he had written brief details of several days at a time, whenever he had leisure. The dog and the swimming he recorded briefly and mentioned Kit's reservations and his grief at his parting with Celia and hope that a reconciliation would follow if time allowed.

That and other mundane issues left him some time to write and, with increased calmness, he began to play with words and feelings as one does. Sometime later he found a page covered in several directions with words and phrases and clumsy rhymes and Celia, written large and small with curlicues and in beribboned boxes and began to sort the ideas. "Your lips and loving heart" rhymed well with "warmth of your tender parts" and there were other references and phrases which he used at first before putting them aside as dubious reading by a parent or friend e.g. "the gentle touch of your warm hands" or "the glowing beauty of your breast".. Further effort produced something less explicit, (though he might perhaps show her his first thoughts later!) At some opportunity he thought he might slip a package, containing the poem and a gift bought, into her hand. He copied it out and re-reading it, decided it needed further work;

Celia's Coronette.

This trivial gift you graciously receive
For it is kindly given:
These gaudy beads do not deceive-
Their tints are those of heaven.
Truth, Faith and Eternal Love presenting.

Their filaments entwined are ties that bind our hearts:
When doubt and danger stir your fears
Know they will form a stronghold firm
And strengthen you and dry your tears.
Saving you from all harm.

"Well", he thought, "my mother might regret forcing me to read Michael Drayton's poems. Fortunately, she will never see it!"

* * *

He and Gideon made a rapid end to dinner on the unexpected arrival of a small deputation consisting of Mr. Smith, Mr. Larke, the Lawyer, Alexander Menzies the fur-Trader, and, to his consternation, Mr. Arblaster. However, the latter shook hands with his usual firmness, so George decided that the anger Celia had displayed, had not been displayed at home.

Over cheese and cider, a difficult situation was discussed concerning the behaviour of the surly Businessman, Mr. Gregory Spalling. He had recently returned from an expedition into the interior of the island in the interests of scientific knowledge. Menzies went as tracker, with Samoset's father as assistant and provider of what Spalling referred to as "bush fare". No expense was to be spared and a half dozen sailors were engaged to carry scientific equipment, heavy packages of scientific paraphernalia, tents and tables and chairs, for examinations of specimens.

* * *

Despite the advice offered, that the best areas were towards the small northern settlements, Spalling insisted that they would go inland, then south towards the headland referred to on sea charts as Burin Head, at the end of a long peninsula. He was not concerned when told that there was little there and said an expert eye and judgement might show otherwise. Since they were well rewarded, they gave him his head.

The area was inhospitable and thrashed by rain and gales despite constant sun. They made regular pauses while Spalling, armed with hammer and chisels, collected rock and vegetation samples which were examined on the tables and, in the main, cast aside. Some were added to the loads. Spalling seemed impervious to rain and cold. Casting about with his hammer and a telescope, he commanded that a tall contraption fitted with blank boards and polished sheets of copper be erected. When the sun rose, he began complex adjustments so that mirrors flashed their light across the sea. There was much consultation of a book of tables. When Menzies questioned him, he was told he was developing a warning device for ships at sea where rocks were hidden.

Menzies and the sailors felt that since sunlight was essential, it would not work in poor weather, but it could be used to send messages to ships at sea. Menzies knew that beyond the horizon were the St. Pierre and Miquelon Islands, where the French had set up a fishing base. Menzies

129

reported these matters to Smith, with his suspicion that the French might be planning to establish a base to rival or capture St John. He and Arblaster confronted him with their suspicion which Spalling forcefully denied, though he admitted that it might encourage French ambitions.

"Was not competition to be encouraged in trade and business?", he enquired. "I have always believed it was so!"

George offered to leave the room, but Gideon indicated that he should remain. Mr. Houchin, his landlord, remarked that Spalling paid his rent, and attended prayer meetings regularly; he had no reason to complain. A silence followed then Menzies spoke.

"I am convinced that he is devious and unconcerned about endangering our interests, thinking only of his own advantage."

"That in itself is not a crime," Gideon remarked. "Mr. Arblaster. Can you see any possible infringement of the law? Is there a treasonous act in preparation? He said that he was attempting to send warning signals, whereas a lighthouse might be more useful, or a warning cannon to be fired. French "M'aidez" for example. Can flags spell out, "Land here: there are no rocks? George. You have heard him and worked for him; what do you say?"

"I think he cares little for others or their opinion and disregards the advice offered by Michael Ramsey, whom he overrides on all occasions. His trial of the clocks for use in navigation is a good one. The signalling cannot work unless the French have knowledge of his purpose. If they wanted to land invading forces, for which they would need good weather, prearranged flashes of the mirrors could indicate whether or not the landing attempt had been seen."

Another break was called while Mrs. Smith brought in small, hot pancakes. Gideon took Arblaster to one side, to return brushing sugar from his cravat.

"I have a proposal that, as a safeguard, I should take Spalling to Plymouth with his signalling material, where expert scientists can assess his work. Ramsey will return with Carteret and the clocks to complete that exercise to his satisfaction. Spalling is a wealthy businessman and the Royal Society are paying for his Time experiment."

There was general approval, and Arblaster proposed to escort him to Plymouth in two days" time. The meeting ended, they retired for the night.

"George," his cousin exclaimed, "tomorrow I am going to buy new linen and shirts for myself and you are coming with me for the same purpose. No. Do not argue! Mrs. Smith says that the laundry woman refuses to attempt to clean your shirts and - look - the back is splitting! You are growing like a beanstalk: three inches in the last two months, I think, and your chest is stretching your shirt to bursting. As for your backside! - Your breeches are about to burst their seams and the codpiece hanging by a thread is as bad. You're a growing lad and need more room for comfort and unexpected stress. You take my meaning, I'm sure."

Grinning sheepishly George peeled them off and leaped into bed.

"Good. So tomorrow you say goodbye to your stinking gear and stop looking like a dockside urchin. Your observation concerning the state of French awareness, was helpful. I have been thinking about our discussion about right and wrong churches. I still cannot answer your question and I don't think there is a plain answer. Beliefs seem to swing from one extreme to another and are different in different places. Best I think, to avoid taking sides, but fit in with what people expect of you. I feel sure that we share the same deep convictions about the best way to live. I enjoy talking to you and our host thinks highly of you: so, of course do all the girls."

* * *

Woken by the sounds of carts moving in the streets, George remembered Celia would be leaving the next day. They had not arranged to meet, but he decided that he would walk casually in the direction of their rock. She might be looking for him; he hoped she was. Breakfast eaten, George left the table, Gideon reminding him that their departure was to be soon after nine. Passing a hand over his hair and brushing at his clothes, he hauled up his breeches and went down to the waterfront. Only small boys were there, so he kicked a ball about with them, before wandering down the shoreline.

Reaching their familiar rock, George looked back and around, but there was no sign of her. He felt deflated and guilty. He was wrong to tell the puppy story and should have asked her what she had done that day, or said he was pleased to see her. Oh! How pleased he had been! He sat for a few minutes chewing at a split fingernail and decided to return to their lodging. Close to the Smith's house he thought he might see Matthew, but he did not appear. It was Jane he saw leaving the house. Seeing him, she changed direction swiftly and smilingly began to regale him with Sammy's latest accomplishment, and her earnest wish that he would come to see for himself. George congratulated her on her skills and learned that Matthew was down at the fish sheds with his father.

Time was moving on, and Gideon would ask why he was so late. On impulse he asked Jane if she would do a small errand for him. The girl blushed, and he asked her to go the Menzies' house and deliver a package for him. She smiled and agreed at once. took it and walked off, saying goodbye. They went their separate ways and Gideon appeared at the door as George arrived. Jane in the meantime had read the address, "For Celia", and her face crumpled: She walked on, eyes streaming, but had recovered before reaching the house. The door was opened by Lyall, who Jane did not like. He said he would deliver the package and closed the door.

"Where is Celia?" he shouted.

"Out on the beach," his sister replied.

"Will you give Celia this package when you see her, Ennis? Tom is waiting for me to go to school. I must go."

Ennis silently fled to her room and, having read the label, flung herself on the bed and sobbed and sobbed.

"Whatever is the matter with the girl?" the mother asked the furniture, as she collected the plates. Outside, another lovelorn lass crept to a quiet place behind a boat and cried as though her heart would break. In the meantime, George was being sized up by the tailor for two pairs of breeches and two sturdy linen shirts. While they were there, he inserted a gusset in George's old breeches and cobbled his shirt together. His new clothes would be ready in a day or so and in the meantime, he could wear his favourite old ones.

"If you are going to the cove for a ballgame later, enjoy it, for we will be leaving shortly if the wind holds while we load. Stay a moment. Have you been offering advice to some of your friends? I've had several lads asking to join Fair Haven. I have accepted them, but we cannot take any more; I have no wish to run a naval training school. Also, Seaman Hawkins wants you to know Cabot's Principles. He means to test you and see that you put them into practice."

Chapter 11

Approaching the familiar rock on his way to the cove that evening, he saw Celia was there and smiling warmly. As he approached, running to her now, she fell into his arms. Their relief was almost overwhelming, but at last they subsided onto their rock, to draw breath. They had found their separation intolerable, and now the time left was unbearably brief. Celia would be leaving early next day for Plymouth, with her father and the pompous Mr. Spalling. George mentioned he would be leaving for England at any day. A wave of mutual sorrow and regret swept over them as they promised undying love with more kisses and fevered embraces.

George, however, was unable to ignore the approach of his swimming friends and, to save her possible embarrassment, took a fond farewell. As an afterthought he asked whether Celia had received his gift, which had not been mentioned: he intended to emphasise his deep feeling for her, if it was so, and say that he would never forget her.

To his surprise she said that she thought it was a joke!

"If it was serious you have a strange idea of gifts. What would I do with a piece of Indian filth? It might carry an infection!"

Taken aback, he made the point that its true value was explained in the poem, and that only they, together, would understand its full meaning. Celia appeared puzzled, then asked who wrote it and what it meant.

"No! Don't bother to tell me, George. Life is too short, and we will be leaving at 10.00 tomorrow," she said, and added, "If you want to say goodbye properly, I'll probably see you if you come to wave us off."

As he walked away, stunned, she smiled and gave a friendly wave.

Pausing for breath later, between matches with his swimming team, he noticed that Celia was sitting talking with her friends on the bank; she turned and waved to him.

* * *

The following morning, he was walking back to their lodging and noticed the passenger cart waiting outside the Menzies' house. Hesitating, while he decided whether to wait to see them off, or go on his way, he saw Celia emerge from the house, escorted by Mrs. Menzies and her daughters, carrying a number of curiously shaped packages. Noticing him, Celia gestured that help would be appreciated. Walking forward, he almost collided with Edward Smith, advancing with the same intention. However, it was Mairi Menzies he went to, leaving George free to assist Celia. He and Edward stood waving side by side as the cart rolled away. Celia had merely said goodbye while climbing in beside her father.

"Mairi and I are thinking of getting engaged, George. I see you have made a friend of Celia; she seems a quiet girl. Have you noticed that Ennis is giving you friendly glances, George? I thought you might have got to know her better; I know she likes you! Don't forget your Uncle and the fleet will be leaving any day."

The time for departure had come. Two days had been sufficient to get the ships loaded and crew members redistributed among the ships. At any moment they would be sailing, the larger ones mingling among the smaller boats, to lend possible support in any emergency that might arise on the two-thousand-mile return trip. He and Pierre were now to be regarded as Midshipmen, though on such a small boat, it was only an honorary post. It meant that they could now take their place as crew members, expected to search out occasions for using initiative rather than waiting for instructions.

Kit came up to him later to say that he and his girlfriend had reached an agreement, and he was going back to see his family.

"Saw you waving goodbye to that Celia, George. That'll give all your other admirers a clear field. Good luck to you. What have you got that I haven't?"

* * *

Seaman Hawkins made it clear to them that he knew their activities in St John and praised them for their efforts. Then, as Gideon had warned him, he was questioned on his knowledge of Cabot's Ordinances. Sebastian Cabot, son of John Cabot, had been responsible for the discovery and settling Labrador as a British territory, as authorised by Henry VII. On his second voyage he mapped the coast from Nova Scotia to Newfoundland and laid claim to Canada. The finance for this trip was provided by a wealthy Bristol merchant, Richard Ameryk, and subsequently references to as "America" naming the continent after its sponsor, on 24 June 1497, St. John's Day.

Cabot became "Governor of the Mystery and Company of Merchant Venturers" and issued his ordinances in 1553 for the guidance of merchants and future explorers. George was well versed in these precepts from his study of Hakluyt. When Hawkins asked him to recite the third precept, he and Pierre were able to say "a fleet shall keep together" unless driven apart by weather. The Company operated out of London.

* * *

The first part of their trip went well. George commented on it in his logbook. A week later he wrote,

"a mist rose which seemed to increase as we sailed easterly. After another day, Tuesday, at south west sun, we thought that we had seen land; which afterwards proved to be a monstrous heap of ice. Within a little more than half an hour after…. we were enclosed within it before we were aware of it, which was a fearful sight to see: for, within the space of six hours, it was as much as we could do to keep our ship aloof from one heap of ice, and bear room from another, with as much wind as we might bear a course."

They escaped somehow without harm and went on their way. None of the men had seen ice bergs on the return the previous August. More danger was to come for on 15 August, St Mary's Day, an enormous whale rose to swim alongside the Fair Haven.

"It was so close that it was within a sword's length of the port side. The creature was perhaps the length of our ship and might, if it chose to, swamp and overturn our boat. There was considerable fear for if it suddenly rose up our vessel would be immediately overwhelmed. My Uncle Gideon saved us with an unlikely plan which, hearing him in discussion with Mr. Tull on the best course of action. I remembered that in a similar situation, Hakluyt had reported, that a Captain had resorted to noise and shouting. I showed my uncle Hakluyt's words in my book.

137

My uncle ordered the crew on deck and gave orders that they were to stamp and shout. The noise made him depart, to our great relief, and his back rose up out of the water as high as the width of our ship. As he dived, he made such a terrible noise in the water that any man would greatly have marvelled.

My uncle commended me for my knowledge of Cabot's words and Mr. Hawkins, who had been surprised that I knew several of Cabot's Principles by heart, applied himself with renewed vigour to our training. Pierre, seemed to be a receptive student, and, in confidence, stated that he had decided on a naval career, though he feared that his father wanted him to be a farmer. I remembered that Pierre had two younger brothers and kept it in mind. I asked him if he had thought of being an artist: he spent his spare time drawing.

Together we learned the use of the Quadrant and how to interpret its sightings, Hawkins giving us daily examinations. Similarly, he taught us to read the skies and clouds as forecasters of weather, and to judge which protective measures were appropriate, and to assess the speed of the wind. We learned to take soundings when we came upon headlands or islands and stood by the helmsman and learned to make measured judgements.

In addition, we assisted Mr. Ramsey, who was determined to bring the Timing Experiment to a successful conclusion and our ship's clock found to be in accord with English time as well as could be estimated in Falmouth, or wherever we made landfall. His Uncle was as keen as Ramsey that the Royal Society should be encouraged to make further trials, using his experience. He, Gareth Jones, the surgeon, his uncle, Pierre, Mr. Tull, Hawkins, and any of the crew at leisure, formed a small University of the sea, learning and sharing knowledge with Hakluyt's book as a Primer."

* * *

The remainder of their voyage was relatively uneventful, though they had to contend with storm force winds as they entered the Channel approaches, which provided a welcome coldness for the preservation of their cargo. Channel gales safely negotiated, they sailed at last into Falmouth Harbour where the Fair Haven unloaded most of its cargo. The other vessels made for St Helier or other coastal ports where orders for cod had been placed.

"Our ship and two others delivered stockfish to Penzance, Plymouth, Dartmouth, and some to Lymington, before making the Channel crossing to Jersey. Assembling finally at St Aubyn, our own fish were unloaded. The other ships had already sailed off to their destinations on the Normandy and Brittany coasts, and as far south as Porto. Broad agreement had been made between the Captains that the trip would be repeated the next year."

Pierre went home to help with the grain harvest and to rake up vraic for manure, on the family farm, and Kit joined the men working on the Rope Walk, work which Elie had found him, and where he was happily employed. Ships not propped up on "legs" for repair, were at sea once more: the salted fish divided, and the proceeds allocated among the crew. George went home with a leather pouch laden with the gold he had accrued, and firmly resolved that he would return to the Banks next year, now demonstrating his newly acquired skills in their normal Channel fishing. Kit was happy and would return to Jersey after visiting his family. Conveying goods and produce between the islands, and English ports, George might learn more about Falmouth and Cornwall and renew his friendships. Above all he intended to show his father that he would be able to command his own fishing boat and crew within the next few years.

He made a point of thanking Hawkins and spoke to his father of the man's excellent qualities and asked if he could be given some financial support in his wish to join the Royal Navy. He would need to find sponsorship, financial and influential, to take his exam and find employment. Carteret's influence and opinion were beginning to carry some weight and might be used in his favour. Elie listened, and agreed to give serious consideration to George's request.

George was welcomed with tears of joy by his mother and loud and boisterous greetings by his brothers and sisters. The small gifts he had wrapped in oiled paper at the bottom of his backpack, were distributed, including a beautifully woven headband for his mother and bead rings and bracelets for his sisters. Small wood and bone carvings of puffins, seals and fish were admired and played, with and his stories of hunting and fishing were received with open-mouthed wonder. His mother was concerned about the condition of his linen and noticed that he was already growing out of the trousers made for him in St Johns. His father turned George's face to the light and claimed that he had the beginnings of a beard which, when he inspected his own face later, he found to be true, though it was only a few whiskers!

* * *

A day or two after his return, George made a visit to St Ouen where he was eager to say how much he had enjoyed being involved in the fishing fleet.

"I have to admit, George, that Anne and I were fearful that you might come to harm on the trip. I'm delighted to see how well you look and how much you have grown. Your shoulders are broader and you have developed a sailor's rolling walk. If you have made some sketches, may I see them?"

"I was afraid that we might have bullied your parents into a change of heart and be blamed for any harm you suffered. I was sure you knew what you wanted to do, would go well for you. Do you still want to join the Navy?" asked Anne.

"I'm more certain than ever I was. I've decided not to go next year because I am not strong enough yet to take on all the fishing and filleting, I hope I shall be more able after two years."

"That seems to be a sound idea. It would bring you to the right age to try the Lieutenant's tests. What will you do next year, George?"

"I thought I would work for matriculation with my brother and spend time gaining wider sailing experience and perhaps helping father with his work; he is Attorney General and has to spend too much time building stone walls. He might let me do some of that with some of the lads who have no work."

* * *

"So, Lizzie, what do you make of George? Hasn't he grown! I think he is going to be a handsome man before long!"

"Oh, Anne! He's so thin, he looks half starved: I shall have to feed him up or he won't survive, handsome or not. And the state of his clothes....! Quite disgusting. I'm surprised Gideon allowed him to go about with his clothes in rags. What must people think?"

"He will recover, Lizzie! Before you know it, he'll be looking for a wife: the girls will be all over him!"

"Anne! How can you say such things?"

"Would you rather he didn't marry? Surely you don't want him tied to his father on a leading rein like Prince Charles. He must be twenty-five and still no sign of a wife. Of course, most of the Princesses abroad seem to be Catholic, and therefore enemies, but it didn't stop his father. I expect he will have to settle for a Duke's daughter, if he can find a wealthy one. Perhaps Winchester has a young grand-daughter; I must ask Rachel; she's bound to know."

* * *

George also became an increasingly valuable crew member on fishing and commercial trips, he gained a number of new acquaintances in the wider community and developed new friendships. Gaiches and Robert appeared together on the day after his arrival and James Pallot, and Hion Storace, who had served on Fair Haven with John Merson, Dick Archer, Hugh Mallet, Jean Du Quesne, all local and shipmates. Their friendship led to them becoming regular crew members in his future exploits, as well as others whom he had known from earlier in his childhood. By the next spring, George was given charge of a boat and chose his own crew, He began to spend leisure hours at the Broad Street house, and enjoy the company of the younger citizens of the port and to appreciate the grim determination to survive on the narrow range of produce gained only by hard and unrelenting labour by men, women and even children. The young seized any opportunity for enjoyment though it was limited to Saturday and Sunday evenings after church. In his spare time, he worked with his brother on Latin textbooks and satisfied his father that matriculation was certain, if he wanted to pursue that way of life. He was quite certain he did not!

George began to be welcomed on board other ships as a reliable team member. Many of the Jersey boats were under Carteret ownership, but over the following months a hierarchy evolved headed by George and Hugh Mallet. The Mallets owned several parcels of productive land and were also traders. They were the first to see what needed to be done and George's sheer energy seemed to have no end. This was the source from which came the tremendous drive and qualities of leadership which led him to the great Offices of State, and the friendship of a King.

Chapter 12

In the meantime, the returning mariners found that the normal everyday tasks of exacting food from the stony soil of Jersey had to begin again, or there would be nothing but fish to eat. Stones had to be gathered and heaped along the sides of fields so that crops could be planted. Potatoes and turnips were the principal root vegetables, since both helped to increase the fertility of the soil, and animal manure was never sufficient in quantity. From every farm, carts drawn by donkeys, made their repetitive way to the beaches. Particularly after storms, banks of seaweed were built up by the waves, and left behind, soggy with sea water, and giving a pungent odour of iodine, a material named "vraic". It was raked up and loaded onto the carts and taken to the farms where it was spread of the soil to rot away until the time came to plant the new crops.

Everything had to be dragged from a reluctant soil and stored for winter, where possible in barns, and apples came ready for harvest to be taken to the cider presses on each farm where the cider press would crush them under heavy wheels propelled by overworked donkeys. In the quarries, men would be performing the backbreaking work of detonating gunpowder to break up slabs of granite into usable blocks for building: a granite of a comparatively warm brown colour, pleasing to the eye. It was the season for shellfish, and boats went out into the shallow waters to collect the harvest of lobsters, crabs and ormers which awaited them.

At the first opportunity there was a family gathering at St. Ouen Manor. George's Uncle, Sir Philip had recently returned from London and the Court and Anne, his aunt, were as genial as ever. Young Philip was eager to show George how well he could ride but was happy to have George walk by his side, occasionally adjusting the reins! Elizabeth greeted him with the hugs and kisses of a two-year-old and insisted that he must carry her and her doll and entertain her. George, and his brothers, Philippe and Reginald played endless ball games and hide and seek and George instigated the idea of building a tree house, with a ground floor for those not ready to climb a ladder, and an upper floor for the more agile.

Sir Philip played a full part in the provision of materials and in the construction: these skills were second nature to most Carterets, and from the outbuildings, planks and ropes were brought into service for swings and for climbing trees. Amice and Catherine de Carteret of the Trinity Manor de Carterets, joined them, their son, Philippe, and Joshua, his cousins. Although there are at least four Philippes, the titles "Uncle", "Grandson" and "Cousin" generally prevented confusion and cemented relationships across the generations. When those failed, there were the familiar epithets which several had received in childhood, Gideon was always "Tiny", though over six feet in height, and Sir Philippe was happy to be addressed as "Reynard". The avoidance of the name came as something of a relief and "Sir" and "Dame" were terms reserved for formal occasions, unless a reprimand was uttered!

They were a close-knit family and known as such, generally with approval, though they were at times accused of nepotism; perhaps that was only to be expected. On the whole the family attempted to avoid causing offence. The Carteret young had been marrying into local families for generations so that there was a complex web of relationships in existence, and among them were the de Geht family, the Hamptonnes, the Piports, la Cloche, Pipons, Demaresques, and Morlais families: all closely related. Looking around, Philippe was happy to note that all

145

those present were equal in influence and shared a virtual financial parity: that there was a common feeling of mutual interest and ambition, which he hoped to protect and increase.

Other guests given a warm welcome, were landowners, fellow Councillors, and Jurats. Sir Philippe was conscious that his good fortune might be a cause of envy, and on this occasion, he spoke to them about his wish to invest in the enterprises of others for the benefit of the island. St Helier would benefit from providing a higher standard of accommodation for visiting traders, and main thoroughfares might be improved by paving. Public buildings needed improved facilities and their improved status, demonstrated by two storied homes with separate accommodation for animals and storage. Thus, agricultural growth could result. He proposed to make a start on the homes of his tenant farmers in the near future.

If George harboured any doubts regarding that assertion, the events of the following weeks would have dispelled them. His father surprised him mentioning events and problems of local significance, asking whether he could give thought to the matters raised. His opinion was even sought on farming and farm management issues, and he was introduced to Raulin Crookshank, who, with the help of his son, Guy, served as Farm Manager when Sir Philippe was away on business. Raulin was at this time, a constant companion. It seemed that his father required their assistance also at Mont des Vignes and Crookshank, whose legs were perfectly normal, had been asked to introduce George to the management work he did. George, who knew that Guy was a friend of Amyas, agreed willingly. Elie commended him afterwards when he accompanied him on a visit to Orgueil Castle which had been gifted to them by Queen Elizabeth herself, albeit at Raleigh's suggestion!

As they neared the building, Elie asked whether he could see any changes.

"The curtain wall is higher than I remember it. Have you raised it?"

"Well done! You can't see into the courtyard from the land any longer, but only from the sea. Tell me if you see any other changes as we come nearer."

The next thing he noticed was the strengthening of the gatehouse and, once inside, some openings had been blocked and others opened, for the convenience of those inside.

"It looks less like a toy and more capable of use for defence or attack."

His words were received with approval and his father confirmed both these suggestions as they inspected the interior. George felt compelled to ask why the precautions were necessary. His father looked a little evasive but remarked that it might discourage pirate raids. He drew attention to the new gun emplacements, to increase mobility if it became necessary to move the cannon, and the improved cover for defenders using a harquebus. He refused to be drawn when asked whether he expected raids to increase. George reflected that, if the island was overrun by the pirates, they would gain a secure base for their nefarious activities.

"We need it for defence, which I fear may be required quite soon," Elie stated. "You won't have heard of it, but Lundy Island and St Michael's Mount are established pirate strongholds both recently captured by the Moors. When we have time, I'll show you the new barrack block I've built at Elizabeth Castle and other coastal defence works."

"This work must have cost a fortune, Father."

"Some of the cost was covered by a tax raised by the States, but we paid for Orgueil ourselves, because it is our property. If the wind is right, we'll sail over to Sark sometime soon and stay with your aunt in

147

the Manor House. I expect she would like to see you looking so grown up. I've made some changes there too which I would like you to see."

"Father, you say that the Duke will send help when we need it. Has he sent any money?"

"It would be very welcome, George, but the Duke is also the King and has empty pockets at present. Sir Philippe and Sir John have been asking him for months, but his daughter will probably lose her throne to the Emperor's armies, and his money is spent on her and her family."

* * *

Two days later they made a rapid crossing, where George took charge, and with no visible danger, until Sark came in sight. His father was very pleased with the engineering works, in which he had played a part, laying brickwork and stone walling, mixing mortar with labourers taken on from the unemployed. Carterets had always had a reputation for being prepared to play an active part in construction work.

George concentrated on sailing, but his father was seated between him and the bow. He noticed that his father looked much older, though he remained strong and healthy. He calculated that he would shortly celebrate his fiftieth birthday and his hair was grey. The sobering thought occurred that he was his father's heir and that he was being shown the inheritance that might be his at almost any time. He noticed that his father's left shoulder seemed to give discomfort and that he favoured his right hand. He might mention this to his mother, he decided.

His father had become suddenly watchful, shading his eyes and George, looking into distance saw a number of small boats offshore.

"Not pirates, I hope," he remarked.

"Too soon to tell," Elie responded. "We may have to take evasive action."

Some minutes later, Elie visibly relaxed. "They are pirates, George, but they are our pirates for the time being. They are Dunquerkers and I recognise the boats. They owe us a lot for the care we took to get them to The Banks and back."

When they came within hailing distance, friendly greetings were exchanged:

"Cart'ret, you rogue! Thought I'd seen the last of you! Come to steal the food from our children's mouths again?"

This challenge was delivered with a loud roar of laughter and its response was in similar jovial style: "It'd take more than you and your scurvy crew, you lousy French Bluebeard, to scare my lad and me!"

Further insults and foul oaths were exchanged for several minutes until "Bluebeard" Finch, as he was known, suggested that they should moderate their oaths to protect delicate young ears.

"George will have heard worse talk on the Banks I'll wager, you heretic!"

"Thought he must be your lad. I hear he got up to all kinds of mischief behind your back. Isn't that so, lad? However, I can see he's a good helmsman keeping the boat steady- "

" — and none the worse for the experience, eh, George?"

So, George was introduced. Finch, it seemed had heard favourable remarks made by his friends about George's exploits in St John's, and his group of female admirers. Finch recommended George to consider a life of piracy considering his reputation and talents. George felt a little embarrassed, but no harm was done, and his father was amused.

* * *

149

The landing at Sark's main harbour was managed by Elie, since it needed skilled steering to prevent swamping those on board. Their arrival attracted a growing collection of children and women, all of whom George and his father knew by name. The population had settled on Sark only forty-five years earlier when Elie's father had obtained Queen Elizabeth's permission to possess the island and settle it with forty families in two years. It had been an abandoned wilderness since the Black Death and making it productive had been hard work and involved many hardships, but it was now flourishing under the active care of Elie. The Queen had made it self-governing under permanent Carteret control. This power could only be rescinded by a Carteret application to the Queen.

Several of his mother's de Maresque stepdaughters had married islanders and settled there and George rapidly escaped from the fond embraces of his aunts to spend time with his cousins and other friends. Amyas was the brother of his aunts. A visit to la Coupée was his first requirement, the challenge of crossing the rope bridge with no handrail being irresistible, and this was followed by a descent to the small pebble beach giving access to the Grève de la Ville cave, accessible only at low tide. George resisted the many opportunities for cliff climbing, in favour of returning to Le Manoir for a filling dinner. Le Manoir was a fine stone building designed by Elie, who had worked alongside the other men in its construction. His grandmother was at home in le Mont, but his Aunt Mabel, helped by her sisters, Colette and Elizabeth, were unstinting in their care. Colette was a particular favourite and told local gossip with such colourful description that his father laughed until tears ran down his face.

Before they left the island, George saw the Island Militia drilled and were inspected by Elie, who then had the Captain show him the six cannons given by Queen Elizabeth for the defence of the people. They were in good condition and could be moved about by donkey power. Next, visits were made to the fortifications which could be manned if the few accessible landing places were attacked. Finally, they viewed together Le Creux harbour and considered ways in which it could be made less hazardous to passengers while remaining secure from attack. Several solutions were discussed, but they decided that any solution would be extremely expensive and would have to be delayed.

As they sailed for Jersey, George realised that his father had been happy and enthusiastic throughout their visit. He told his father how much he enjoyed Sark and the friendliness of the Sarkese. Elie, visibly pleased to be told, confessed that if he was ever able to hand over his Jersey responsibilities, he would settle permanently on Sark and put the problems of the wider world behind him. George found a strong bond of fellow feeling with his father's wish, which was never broken. The protection of Sark was paramount for Carterets for years to come.

They were reminded that a water fête would take place shortly in which George, now that he was older, might like to take part. There were swimming competitions, carrying a "Drowning Man" to safety, races swum, while wearing clothing, and diving from a tree-trunk suspended over the harbour. George expressed his willingness to take part, but Elie felt that next year would be a better choice, when George returned from St John. There was some discussion about competition between Jersey and Sark teams. This would need to be thought through, however.

As they sailed, his father quizzed George on his impressions of Newfoundland. George spoke enthusiastically about the kindness of the people, including the Tribes people, the hunting and wildlife, the variety of crops grown and the wonderful summer weather. His father asked about the winter and George said, though it was very cold, it was often sunny, and he was told that, though the fogs were thick they soon cleared. With great seriousness, his father asked if he would be happy to live there. After seeking assurance that he was not about to be banished overseas, George said thoughtfully that he believed he could be as happy as those who had settled, although he wanted to know Britain, France and even Africa before he settled anywhere. His father nodded thoughtfully, then remarked, " —then Sark, eh!"

Chapter 13

For George Carteret, 1624 was a turning point; from childhood to youth, then manhood; from a happy and carefree childhood, to adult responsibilities; from being subject to care and concern, to bearing responsibility for his own safety; from caution to the confidence to assess dangers and possibilities, and then to take risks; from uncertainty of his own capabilities, to the ability to encourage others to develop abilities; to move from narrow securities, to imagine new possibilities and inspire others to trust his powers of leadership, and, above all, to gain self-confidence and to earn the trust of others.

He was fortunate in being surrounded by relatives possessing imagination, persistence and resilience, and strengthened by the knowledge that his increasing abilities were being noted with approval. He had made a number of strong friendships and enjoyed the company of people from all walks of life. He had the warm and outgoing personality which brought him success and happiness in his work and family life and would make him a byword for kindness and loyalty. All this was to come later: he was yet to gain strength and confidence and become self-reliant.

Sir John, the Governor, and his wife joined the family party at St Ouen for several days, probably to form an estimate of the loyalty and views of these significant people. It was clear to Sir Philippe that this was in accordance with instructions from His Majesty, and the equivalent of a Royal Inspection. He made it clear to Philippe and Elie that he would be reporting back to Court but would convey a good report and, as a sign of James' approval, he announced that Sir Philippe would be made a Baron so that his male heir would inherit the title. In addition, he was made Bailiff of Jersey, when the present holder resigned, and his heirs would hold the Office in perpetuity. He felt that these changes should be announced only when the need arose, since islanders might suspect nepotism.

George heard of the Baronetcy, which made no difference to daily life, as far as he could see. However, he noted that his uncle made much of Elie, his younger brother, praising him for his tireless attention to the Island's defences. Meeting privately, the Governor and the two brothers made a more measured assessment of the new posts. Sir John made it clear the promotion had come because of their strong defence. Philippe had made clear the Island's privileges and given his report on the military improvements in response to modern weaponry. George had also noted the inclusion of his generation in these arrangements.

Their satisfaction expressed was muted though His Majesty's pleasure was welcomed. On the other hand, they all saw the problems it presented. In effect James, who had an empty exchequer, was giving the Carterets full responsibility for the defence of the island from attack by external or internal forces, and in perpetuity. They should no longer expect the King to send an army to protect them. They must defend themselves. So, the task of combating the pirates was theirs, with the aid of other islands and coastal towns, if they could be persuaded. Heads were shaken, though it was agreed that their homes and families must be defended, and it should be borne in mind that they had never, historically, received any assistance from any monarch.

So began an active campaign of attack on the pirate fleets. These continued whatever weather was thrown at them, and it was never entirely successful, for their Moorish attackers were desperate for gold and plunder to finance the building of a new Empire intended to destroy Spain in revenge for their relatives who had escaped burning as heretics, or had been expelled, and deprived of all their property. To achieve this, their ruler needed gold to pay for invincible strongholds and a powerful navy. Spain, with a steady supply of ships, many built in Venice, had a fine navy: Louis XIII was building one on foundations laid by Henry IV, but Britain had only a few naval vessels and a few merchant ships, forced into service, with reluctant crews, when the losses of the merchants became insupportable.

As the ships of the channel ports began to gain success, their plunder, and the captured vessels added to their fleet, added to the wealth of the islanders. Effective piracy brought wealth and new trading ports for their goods. Carterets owned most of the shipping, and Elie and Gideon in particular, were excellent planners and strategists: there was hardly a man on the island who could not handle a boat! The pirates widened their range in the coming years, and every harbour in Britain was under constant threat. Cross Atlantic traders and immigrants alike were captured and enslaved, and also citizens of the new English, Dutch and Spanish American colonies.

These were the conditions in which George learned his trade. Variously as crew, officer or captain, he went on numerous trips, bringing home ships, plunder and captives. Each was marketable and had a price. Many captives were sold to traders in Spanish America to harvest sugar; or the Republic of Venice, to satisfy its permanent need for galley slaves. Many were sent to merchant ships as unpaid crew to join the convicts supplied by the English legal system, or the many men "pressed" in the seaports of Britain. Among the somewhat motley crews

155

of their ships were old friends and fellow sailors, such as Person, Mallet, Archer and le Montais. With his core group of Jersey men, and friends from Newfoundland days, George mastered the skills of leadership. His men were always rewarded fairly when their exploits were successful, and so his reputation grew. As trade improved, so did the wealth of the merchants, and Elie's fine new house in Broad Street was joined by other fine stone-built merchant houses.

It was probably at this time that George had a speedy and slim-lined vessel, built to attack raiders and armed with a modern cannon. His crew were trained to work silently and obey verbal instructions and prided themselves on the speed at which ships were approached, boarded and overcome. The cargo captured was variable, for the Channel was the main Transport artery of Europe, and goods were bound for the Indies, Muscovy, Africa, Britain and the many new American colonies. Ships carried no flags at that time to announce their country of origin, and many legal cargoes would change "ownership" by capture, more than once before reaching a port. Precious metal work and pottery, barrels of wine and spirits, oranges, animal feed, flour and dried fruits, were among cargoes finding buyers in St Helier, and the Islanders remained unthreatened by invasion. Guernsey benefited from these activities, and St Peter Port was an excellent harbour, better sheltered from Channel storms than St Helier, and still continuing, through the authority of its States, to regard the King of England as its protector.

Even though the efforts of Channel islanders had only a moderating effect on the increasing frequency of pirate raids, their efforts did not go unnoticed in the Coastal ports and by governors of ports such as Portsmouth and Plymouth commented with appreciation to Carteret and to the Admiralty officers in Whitehall. There would be benefits to the family from these reports in years to come. A second benefit was gained from the intensification of trade and contact between them. Sir

Philippe and Sir John crossed to the mainland with greater frequency since there were nearly always ships preparing to depart in either direction. Contact with the Court, or at least with those officers instrumental in directing the business of the realm, increased, many of them, like Sir John, recently promoted from City trading enterprises to positions in Government. Financial donations to the Royal purse were generally rewarded with an Honour, and these appointees operated under the direction of the higher Nobility, whose more reckless proposals they could sometimes restrain. Many became Members of Parliament, sharing their national concerns with others from similar backgrounds.

Sir Philippe and Sir John paid close attention to news or rumours from the Court where indiscreet moral lapses were as common as leaked news of confidential state. Officially, to report on the proceedings of the Court or Parliament, or to comment on either, was regarded as treason. For example, Prynne, an MP. and pamphleteer, was also a pamphleteer strongly criticising the excesses of the Court, with particular reference to Queen Anne acting in plays. Dismissed from his post, he continued to agitate for change, despite being pilloried, though, remarkably, he remained loyal to Monarchy as a concept. It was probably Sir John, the Governor, who was able to bring news of a royal marriage. His visits to Court were infrequent and largely ceremonial. When not crippled with arthritis, he hunted and played golf at Royston, his favourite residence. His nephews, Rupert and Maurice, who had been sent to Britain for safety, were arrogant, extravagant, and expensive, and were not restrained by life at Cambridge University.

The fact was that by 1624, James had begun to relinquish many responsibilities to Charles. The mental deterioration of the King, noted by Philippe and Amyas, led him to leave many important decisions to

Buckingham and Charles, his son. James knew that European allies were essential for Britain's protection, but this could only be secured by siding with France or Spain. If he hoped to assist the Protestant cause and Frederic V, his son in law, a choice must be made. He avoided a decision by permitting Charles and Buckingham to decide.

* * *

George, fortunately, was still involved in fishing expeditions and gaining the knowledge to attempt a naval career. Thus, he played no part in the next humiliating series of military defeats. The 1626 Parliament, summoned to provide finance for another military exploit, enquired about the waste of money spent. This year George made his second trip with the fishing fleet. He was now strong enough to play a major role in the command of their boats and support Gideon in his work. The friendships made in the coastal ports were renewed, and he was given a warm welcome at St John, where he found that Edward was engaged to be married to Mairi who had overcome her feelings for George. During their stay in St John, George became the centre of new feminine suitors from whom he finally managed the difficult task of severing connections without recriminations, although much justifiable grief.

Charles responded, following Cecil's disaster, with a proposal to free the Protestants of La Rochelle, threatened by Richelieu, which would necessitate a war with France. Parliament, in reply, demanded the impeachment of Buckingham for reckless extravagance, as a first step. Charles reproached them, suggesting that national affairs were a King's prerogative, and Parliament was dismissed. In 1627, George was in London with his Uncle, studying for the exam and interviews to qualify as a Lieutenant. He had a wealth of experience to support him, written testimonials from reputable commanders, and the support of his family, moral and financial. James Hawkins had passed though the training process, with Elie's support in the previous year, and was now a Lieutenant, looking for a berth. Before going to London, George had fulfilled his wish to take part in the Sark autumn festivities.

* * *

It was in the same year that rumours began to circulate, that the King was anxious to see his son married to secure the succession. The more distinguished of the nobility began to ensure that their daughter were seen at Court. Whoever was the fortunate bride, she would need to be wealthy, to have no previous suitors or lovers, a clean bill of health, and potential fertility. Amyas was the first to mention it and it was Thomas Dowse who supplied more details. He in turn had it from Robert Montague, Earl of Manchester, a strong opponent of Villiers. The King, it was said, believed that his plan to be the peacemaker and legislator of Europe had failed. He fell into a state of depression in consequence. It was probably Buckingham who suggested that, if formal inquiries led to nothing, or envy at home, that a foreign bride might be the best choice.

There was modified interest in the rumour but acceptance that Charles should marry. Sir Philippe had noticed that the King took little interest in politics and relied increasingly on George Villiers to deal with most matters of State. Charles was held to be serious in manner and honest and had some legal training. He might be the right person to the financial corruption rife in the present administration. It raised some concerns about the degree of influence Villiers had with the Prince, some believing that it was malign, though he had helped Charles to become an accomplished horseman and tennis player.

* * *

George at this time was fully involved in developing skills and in management and sailing with larger crews to prepare for his next trip to the fishing grounds. He managed to make a wide range of friendships at all levels of society and, increasingly with the local girls who fell for his charms. The matrimonial concerns of the King or the Prince of Wales would have been of little if any interest to the Jersey people. In London economic and religious affairs were occupying the interests of the City and pamphleteers. Some may have regretted the complete absence of the royal family from public affairs, but it was summer after all, and there was no Parliament to disturb the tranquillity.

Things changed suddenly in August 1624, when Charles, on behalf of his father declared war against Spain and their territories in the Netherlands. An army of 7000 men was dispatched in support of Maurice of Nassau and led by Cecil and in February 1625, was overwhelmingly beaten by Spinola, and the Protestant town of Breda, which the war was designed to defend, was recaptured by Spain. Charles' army, of which there were few survivors, crept home in the coming months. Undeterred, Charles and Buckingham launched a second attack, this time on Cadiz. Leaving England in October, the troops met heavy weather, landed far from Cadiz, many died of sickness and lack of food and Cecil lost control. The survivors returned in time for Christmas.

These campaigns had been under the direction of Villiers and neither he nor Charles had any direct part in the affair. The King's health was deteriorating and his depression increasing, due in part to anxiety over finding a wife for Charles. Somehow an agreement was reached that France was a greater threat than Spain and that their sickly King had a marriageable sister, Maria Anna. Eager to solve the difficulty before his father died, it was agreed that Charles and Buckingham, accompanied only by two gentlemen and a groom, would ride post haste to Madrid,

160

and bursting into the presence of the Infanta, Charles would sweep her off her feet by declaring his undying love and return with her to England and a Royal wedding. This was an entirely secret enterprise which would have caused national outrage had it been known.

This incredible farce took place while the Breda and Cadiz attacks were taking place and it remained a well-kept secret shared by only a few, which in itself was quite remarkable. The mission itself was a failure to the relief of James, who had feared that his son might become a prisoner of the Spanish! King James died in March, 1625 and following the obsequies, Charles summoned his first Parliament having first, supported by his new Ministers, announced a great Diplomatic victory over the treacherous Spanish whose latest plot against Britain had been foiled by his own visit to Spain where he had unveiled the depth of Spanish duplicity. Charles made a ceremonial entry into London, where he was met by cheering crowds celebrating a superb British victory. Shortly after, he met his Parliament in the House of Lords to receive his official acclamation and his Coronation Financial settlement. It was quietly revealed that before long there might be a Royal Wedding. The general feeling was that a new age of peace and plenty was beginning. In the meantime, illuminated Addresses were dispatched to the Privy Council congratulating the King on his Accession and offering assurances of Loyalty.

In Jersey some of the news came through, and the setbacks of the Breda and Cadiz campaigns seemed to be contradicted by the King's direct diplomacy in Madrid. Their King had gone alone into the camp of the enemy and returned unharmed and victorious! In public, the Carterets celebrated, but in private they had some doubts. It was far from clear what had been achieved: could it be that a Spanish bride would shortly arrive? It was not until 1647 that something like the real truth emerged, when it was no longer likely that the King's reputation could

161

be harmed. Secrecy and disclosure of only favourable news were to be Charles' guiding principles. Discussion of the King's business would be a treasonable offence. George was spending much of his time at sea collecting charts for further study and enjoying the usual pleasures available to young men of spirit and to the detriment of no-one. How much notice he took of these matters puzzling his elders is not known and did not affect his firm determination to serve the new King loyally in his Navy.

* * *

"Lise, my dear, you haven't heard a word I've said. What is worrying you? You are flushed again: let me open the window: there is a cool breeze."

"I blame my age for my sudden sweats. I'm afraid I was worrying about George again. Don't remind me that I never worried when he went to the Banks. I knew he was with dozens of other ships and would be safe. Now he is sailing with one other boat and the channel is crowded with pirates. I cannot bear to think of him being made a slave in Sallee, or another of those dreadful places."

"He has made so many trips recently, and they are always armed, and prepared. You must let him grow up and learn to avoid danger or deal with it. His father and Gideon have great faith in his ability. I can hear the children arguing. Let us make them a cool drink and perhaps we could take them for a picnic— I think the water is warm enough for bathing, too. There is always something new to see and the children are happy watching the builders, and the lobsters being sold. Everyone is so friendly. It is so nice to be so close to the sea and have friendly neighbours around us. St Ouen can sometimes feel quite lonely and my children love being with their cousins and friends.

"Anne, you always come to my rescue; one word from you and they become perfect little angels. I am driven to my wits" end sometimes. I want to talk to you about my daughters, if we have time: I must try to find them husbands, Elie is so good to them, but they are a burden and he is beginning to look old. They say the King is trying to find a wife for his son: children are a problem! Then, of course there's Gideon, he works so hard, and we hardly ever see him. He sailed to Guernsey last weekend and I've no idea when he will return. There is so much here he should be doing! The children miss their father so much."

"Elisa, you worry too much about things you can't change. Try to be optimistic: everything will be well I'm sure. No— don't sigh any more. Perhaps we will see Gideon: he seems to be taking on a great deal of the shipping business. Perhaps one day they will ask us to sail over to England— I would love to see London!"

* * *

The bathing beach, popular with the young of St Helier, was to the east of the quays and jetties and provided clean bathing. There were rocky pools to engage the interest of small children and the sand could be shaped by small hands. When the weather was sunny, this was where the water soon became warm enough for paddling. When the sea was calm, there were always children paddling there and no social barriers ever separated children!

When the trading day was over, and the stevedores finished their work, families came there on hot evenings for air and to socialise, and the hostelries made a good trade. Saturday afternoons and evenings were particularly busy, and when the adults departed with the little children, the young unattached lads and girls congregated to size up each other, and sometimes stroll off along the quay to know more about each other.

163

On Sunday, obligatory communion attendance over, the young, in their smartest twill suits, and lace-trimmed dresses and bonnets. would wander about, to gossip or introduce friends, and make any future assignations. There was little leisure time for anyone in Jersey, and its brevity was precious and jealously guarded. and carefully managed.

George, then about sixteen years of age, making short boat trips and the business allocated to him by his father, spent increasing amounts of shore time at the Broad Street house. From there it was a short walk to the boats and quays or to the bathing beach. Here he met his friends and ex-shipmates, sitting on the sea wall or stacked crates, exchanging ideas and hopes for the future, and assessing the finer qualities of the young women, strolling past with linked arms.

Comments were exchanged and passing girls noted and praised- or pitied. The popularity of a girl was approved, or questioned, and strategies for navigating an introduction planned, and the most effective remarks to convince the chosen girl of their favour. Jersey was a small island, most of the boys and girls knew each other, or had friends and relatives in common, and the arrival of a newcomer, staying for a visit, or living with relatives, roused considerable interest.

George was already among the tallest boys, and with his sturdy physique, dark, wavy hair, and aquiline features, an object of considerable interest to the young women. In common with other young men, younger brothers or cousins, could be bribed to be intermediaries in the game, and meetings often happened before and after services, since this was the best opportunity. Those who did not attend a church or chapel laid themselves open to gossip. Public opinion carried weight and gossip was rife, open criticism of moral backsliding supported by social sanctions or comment. Heinous crimes of murder and repeated assault were punished by public hanging from the gibbet situated at Charing

Cross in the town centre, where corpses were left hanging as an example to others.

Much later in the 1630s, the stout beams of the gibbet were found to be rotten. Since no-one accepted responsibility for repairs, Elie justified the cost of rebuilding, writing, in the official record, that he was providing "a benefit for their children and their children's children". Capital offences included piracy, murder and theft, and the gibbet was in constant use. Nearby were the stocks, generally used to expose to ridicule those whose conduct scandalised public opinion or the strict moral and legal codes of behaviour. For lesser crimes by the young, or recalcitrant employees or apprentices, strokes of the birch or a whip were imposed. Justice was performed rapidly, and Mont Orgueil Castle provided cells for major criminals awaiting trial or execution.

Spring and autumn were times for weddings and celebration, couples generally leaving after the brief exchange of vows, and making their way to the main street or quay, where family and friends met to offer congratulations. Perhaps the bridegroom would take his bride and their families to inspect the fishing boat whose purchase would demonstrate the ability to support a wife and family. Sometimes support was provided with the gift of a few vergées of land, or an unused cottage, to ensure the future of the couple. For George, this had been the year when he was able to visit Sark to join in the harbour festivities. All these events provided welcome and enjoyable breaks from the hard labour and grinding poverty of everyday life.

This was the year when he won the greasy pole competition luckily regaining his balance when almost within an arm's length of the fine leg of lamb attached to the end of the pole. In the previous year he had fallen in spectacular fashion into the deep water of the inner harbour like all but one of the many contestants. The succulent leg of lamb was borne in triumph back to Mont des Vignes, to the delight of his siblings and the friends who had joined him in Sark. George was becoming an object of envy mingled with admiration among those of his generation. Perhaps it was because he had no cousins close to him in age, that he sought the companionship of others. He was fortunate in having an open disposition, and a genuine interest in the lives of his contemporaries that his company was welcomed when he came back from sea.

He spent considerable time at St Ouen where he and his brothers and sisters were always welcome and Anne's children Philippe, Gideon, Francis and Elizabeth and their younger brother s and sisters formed a cheerful and active gang of varied interests which changed as they grew older. George constructed hobby horses, sledges and provided materials for the construction of camps in the woods, and in bad weather, there were card games like snap and card turning from memory. Later there was backgammon and whist. In summer many hours were spent on the beach at Greve de Leque, swimming, rock climbing and picnicking. George, Elizabeth, and Philippe were joint organisers, leading teams of explorers or pirates as required. Once Philippe was at College in Coutance, George and Elizabeth formed a good team finding that they worked well together, enjoyed small children, and were amused by similar events.

He experienced real dangers at sea, ranging from possible capture by pirates, to furious Channel gales, in which ships were often lost. He was regarded as one who could challenge and overcome hazards at sea, and yet remain confident. No other life, less subject to chance, tempted him to change his decision. Rarely without an attractive girl on his arm, and a range of increasingly close relationships, he was always clear that he was not to be counted on for a long relationship. However, though other lads envied his frequent changes of partner, none of them seemed to be resentful when he moved on or withdrew their friendship. Despite the strictness of moral conduct in public, there was no doubt that many young women gave birth to a first child within a few months of marriage, their husbands accepting the child with forbearance, since it might well be theirs, or that of a friend. George was always happy to stand as a godfather, and remained a generous benefactor, especially in times of need.

He was equally generous with his brothers and young cousins and was always ready to join in their games. His uncles taught him the basics of swordsmanship and soon after his sixteenth birthday, he was enrolled into the St Helier Militia, whose duty was to defend the island from invasion or the ravages of pirates. This skill he passed on to the younger boys and, knowing the preoccupation of his father with defence matters, and Sir Philippe's dislike of the sea and outdoor activity, he repaired a small rowing skiff which could carry a mast and sail, and taught them to row and sail. The girls of the family were eager pupils and became no less skilful. Starting with the safe beach at St Helier, most also became adequate swimmers. Many were the picnic meals prepared over an open fire and eaten in the treehouse which grew in size as the family increased. Every trip to sea produced small but curious gifts, found by George: perhaps the white skull of an albatross, or a beautiful seashell concealing a mother of pearl inner coating. In all these activities he had the full support of Aunt Anne, and the servants.

* * *

Amyas, during this period, was spending most of his time in London, building up useful contacts among those at the Inns of Court and in the chocolate and coffee houses. Outwardly sociable, and welcomed into those circles where trade, scientific and philosophical matters and, for that matter, racing and hunting were pursued, he was involved in the licentious and extravagant excesses of many of his contemporaries. He

167

was welcomed in drawing rooms, and enjoyed dancing, card games, and was always willing to play the flute or take part in chitchat. He was fortunate that Sir Philippe gave him generous expenses, and in return Amyas provided information about everything he heard or observed. Some of his businessmen friends crossed to Jersey and found it advantageous to expand their trade with France and the Low Countries through a sea route which was under protective surveillance.

It was late in the month when Amyas wrote an open letter to his Uncle to announce that the King had summoned Parliament to report the news that Prince Charles was returning from a very important diplomatic mission on Britain's behalf, and that a full public welcome should be prepared on his progress from Portsmouth to London. In retrospect it may have been apparent how confused and confusing news reports were, Last month's certainties were contradicted or represented in a more favourable or unfavourable light, according to the prejudices of the informant. It was difficult to know what was true. His visit to Spain had been entirely successful and it was clear that the Spanish still had plans to conquer England which Charles, and the noble Duke, had been able to foil. While they had been distracted, Cecil had been able, to destroy the Spanish fleet in Cadiz. Spain had been outwitted! It was only the return of the fragments of the force sent to fight of whom so few returned to tell the tale of mismanagement and poor food and equipment, which was certainly noticed and blamed on Buckingham.

* * *

This was not the only account received, however. Peyton, the Governor, had taken the Island's congratulations to London himself and met new members of the administration. He had relatives in the City but spent time in the company of Sir Francis, who was an old friend. Sir

Francis as MP for Southampton had been present at the first meeting of the new Parliament. The first meeting with the commons was not an easy one. Charles reported the success of his mission to the Spanish court explaining that the Naval attacks on Breda and Cadiz had set the standard of conduct for concessions on the part of Spain. Britain's authority had prevailed, and Spain was no longer a threat. Therefore, he wished for a grant to launch an attack on France to relieve the persecuted Huguenots of Gascony, previously an English possession. A naval attack on La Rochelle was being planned.

Parliament agreed to a grant much smaller than the King had demanded and expressed a wish for a different leader than Buckingham. Charles stated his full support for Villiers and was reminded that he had not been present for Cadiz and that Cecil and de Vere had failed at the cost of many lives.

Charles turned to the subject of the annual grant which Parliament made for a new King which must allow for the full cost of an effective navy and to equip the army to prepare to defend the realm. The members asked which country the services were about to attack, and Charles reminded them that matters of state were for him to decide. They awarded a coronation grant which was much smaller than Charles had expected. Charles asked that it should be increased to the amount requested, which led to questions about the uses of the money. Again, the king refused to answer; he asked that they should act "according to established custom". Since no response was offered, he asked them to give the matter more thought and do what was always done.

Coke, the Attorney General, led the members asking for the dismissal of Buckingham, which Charles refused to consider and repeated his previous request. Further details were delayed for fear that spies might learn of the exchange. So much Sir Francis was willing to impart, and he finished with the hope that this small difference would be easily resolved. No doubt parliament would do what was expected.

* * *

Later, Sir Francis arrived with an eyewitness account of the official Mayoral welcome for Charles and the Duke of Buckingham, when they returned in October, and the size of the crowds greeting them. Charles claimed valuable insights into the wicked schemes of the Spanish court, and that a possible attack on Britain had been averted. In fact, the main interest of the Spanish, was the extermination of Protestantism in Hungary and Bohemia. Frederic, King of Bohemia and his Queen Elizabeth, the daughter of James were abandoned by the English, from whom support had been promised, and would have to be content to live in the Palatinate of Heidelberg. They finally accepted they would never return to Prague following the Battle of the White Mountain. With this massacre the forces of Reformation suffered a fatal defeat. The ruthlessness of the victors, in flinging the defeated Government from the windows of Prague Castle, gave extra impetus to the fear felt in the Low Countries at the resurgence of Catholicism. Few in England were disturbed by this event in such a far-off country.

The Spanish had been shocked by Cecil's attack on the Cadiz fleet, and pleased by Charles' refusal of a marriage to Anna Maria, but events had moved on. The Infanta had chosen the conqueror of Protestantism as her husband, and married the Austrian King, and when he inherited the Imperial throne, she became Empress of the Austrian Empire. Parliament had hardly noticed this event and had been pleased to be told of Charles' triumph, and rewarded money the King equipping a Fleet to rescue Presbyterian allies, persecuted on the Isle de Ré. Buckingham was, inevitably, the man chosen to lead the fleet to victory. In their joy that a

Spanish "plot" had been foiled, the City overlooked the complete failure of the first La Rochelle campaign, and Charles and Buckingham planned a second attempt. In the event, a naval force under Buckingham was assembled and set sail. News of parliamentary actions came by means of Sir Francis and Peyton and led to much discussion

At their next assembly, the States of both Islands were informed of these events and loyal messages of support were dispatched to Whitehall. There was general relief that, since a fleet was about to rescue their fellow non-conformists in France, the chance of an attack on the Islands, was probably decreased. They would surely benefit from the campaign. As was frequently the case, that conviction was stronger in Guernsey than in Jersey. George, as a loyal Jerseyman, had always been aware of the timeless antagonism which existed between them and Guernsey. Ships from both islands fished the same water and fished the Banks where boats competed for the best catch and the men occupied quarters. Jersey people worshipped in churches if they were Anglican, and in meeting houses if they were Presbyterian or Calvinist. Both islands had traditionally been under the authority of the Bishop of Coutance. The reformation had made Anglicanism the orthodox sect for all the islands. The Catholic Church had few supporters who either temporised or emigrated. There was a dispute between the bishops of Winchester and Salisbury for a responsibility neither really wanted as a result Winchester appointed a Dean to appoint and discharge clergy as appropriate. The outcome was that lively discussion took place in Jersey while Guernsey was served by strongly Calvinist preachers from France, seething with anger at the persecution of Protestants in France under Maria de Medici.

George had met his uncle Amice de Carteret and his two lawyer sons at family gatherings over the years and accepted them as family. He now learned that Amice had, for some time, been active in stamping out any sign of superstition or Catholic observances. At this time Amice had accepted the office of Bailiff of Guernsey. As such he gave warning to idolaters and Satanists that if they did not renounce these abominable practices, they would be brought before the court for judgement and condign punishment. Later, finding that French Catholic Bibles and Missals were being brought from France, the Privy Council, supporting the "Daemonologie" written by King James, who had passed a law in 1604, making Witchcraft a crime to be punished by death. Nine witches in Pendle, Lancashire, had been the first to be burned at the stake.

Other trials took place throughout the country, though they were not popular. Dr Harvey, of the circulation of the blood fame, suggested to Charles that such charges were impossible to prove in a court of law, since the devil could not speak in defence of his followers. Charles accepted his suggestion that tangible evidence of devil worship would make a better case. Amice as a result, used the possession of Missals etc. as the clearest evidence possible. And between 1629 and 1650, seventy-seven witches were tried before him, of whom thirty-four were burned alive at the stake and twenty-four sent to exile in the New World. From that time Guernseymen were called "donkeys" and Jerseymen called "toads". George received a valuable lesson of the extent to which religious differences could be politicised. What he had learned of the activities of his uncle Amice had prompted his discussion with Gideon in St John. There was a tacit agreement between them that such a position must be avoided in Jersey.

* * *

At the earliest opportunity the senior Carterets and other influential leaders of Jersey met with the Governor for a more complete briefing. There were many questions requiring answers. Why had the Parliament, formerly reluctant to award any funds to the King, suddenly changed its collective mind? Amyas pointed out that many of the members were new to the role and may have been picked for their known support. Those in public life knew that trade was poor, with most of Europe opposing England, and the only encouraging sign, was the trade with our American colonies, though it did not make up for lack of trade with Europe. The fear of an attack from Spain, after the Armada and Gunpowder Plot, was deep and widespread. That alone would have assured Charles a welcome. In confidence, it seemed Charles had reported that Philip IV was little more than a fool and completely at the mercy of the Church and of an incompetent courtier named Pombal. (Elie at this point was heard without reproof when he muttered, "We know all about incompetent adventurers like Carr and Buckingham, don't we?") He was not called to order!

"I know Buckingham has a flexible mind," said Sir Philippe. "Has he experience of Military affairs, Amyas?"

"I have not heard that he has battlefield skills, but he goes to a fencing master every day and is an excellent leader of a hunting pack. There is no doubting his physical courage, and he faces down speakers who oppose him with great skill, without losing his temper."

"Was Admiral Pennington not asked to lead the raid?"

"Apparently not, for the King has chosen his own man. Buckingham has been appointed Lord High Admiral and will direct the campaign."

"I suppose we will have to await the outcome with patience, but I am not convinced of Buckingham's ability. Perhaps these plans will come to nothing, like the Spanish wedding. Are you confident than this intelligence is genuine?"

"You may take it that my source is reliable and a close member of the innermost group of courtiers. Of course, it may not come about, but I expect I shall be informed by a reliable source."

"Further to that matter," said Sir John, "you had it on good authority that His Royal Highness had agreed on a binding contract of marriage to the Infanta and had taken an oath in the Cathedral to obey the conditions of the contract. Was I misinformed?"

He looked to Philippe for a response. The information seeping through to Jersey always came piecemeal and needed to be constantly reviewed to bring everyone up to date.

"No. Amyas tells me he did indeed take the solemn oath as he had promised. Two days later he left his lodging and rode post haste for the French border. He spoke in London to the Paris Ambassador's Secretary on this matter, and the Prince told him that had only sworn the oath to win his case. He maintained that he had no intention of abiding by any oath if it was contrary to his wishes, and his word as a King anointed by God. He had shown them that a British King must reserve the final decision for his own judgement and would never keep an oath forced upon him by another party."

This statement was created by shocked silence. Faced then with a chorus of questions, Philippe affirmed that these events had occurred and that the King, when Charles told him of his breaking the oath, and congratulated him on his strength of purpose and refusal to be bullied. It was agreed that Charles's contempt for any oath imposed on him should be borne in mind for future promises. Philippe recalled that he had always felt that Charles would never be swayed by others, however rational their case.

Drawing his chair closer to the table, Sir Philippe asserted that having heard a number of accounts of the Prince's behaviour, he was more than ever sure that they must always take the apparent approval or agreement of the King to undertake some object or other with a measure of caution since Great Ones have a reputation of changing their minds or policies in a peremptory manner. This he recommended they should all keep in mind and that they should not expect a King to abide by a handshake agreement, such as might be expected of a tradesman. It remained to be seen if he showed willingness to keep to a signed agreement. The years following were to demonstrate the value of his caution and young George would soon come to appreciate the warning.

The truth of the account given by Sir John received further confirmation from family visiting Jersey or Southampton when their business took them there. Anne, leaving her children in the care of her sister- in- law, travelled to London to stay with her father, Sir Francis Dowse, a lawyer whose duties included the care of Wards of Court and their inherited wealth, which he invested until they ceased to be Minors. In Parliament he had supported actions to dismiss Buckingham. So far, they had successfully brought an embezzler, Guy Mompesson, to justice and confiscated the wealth he had acquired illegally on behalf of the King. Mompesson was the brother in law of James Villiers, the younger brother of Charles, Duke of Buckingham.

Francis reminded Sir John that Buckingham himself had persuaded James to put Guy in charge of new taxes on the income of innkeepers and impose licenses on London jewellers who were required to pay new taxes on gold and silver thread. Buckingham was the next target in the view of MPs, but it could only happen if Parliament found a way to overrule the King. The evidence suggests that James's mind was failing. Was this possibly the reason for these inept decisions? Francis found the whole issue deeply worrying.

Sir Francis was married to a Paulet and was a Magistrate holding manors in Hampshire. Anne returned to Jersey escorted by her father, pausing at his house, Moore Court, near Romsey. Sir Francis was devoted to his daughter, and his increasing number of grandchildren, and liked to be present for Christenings. It was however Sir Steven Peyton. brother of Governor John Peyton, who was able to confirm the actions expected by local authorities for the performance the King's intentions. Admiral Pennington was definitely to be rejected in favour of Buckingham.

Chapter 14

T he remainder of the year brought increasing trade to St Helier, despite some exceptionally fierce storms, and goods in increasing amounts passed through newly built warehouses, and the goods included an increasing number of slaves. In part, slavery was a convenient and practical way of disposing of the crews of captured ships who, whatever their country of origin, were likely to have been already enslaved before arriving in Jersey. Jersey law was severe: fines, confiscation of property and whipping being generally employed. Three people who had spoken against Catholicism, had been burned in the time of King Philip, otherwise pirates were sometimes hanged. There were cells in the Castle for those awaiting referral to Senior Courts on the Mainland, but this was rare, though the drunk and unruly were sometimes confined briefly to await sentence or release. There were no facilities for the feeding and accommodation of long-term prisoners or captured slaves, and to sell them on as soon as possible was the favoured solution. Money often changed hands in the process and so slavery benefited many islanders.

Following the social turmoil of the Middle Ages, and the death of a third of the population in the Black Death, serfs had acquired freedom, because plagues and wars reduced the working population so that the most humble labourer could expect to receive a wage, and apprentices were trained, and kept, at their master's expense. It was essential that the young should be trained to replace dead craftsmen. The Craft Guilds received a new lease of life as trainers of new craftsmen and, though their religious affiliations were ended, their function was essential. Feudal serfdom continued to be the rule in Europe, where the Papacy had banned the sale of slaves throughout their overseas colonies. Since there were no slaves remaining in Britain, there was no need for laws forbidding slavery, or the trade in slaves. This loophole was already being exploited in English ports by English traders.

Historically, it was probably Sir John Hawkins who traded first in slaves when he captured a Portuguese ship carrying 300 slaves to Haiti and sold them to Spanish merchants. On later voyages he found the transport and sale of slaves brought good profits, and frequently traded them in Portsmouth, making it the first slave trading port. Angry diplomatic exchanges followed from Spain, but he continued to trade in slaves and other articles of value to the English. In the 1560s, he was given a Knighthood and permission by Queen Elizabeth and encouraged to continue. With Britain and the European nations engrossed in war, the trade flourished and the Moroccans of Salee were conspicuously successful in the capture of slaves. It was asserted that the impenetrable walls of their Capital were largely the work of the many slaves captured in Britain.

When George was a boy, he would almost certainly have heard of the wealth gained by John Ward of Bristol, the first merchant to trade primarily in slaves, and of John Colston, who used his enormous accumulated wealth for the benefit of Bristol, which in size was second only to London, Britain's largest slaving port. By 1624, increasing numbers of British merchant ships were plying a regular trading route from the Guinea Coast of Africa to central America and bringing chocolate, coffee, rare spices, coromandel and other fine woods to Britain. On the whole the British believed that it was good to remove black people from the tyranny of their heathen rulers to civilised Christian owners and luxuriated in the falling price of the luxury goods it provided. Traders had not yet latched on to the possibilities of sugar production, although in the 1660s it would make Britain the world's richest country.

While George was travelling with the fishing fleets to Newfoundland, armed British ships were attacking and, finally capturing, San Cristoforo, later re-named St. Kitts, then, Nevis, Antigua, and Montserrat were added to the list. These islands, though small, produced quantities of sugar and spices for the home market, while providing a pleasant climate for settlers as well as a source of considerable wealth. The much larger island of Jamaica, where Port Royale had been captured from the French as long ago as 1605, was now beginning to be planted with the vast sugar plantations which would supply the world with sugar. Slavery was gradually to become an acceptable corollary to economic growth, and for the supposed betterment of the slaves.

With the increased frequency of contacts between Jersey and the mainland, not only were her ships relied on for deliveries of essentials, but they also provided a passenger service between Britain and Europe. Correspondence between Government and agents abroad and demands from the Carterets for payment for passengers and goods carried in safety, and for their food, feature in the records. Government made the unwarranted assumption that such items were a patriotic obligation and freely provided. One letter of 1626 takes the form of a Petition from Hon. Hugh Paulet for the payment of expenses incurred during his travels in Europe. This journey was part of the wedding preparations of Charles and Henrietta Maria and involved the sale of some of the Crown

Jewells. As he was a kinsman of Sir Philippe, it is probable that Carteret money financed the trip.

This and other correspondence show a contradiction in Government for, though it was illegal to speak of "the King's business", if his decisions were to be enacted, they had to be explained to those who brought them to fruition. This was put into the hands of ordinary members of the public. As a result, without newspapers, or by illegal pamphlets, confidential information often become public within hours. While George continued to gain experience in seamanship and man management, he could not have been unaware of the increasing extent to which new threats were being planned which would be likely to affect the islanders.

Charles's repudiation of Spain was broadcast as a triumph of clever diplomacy. Parliament, lacking the full story, was happy to reward Charles for not marrying the Infanta and awarded a special grant to provide new ships for a war against Spain. Ships were built, and existing ones renovated, and Charles was acknowledged leader of an anti-Spanish party in England. In 1624, Parliament made a £300 grant for an invasion to expel the Spanish from the Low Countries and restore Frederick to the throne of Bohemia. Charles needed the tacit support of Louis XIII, and Hugh Paulet may have played a part in the meeting of Charles and Louis, to make this alliance. During a ball at the French Court, Charles danced with the 14-year-old Henrietta Maria, the King's sister, and found her company delightful.

Charles saw this as a potentially advantageous marriage, since Britain needed strong support in Europe. Embassies were sent to Paris, and an engagement to make a treaty, was signed by Louis. Charles agreed in the secret document to rescind the penal laws forbidding Catholics to attend Mass, which had been in operation for the past few months. Possibly, Charles expressed concern that a rapid legal change might be difficult to enforce. Louis proposed that, provided the intention was written into the Marriage Contract, he would not hold Charles to a precise date: political convenience would be considered. She must, however, bring her own priests and confessors, Charles agreed since there were no English ones. Richelieu saw the marriage as a means of attacking Spanish provinces in the Low Countries and was eager to have Charles's support against the Emperor, who wanted to replace Louis with a Habsburg king in France.

* * *

For most of those in positions of power, James's death led to hopes that mismanagement and incompetent government would end, and great hopes were invested in Charles, whose behaviour initially showed moral strength combined with firmness of purpose, which had made a favourable impression. The new Parliament was determined to keep him in check, preferably by gentle means and efforts to restrict unchecked freedoms which James had acquired. Charles's plans were quite different: he would follow the principles laid down in his father's book, Basilikon Doron, and ensure that no law fell into abeyance which might strengthen his authority. These principles included the freedoms which James had claimed. Charles regarded his father textbook as legally binding and refused to deviate.

With the Carteret connections at Court, and through commercial transactions, they gained collective insight in these matters and George, though an onlooker and concerned primarily with the next trip to the Newfoundland Banks, must have learned of his family's concern. The events of the following two years affected him directly, just as the King's firm decisions were to affect the whole country.

Trade between Jersey and Cornwall flourished during this time. Cornish tin and lead and some silver was in great demand among the competitive and warlike nations of Europe, With Welsh copper from the foundries, they were producing ever larger cannons and other weapons. Ships required ropes of many varied gauges and lengths, in consequence, sisal and hemp, and even reeds, were in constant demand. In addition, longer masts were required by the new "Ships of War" capable of conveying regiments, and their weapons, as invasion fleets. Jersey merchant ships were commandeered in these preparations for war and the ageing British fleet, neglected by King James, required new ships in addition to those foreign ships captured at sea. George Carteret sailed his father to Falmouth to gain the support for the tin miners and Elie, during one visit, was elected to honorary membership of the Stannary Court.

* * *

It was sometime later that, during a visit to Sir Francis in his London house, that Philip heard the full story of the marriage of Henrietta Maria and Prince Charles. They had met, he had been told by Lord Herbert, the Ambassador, following his escape from Spain, where he had rejected a marriage to the Infanta. There had been a Court Ball in Paris at which Charles had danced with the sister of King Louis who, at the age of fourteen, he found quite enchanting. He had proposed marriage the following day and Louis had been pleased to agree. The French Marriage plan became general knowledge. In mid-April, Buckingham was despatched to France to bring Henrietta Maria to England for a Royal Wedding. Louis refused to send her and insisted that Charles must go to France to claim her hand in marriage. Charles, knowing that this would seem like a French victory, appointed a proxy. The Catholic marriage of the Royal couple was celebrated in Notre Dame Cathedral on 1 May,1626. It was witnessed by the crowned Heads of Europe. Sir Henry

Jermyn stood in for Charles. Henrietta, his bride, aged just 15 years, would follow him to England, later in the year. Jermyn played a large role in Henrietta's life, and his death, many years later, caused her much distress.

Since it seemed a good opportunity, Sir Francis provided a blow by blow account of the meeting with parliament which he had been loath to discuss previously.

Charles's first meeting with his new Parliament came shortly after the wedding and began, with a loyal greeting by all present.

"We knew that the first business was discussion of the Kings financial requests and future income. Charles made his claim to cover the expenses of government for the following months and the members greeted it with silence after which they responded with a pre-agreed sum considerably less than had been requested. The King was visibly surprised, but we had been eager to impose a degree of control after the extravagance of King James."

"Was that wise, Sir Francis? Why did he need so much?"

"One member asked, "Your Majesty. How do you intend to spend the money?" We wanted to ensure that money was not wasted on favourites and expensive works of art."

"Without it, I shall be unable to defend the country from our enemy", was the king's reply.

"Which country is our enemy, in your opinion?"

The King stated that this was his concern and the decision was his alone to make.

"His response was greeted with puzzled and indignant comments. Having spoken he surveyed the House carefully, looking at individual members firmly as though expecting a general agreement.

"No answer being given, the House moved on to the next item: The Royal Coronation Gift. Charles expected a large sum in gold as a gift. which was generally awarded to a new monarch. He would certainly expect a larger sum than that given to his father. However, Parliament, eager to impose restraint on Royal extravagance, awarded a quarter of the amount previously offered. Charles reproached us for breaking with tradition. We moved on the next item; the award of Tonnage and Poundage. We announced that in a time of austerity, the tax would be needed by the Government to cover its costs.

"Charles was deeply offended and protested strongly at their parsimony. A lengthy pause ensued as he surveyed individual Members once more, with an expression which seemed to convey sorrow, disappointment and scorn, emphasised by his downward turned features His survey completed, he spoke briefly and clearly, saying, "The traditional practice must be observed," and indicated that he would leave them to reconsider their action. Charles stood straight and elegant, clearly expecting capitulation.

"Parliament, however, was not satisfied, and Coke, Lord Chief Justice, announced that the amount requested could be gained by the "sealing of a great leak". This "leak" was a veiled reference to the Duke of Buckingham, who was held responsible for encouraging James's wasteful rule. The members knew that pamphlets referred to the Duke by that title, as did the King. Charles refused to respond and advised them again "to follow established custom". Parliament was in no mood to compromise and, when the King left, we began Impeachment proceedings against the Duke. In future, John Hampden, a scrupulous lawyer, with a gentle persuasiveness and clear presentation of the central issues of each topic, will advise us on the legality of our actions. As each arose, Members were instructed to take his legal advice on the best procedures for collecting evidence.

"Further developments were halted by yet another outbreak of plague, and in response the Court left for Richmond Palace, while Parliament dispersed to its constituencies to discuss the King's conduct."

"I can understand why you were not eager to give us a longer account earlier. This must be dangerous for all concerned, Sir Francis."

"We will act with great caution, Amyas. We have most of the City with us: they are being constantly penalised by Royal negligence, and we should be governed by experts not by whimsical courtiers."

* * *

Charles was soon to find the cost of marriage expensive. His wife had brought her own three hundred courtiers, installed in Whitehall Palace, which was much in need of renovation, and in surrounding buildings, which his wife found inconvenient. No allowance had been awarded by Parliament for the marriage, and Charles was forced to dismiss all but a handful of her attendants, whom he would retain at his own expense, and paid for the return of the majority to France. His bride was outraged by her husband's decision. He had agreed to create a Catholic Chapel for her daily worship, and the Priests needed to officiate, but, so doing, he flouted the laws against Catholic worship. His wife found it difficult to believe that her brother had agreed to this move. After broken crockery and windows, and violence towards Charles, Queen Henrietta accepted her lot.

Charles was unable, however, to be crowned with his Queen at his side. She absolutely refused to enter the heathen temple of Westminster Abbey or take part in a heretical crowning conducted by false priests. James" wife, Ann of Denmark, had made the same refusal and, like his father, Charles went alone to his Coronation. This information was leaked discretely to radical Members of Parliament to the City fathers, in whose hands the future of the monarchy lay.

* * *

Those in the Channel Islands who would have received this news were, in the main, leading citizens on whose lives it would have been seen to have little relevance. They had little interest in the politics of Government and were mainly concerned with gaining a living and disputing the decisions of the States and its legislators. George and his relatives would, however, have realised that increasing numbers of ordinary families were making the hazardous crossing to the American colonies to earn a decent living by using their skills, and avoiding religious interference. Each settlement seemed to sponsor exclusively Catholic or Protestant worshippers. These emigrants were prompted by a deep longing for the old religious "freedoms" to be reinstated and enforced by law, whether Catholic or Presbyterian. With them travelled their domestic servants, experienced farmers, ploughmen and carpenters. Unwilling to abandon their beliefs, they preferred isolation to persecution. They were by no means prepared to move with the spirit of the age in spiritual matters; a determination which had long-term consequences.

King James, previously, had managed to gain acceptance for his new Bible and forms of worship. This toleration was to be ended by the new king. Each small community had governed itself for many years without regard to the London Courts or Parliament. Total conformity to the doctrine of a new broad-based Church of England was to be enforced on all. Over twenty colonies were settled by the British in the Americas in the years between 1620 and 1660 as a result of these arbitrary decisions. By the end of the decade the trickle of immigrants had become a flood.

Each new community required imported goods from Britain or France. The French Colonies of Canada were also growing, often driven by poverty and religious persecution. The people of Jersey, if they were aware of this, would have been thankful they could remain aloof with a degree of freedom of worship. This would not last much longer, however. Charles, as head of the Church of England was perfectly entitled to impose religious conformity throughout Britain.

Despite his parliamentary setback, Charles was confident that a successful attack on France would encourage Parliament to be more supportive. The restoration of Britain's naval power would be a popular move. "Orders in Court" were issued instructing merchants in all southern coastal ports, to provide ships and armed men for this campaign. County Sheriffs and port officers were obliged to obey these orders. Buckingham in the meantime, appointed Admirals and Captains for the new fleet, from among the Courtiers of the counties involved. Scarce finance went on new equipment, though it was insufficient, and many ships were unable to put to sea in consequence. His Majesty had instructed all coastal counties to enlist hundreds of men to create an invasion force to relieve the Huguenots of La Rochelle, but no financial support was offered, though the King maintained that the people had an obligation to help in the defence of their country.

George was gradually introduced to the responsibilities expected of a member of his family. He had accompanied and assisted his father in his regular programme of inspections of the defences of Jersey and Sark, and in his active concern for Guernsey. He had taken an increasingly active part in the fishing trips which provided the main source of income, and in developing relationships with the American colonies, and their leaders, and those of the Channel ports, British and European. He took a leading part in the actions against pirate raids and strengthened the wealth of Jersey with captured contraband and ships. With his father and

187

Crookshank, he gained knowledge of finance and book-keeping, and understood that security for the island made necessary a constant search for new sources of income.

His family was successful because they were adventurous and believed that income must always exceed expenditure. Now, past his mid-teens, he realised that, increasingly he was playing a variety of essential roles in the family success. He was the inheritor of the family traditions. Yet, despite this, and the fact that the family held him in high regard, he sometimes, as he grew older, began to feel that his life, though comfortable, was in the hands of others. His family, large though it was, consisted of uncles and aunts well into adulthood, and a growing crop of siblings and cousins many years younger. His voyage had gained him new friendships, some of whom lived lives of less freedom and privilege than his own. There was a general contentment among the Jersiaise with the farming and fishing life which supported them. He sometimes felt trapped by the expectations placed on him.

He had seen a new world and wanted more of it: his determination to enter the Royal Navy grew stronger as the years passed. He realised that he was an object of considerable interest to the sisters of some of his friends, and though at first he felt perhaps, that their admiration was his due, it sometimes led to quarrels with them, who knew that the girls were always flirting with George, or telling other boys how much they admired him. Even in St John, for subsequent fishing trips, he realised that the women of the community were beginning to look on him as a desirable marriage partner for one of their daughters.

Naturally George, was increasingly aware of his own healthy response to their attractions, and they were quite aware of the impression they made on him and was perfectly happy to pay them the attentions which he found, gave mutual pleasure. He enjoyed caressing a smooth breast and found that his attentions were welcomed. Realisation dawned gradually that this was not merely a new and enjoyable pastime to be indulged at random, since it had the capacity to lead to quarrels and even fights with others. He began to spend more time in the preparation of the fishing or in lengthy tours into the interior or hunting trips in which he developed his skill and learned the skills of living off the land: skills gained from his Scottish and Indian friends. He had no wish to confine himself to the new world, when the old world offered the variety which he regarded as a personal challenge. He grew increasingly self-confident and convinced that the navy would bring him the new experiences he sought.

Chapter 15

Returning from his first year's fishing trip to the Banks, he had noticed how often Louise, one of the girls employed about the farm, seemed to cross his path and what a fine young woman she was becoming. He had known her for years and she was part of life at Mont des Vignes but he found her generous bosom, and the movement of her hips as she walked, so affecting that he found it difficult to suppress a desire to call her to him, with some excuse. She often went home at the weekend, if his mother could spare her, and on impulse he took the opportunity to escort her most of the way. The habit grew. Louise was not only attractive, but was a lively and amusing companion and over time he began to seek her out during the day, and found that she was happy to be distracted from her work, though he insisted on helping to carry heavy pails and she was willing to reward him with a kisses and a cuddle. Of all the girls of the community, it was Louise who gave him most pleasure, and most anxiety when she was too busy to see him, or when she had to remain at home. Was she seeing another boy? The very thought became torture. Why was she so eager to leave him? The horror and anger he experienced, when one of his friends from St Aubin, mentioned how pretty she was, led, almost to another fight. George was consumed with grief and, reluctant to punch the speaker for his impertinence, walked off at speed to hurl rocks at the unfeeling sea. Celia was long forgotten and Mairi in St John. All that mattered was that he should assure himself that Louise was not secretly walking out with someone else.

190

Two years later, aged seventeen and the eldest of his generation, he was included in family discussions on all their concerns. He was surrounded by adults, male and female, whose future wealth and happiness was his responsibility. In addition, his own future depended on his own efforts, and the future of his own family, when eventually he had become a lieutenant. He enjoyed an active life and was regarded as quick-witted and able to deal with emergencies when they arose, as so often at sea. He intended to pass the Admiralty's Examination for aspiring Lieutenants. His uncle would lodge him in London with Amyas, in his Uncle Philippe's town house, and Thomas Dowse the lawyer, son of Sir Francis, would accommodate James Hawkins, George's old mentor and friend, whom his father had agreed to sponsor at George's request.

The coming events, viewed by George in tranquil old age, would have seemed a turning point in his life. It was not any one of the developments just outlined, although each contributed to making him the man he became. His natural inclinations, combined with his basic good-nature, openness to people and ideas, and adaptability, might alone have secured his survival during the years of political vindictiveness and the brutalities and viciousness produced by the coming ten years of civil war. To have survived the years of political chaos which preceded it, followed by years of social confusion and uncontrolled revenge, which ruined the lives and hopes of many, was an achievement. George Carteret had to rely on his own skill and resourcefulness if he was to survive. He was certain of one thing. He enjoyed a challenge and had decided that he could look after himself and would take what came if he made a mistake and move on to the next opportunity.

As always is the way with opportunists, questions would often arise regarding the morality of some of his actions. These arose in his lifetime, but his active part in the slave trade did not arouse moral concern until long after his death. His contemporaries would have asserted that slavery did not exist in Britain and what happened in other countries was not theirs to question, except to question the ease with which the British were being captured as slaves and taken to serve in North Africa. Evidence for the support given to our own trade in slaves, may be seen in many towns in Britain, and particularly in London, Liverpool and Bristol. Evidence for the British role in banning the slave trade is also apparent, however, though not until the early years of the nineteenth century. He was held in high regard by his contemporaries, Pepys, a shrewd judge of men, commended George's honesty and capacity for work. This despite the fact that he lived an eventful and challenging life, undertaking tasks in dangerous situations which would have defeated a man of less resilience. In an age where many public figures lost their lives, their wealth and ruined their health with overindulgence, George lived a long life, dying in the arms of his family.

His loyalty to the country of his birth did not trouble him because he was Jersiais, not an Englishman. There were no barriers existing between the English, and French and Germans, since neither of those countries had been created at this time and workers and mercenaries passed freely between them. Religious conflict was the primary cause of the nationhood concept which was to recreate the wars of the middle ages as rulers began to expand their territorial ambitions.

※ ※ ※

The spring of 1627 began with a deluge of letters of instruction, signed by the King himself. These were the heralds to the coming avalanche of changes which were to take George to responsibilities which no-one could have foreseen. One of the earliest was addressed to Elie Carteret, who may have hoped that he would continue to escape Royal notice.

Clearly this was not the case! He was instructed to order his brother, Philippe, to expedite the acquisition of a hundred soldiers to be held in readiness for action abroad. Similar instructions had been received by Sir Philippe himself, Sir Francis, all the County Sheriffs, and the militia officers of the towns and counties bordering the sea. Sir Francis, who had last visited Jersey for the birth of Anne's son, Gideon, in 1625, arrived for the belated Christening of a second granddaughter. There was a considerable amount of support among the working population when volunteers were instructed to report for duty. It was widely known that King Charles was planning to rescue persecuted French Protestants: a war with the French was a tradition which always received support in England, whatever the stated motive. The "Hundred men" were soon "standing by" in Southampton, where they remained, waiting for further instructions.

Orders did not arrive until early July and some of the volunteers had been stood down by then, told to return when they were called. Harvest time was beginning when the call came. Sir Philippe was informed by a government undersecretary, that the Duke of Manchester had recommended Sir Philippe for his energetic response. George felt compelled to ask his relatives what this remark implied. His uncle informed them all that he foresaw difficult events and great expense. On 23rd July his fears were confirmed. Lord Manchester, the Army Commander, instructed him to go at once to Southampton to receive and prepare 200 men who were being sent from Plymouth to join his own recruits. A call up was hastily made, and while he was waiting in the town for their arrival, a further instruction came, instructing him to equip them and arrange their transport to the Channel Islands.

His shocked reaction was echoed by family and the Governor alike. It was agreed that arrangements would be thought about, although "Immediately" they assumed, meant, "as soon as possible". George could understand that the recent arrival of several hundred similar instructions sent to Southampton for embarkation, meant that the Islands were to be the base camp of the new campaign. They could not possibly be housed, fed, and equipped by the islanders. Ships would require time for requisitioning, and a fair wind was essential. In the meantime, a carefully worded correspondence began. Sir Philippe requested a written Order from His Majesty which he could present to The States of Jersey and Guernsey, requisitioning the houses to be vacated and a voluntary tax levied for the feeding of the Troops. While waiting for a response, he sent a second letter requesting finance for feeding and clothing the recruits bivouacked outside the town walls of Southampton.

Many questions were asked, and not only in the islands! It seemed that Lord Manchester had no experience of raising an army. Since the last British military action had been in the reign of Queen Elizabeth, neither Officers nor Men were prepared. Many were reassured by the knowledge that Admiral Pennington, who had trained under Drake and Raleigh, would lead the invasion force. George hoped that his naval appointment would allow him to play some part in the Campaign. The Admiral was an excellent Commander and an old acquaintance of the Carterets. As time passed the news filtered down that Buckingham had been appointed High Admiral for the whole campaign and Pennington passed over. An excellent Vice-Admiral was John Byron, descended from Irish nobility but trained under Pennington. Buckingham had no naval experience, though it was admitted that he was decisive and a fine fencer.

Weeks passed with no response to the letters, although a useful naval ship of moderate capacity sailed into Southampton, to strengthen its naval force. Its name was "Convertive" and was originally French. Jersey's campaign against pirate ships had continued to reap rewards and during the year one ship, the "Diana" also originally French, had been captured. In accordance with the law, this had been reported to the Admiralty and a surprise letter from Mr. Conway gave permission for the sale of its contents, with the good news that £40 could be retained by Sir Philippe to defray the transport of troops to Jersey. George initially thought this was good news, but his elders rapidly disabused him. They pointed out that everyone was out of pocket and that ordinary business was suffering from neglect. It was becoming clearer by the day that a war could not be afforded, and it was unofficially confirmed by Sir Francis and others that a sudden surprise attack by a small, well-armed unit on the fortress of La Rochelle, might be more effective.

Sighs of relief were heard. Everyone had wondered how an invasion force was to be supplied during a long campaign: perhaps the King had realised the difficulty. Buckingham might even be successful. Philippe, his father, and Amyas would need to explain to George that Government was often mysterious and full of contradiction and inconsistencies and, even those who were best informed, were often wrong-footed. Governments and people were often in conflict over the correct policy to adopt. Moral and financial attitudes might help to illuminate the problem, but finally a judgement had to be made, whether or not it met with general agreement. The British system of policy making allowed the King to make the final decision. Rulers guided by their subjects had, on the whole, been more successful than those who had not. King James had at first ruled with care and a degree of statesmanship but had declined into self-indulgence and left policy in the hands of rogues and swindlers. Charles was apparently eager to be a vigorous and effective ruler, and to rectify Britain's low international reputation. It seemed to them that in insisting on a war which he could not afford to finance, and against Parliamentary opinion, he was acting unwisely, or he would not have placed a man whom no-one trusted in charge.

"Are we allowed to disobey the King?", George asked.

"What I think we have done so far, George, is to show Charles that without legally granted money and full popular backing, the campaign will not happen. Therefore, he has decided on a short, rapid campaign. For his sake, I hope it will be successful", his father replied evasively. He considered telling George the truth about the Spanish marriage but felt that then was not the time.

"What will happen to all the recruits?"

"Some will be used for the new campaign, those who are not wanted will have to make their way home, I'm afraid. We won't receive further payments, George, and will not be recompensed for money spent. I'm afraid we must rely on our campaign against the pirates. You enjoy hunting them, don't you?

"You look puzzled, George. I know it's a disappointment, but every naval officer knows that when the King commands him to sail into battle, it is usually quite unexpected. When he is prepared for a great battle, the King may change his mind.

"We have been lucky here in Jersey, most English Kings have pretended we don't exist. We make a good job ruling ourselves, I think. This King seems to have decided to take over control and I hope he soon forgets us and leaves us in peace."

"It means we have to make our own decisions, George," said Amyas. The days of "la clameur Harrou" are over. We can no longer shout, "Harrou! Harrou, mon Prince! On me fait tort!" and expect a personal response. We seem to be expected to come to his aid, which seems a show of weakness."

"Dangerous words, Amyas, though it seems a kind of cruel joke," said his brother, "Time will tell!"

At all times a busy and prosperous port, the constant buzz of activity which seemed hardly to cease until long after dark was sufficient indication that significant moves were. Southampton Water and its expanse of deep water and relatively sheltered moorings had for some years become increasingly somnolent as ships rotted at anchor while their crew, from captains downward, remained on board waiting for payment from the owners, knowing that if they were thought to have left the ship, their wages would not be paid. The Admiralty seemed to feel that the honour of serving His Majesty was reward in itself. Government seemed always reluctant to provide new ships or necessary supplies; ships are famous among those who sail them for their constant need of repair and replacement of damaged equipment. Among the many ships at anchor were some neither commercial nor naval. They were commissioned to convey some of the constantly growing flood of working people wishing for the old security from oppressive rule apparently offered by the many colonies.

Justification for the new excitement stemmed from the rumours of a fresh naval campaign. The Southampton authorities were recruiting again, and many came seeking employment. Chandlers of all kinds of goods began to take stock of their wares, contemplate the purchase of new with the pricing discussed with their usual suppliers, and to prepare lower prices for shop soiled goods. Every kind of trader began to look to a golden future, and Inns and taprooms were in increased demand.

Many unemployed Captains and officers left London and their lodging near the Admiralty, which they visited daily in search of a ship, and travelled to Southampton, which received wisdom informed them was the place to gain a situation. Those in authority, like the Carterets and their wide circle of friends, were followed about by those who quickly learned to recognise them, in the hope of being noticed and chosen. The news that the whole operation had already been scaled down had not yet crept down and it was clear that many would be disappointed. In their comfortable rooms in a well-kept Inn close to the quays and warehouses, the Carteret brothers reviewed the situation.

"You see our problem, George, I hope," Philippe remarked. "So many are seeking work and no decision has yet been taken. It is as well that you and Hawkins have sponsors, and that you are not out of work lieutenants, desperate for money to feed yourselves. Sir Stephen and the port authorities cannot support them; we are still feeding the recruits which arrived a month ago."

"It is not going to be easy for either of us when we pass our test, I can see. Perhaps the campaign will be extended if the first attack is successful, and they will all obtain postings."

"At any rate, I will write your names on the exam entry lists and we will send up a few prayers. Passing tests will not get you a ship, as you see, but there are many pirate ships for you to attack, which earn you good money and you don't have to borrow."

George, with his usual interest in other people, had got to know a good number of those seeking work. They assumed, because of his age and dress, and the fact that he was always talking to seamen and officers, and discussing the finer points of the ships, that he was also seeking work. He wanted to know how those without reliable support managed. Some joined fishing boats, some returned to family homes and earned what they could. Some had recently passed the Lieutenant exam and were hoping for employment.

There were young army officers among those seeking work, several of whom had been recruited by London Militia Brigades. Among them was John Felton, who had served in several places where street demonstrations by apprentices had got out of hand. He was a somewhat anxious companion, whom George had met through using the same Ordinary for breakfast. George expressed sympathy and learned that Felton's father, who had died in a debtors' prison when John was eleven, had been a well-paid procurator, fining those listed by parish vicars as non-Communicants. His father had sponsored his Army career to some extent. Since his death Felton had some support from his father's sympathetic executors, who were also helping his mother and sister. He had served in the first La Rochelle campaign, which he survived, despite receiving a leg wound from a sniper's bullet fired at Buckingham. The Duke, realising that his life had been saved, had assured him that he would support his Captaincy when the offensive began again. The Duke's arrival was expected daily and Felton had written to say that he looked forward to serving him.

George heard his life story and sympathised with him in his brave determination to justify the faith of his trustees, and come to the aid of his mother and sister .He felt that Felton was tending to wallow in self-pity and should adopt a more positive approach, but his own good fortune was brought home to him, since Felton lacked the financial support of influential friends. He felt his word fell on deaf ears but wished him good fortune. He felt considerable sympathy for him and became aware again of his own good fortune in his sponsorship.

Neither of them had a berth, and George was determined to find one for himself and not rely on helpers. At breakfast, George paid for the dishes of meat and cheese and John for the ale they drank; an arrangement made between friends and mutually acceptable. Feeling less guilty, George joked that their food was in fact paid for by foreign pirates and was just retribution for their greed. When they parted, George persuaded himself that John seemed more cheerful, though the cider they had drunk might be responsible.

It was 12 July before Buckingham's much reduced naval force set sail, to land finally on the beach of Sablanceau, close to La Rochelle on Ile de Ré. Their landing was resisted by a force of 1000 infantry and 200 horsemen, despite which a beachhead was established and held, with the

199

loss of 12 officers and 100 men. Buckingham attempted to besiege the whole island, and the accidental drowning of the foremost British siege engineer, meant that they took up a position too far distant for their undersized canons to strike the city walls. Disease had already spread among the British, and a relief fleet of 30 ships and 5000 men was destroyed by storms off the Norfolk coast in October. Only 500 men arrived. Cardinal Richelieu sent a large fleet of supply ships which evaded the British and relieved the siege. A final attack on the Fort of Saint Martin failed because the siege ladders were not long enough and, after a hurried retreat to another beach, the British escaped, having lost 5000 of a force of 7000 men.

The Huguenots of La Rochelle surrendered to Richelieu. Subsequently another attempt was made by the Marquis of Denby who returned the following day to Portsmouth, having discovered that his papers did not include a permit to risk the loss of a Royal vessel! All in all, it was a shameful disgrace, and one which confirmed the low estimation in which Buckingham was held, confirmed by his inability to protect the King's interests. Marechal de Schomberg acquired a formidable reputation with the French and a fair number of English captives were paraded in front of Louis XIII, and the captured Regimental banners exhibited in Notre Dame de Paris. The Authorities of Hampshire and the Channel Islands were also disappointed and angry. It reinforced the general opinion that Buckingham was blameworthy, and Parliament renewed its attempts to have him impeached. Yet another small fleet was sent, which failed to pass the newly strengthened defences of La Rochelle.

The anger felt in Southampton, and by the Carterets and their formidable circle, must have been difficult to contain. George's Naval certification was successful, although he and Hawkins passed their exam in 1628, but neither received a commission until 1629, and by that time circumstances in the country had undergone a considerable upheaval. The impeachment of Buckingham failed to take place because the King refused to call a Parliament and was determined to stand by his chief minister. In justice to Charles, he recognised Villiers' intelligence and ability to see matters through. Though Villiers had neither naval nor military training or experience, those who served him recognised his quick understanding and had no doubt of his bravery. When an attack was made, Villiers was always in the lead urging on his troops. Dozens of fishing boats and pirate vessels, however, had the opportunity to see the English fleets sail, perform ineffectively, and retreat ignominiously. This indignity must have been difficult to bear or to excuse. Nothing more by way of plans for war was heard for the remaining months of the year, and disappointed and angry recruits, and officers hoping for postings, dispersed as best they could, to drown their sorrows or nurse their anger.

The new year brought good news to one member of the Carteret circle. George's great uncle, Sir Francis Dowse, was elected to the administrative post of Lord High Sheriff of Hampshire, following their old friend Sir Stephen Peyton in the post. This must have been a time of considerable satisfaction for this well-established team of local officials: admittedly, they were unelected, but all were well-qualified by education and experience. George was made Lieutenant on the ship "Garland". She had not been commissioned for service and was in fact never fully sea-worthy, but it was a start. In the previous year, the King, who had many reliable informants, decided to launch a diplomatic campaign and send an Embassy to the ruler of Sallee, where newly captured English men were swelling the numbers of his slaves. Charles was aware of the actions taken against these ships by English privateers, but decided that as a Christian, it was his duty to free slaves. Buckingham made the arrangements with the support of the Lords Spiritual and others of similar views. News came that some measure of success had resulted, and Charles' reputation improved somewhat.

It was at this time that new orders were received designating the spring months for another and decisive attack to be launched on the French. The Southampton Authorities were to begin to gather new recruits and ships. Once more no mention was made of payment. Charles by tradition had the right to decide to declare war and the British had an obligation to obey. On this occasion, Charles had decided that victory required a greater and better equipped army than had been recruited previously, and that Ship Money must be levied not only on the counties with a seacoast, but by every county. This tax had never before been demanded and Parliament would not have given approval. Since Charles could not rely on cooperation from Members, he could only use his Royal Authority. Many counties levied a charge on landowners, and some Sheriffs threatened prosecution for refusal: many counties refused absolutely. Charles resorted to recalling a Parliament selecting only those members whom he believed would give their support.

When there was a general refusal to break with tradition on this order, he rescinded that order and asked all loyal citizens to make voluntary donations for the defence of the country. If this was done, he stated, he would never again make this request. It was April, and the war with France was expected to begin. Recruits were assembling and ships being requisitioned and no preparations needing finance had been reached. In May, Charles informed parliament that any financial discussion was forbidden, and Parliament changed tactics and renewed their demand for Buckingham's impeachment. Parliament was dismissed, since it had failed to "Let Right be done", which Charles interpreted as an obligation placed on them to obey his wishes.

Chapter 16

From May onward a new fleet was fitted out with the money raised and assembled in Portsmouth. Devonshire had strong Royal affiliations and a recent High Sheriff was married to the daughter of Sir Francis Drake, first among loyal servants of the Crown. The whole duty of recruitment fell on the coastal counties, including Hampshire and Devon. Dignitaries would lead their own recruits to Plymouth. Sir Francis Dowse led the Hampshire recruits, and took George Carteret, who was eager to try to gain a lieutenant's post on one of the Ships of War. Some ship money had been promised to the Sheriff for the feeding of the recruits and for bivouacs. He and George would be entertaining Sir William Courtney, High Sheriff of Devon, whose mother was Elizabeth Paulet, the sister-in-law of Sir Francis.

George Carteret walked the streets of Portsmouth, taking in the wonders of a town he scarcely knew, other than by reputation, as the place which the invincible Spanish Armada had not dared to attack on their way to certain destruction in the Narrow Seas. His approval of the town was considerably increased as he observed how many jolly, fresh-complexioned girls responded to his admiring glance. One, a charming and buxom dairy maid, asked him whether he was lost. He told her he was enjoying the attractions of the town and wondered whether she knew the public gardens. The girl, Ruby, offered to take him to the gardens of a former nunnery, a popular place for assignations, an offer he happily accepted, and they spent a mutually enjoyable time together there, George finding her a confident and obliging companion.

Finally, they parted company, with some reluctance on George's part, as Ruby distracted his attention to point out the new fleet assembling and insisted that they joined the crowd of sightseers. That the very day, 23 August, Drake's successor, Great Buckingham, would lead the fleet out, and achieve another great victory. The Duke had arrived recently in his Admiral's barge, from a supportive meeting with Charles on board his ship the Anne Royal at Gosport. Bidding Ruby a hasty farewell, as he realised how long they had been together, George found his bearings and their hostelry, the Mitre. Fortunately, his uncle had been fully engaged meeting old friends and a recently qualified lawyer who was there to witness a will of which he was an executor. He had recently qualified and was delighted to be addressed as Sergeant Wallop since he had recently been made a Southampton justice. George was introduced as he was a close neighbour, both holding lands in Hurstbourne.

He and his uncle had chosen rooms on the road leading down to the Flagship, but Sir Francis would first greet the Duke at breakfast in the Greyhound before joining the dignitaries lining the route to the harbour to cheer him on his way. George still cherished the hope that he might hear of a Captain lacking a Servant before the ships sailed. He would stand as close as possible to Greatness as it passed. His Certificate was ready in his pocket.

During that evening, his thoughts dwelled on the events of recent years. His two voyages to Newfoundland remained vivid. He had never seen Celia again, though she had returned to St Johns one year. Other girls had captured his affection in St John, many of whom he remembered fondly, though Marie Lemprière of St Helier was his present favourite. Kit had decided to remain in St Johns when the boats returned. He was planning to marry a local girl and was promised work in the rope walks. George's friendships there had strengthened in the last few years, and Edward was now engaged to marry Mairi, whose uncle was at last prospering as a fur trader, hoping that his beaver furs would adorn the new headwear of the Guards' Regiments. Fido always bounded out to see him when he arrived and stayed at his side during his visit. He was pleased to find that, in spite of her engagement, Mairi was happy to be seen with him, murmuring quietly that she was not Edward's wife, yet! He was tempted for a moment to settle for a life in St John: the dog attempted to persuade him also, but he knew that neither Mairi nor the dog would be happy in Jersey. It was not practicable. Jersey was too small for either of them. Indeed, George was beginning to feel it might be too small for him also. The more he saw of England, the more he wanted to see. Devon was like Hampshire in many ways, and as Portsmouth was a better naval town than Plymouth: perhaps he could find a posting there.

Among the crowds in the street he met several of those young men whom he had last seen six months before in Southampton, and naturally spent time with them, retelling the story of fishing trips and mutual encounters with Pirate ships, while giving them time to tell their own exploits and emotional entanglements, hopes and fears. Some of the newer Lieutenants, were triumphantly boasting of their guaranteed posting: others were still hoping for one, even at this late time. None doubted the success of the new expedition and all looked forward to future advancement. Returning later to their Inn, he caught a glimpse of a half-familiar face and pausing, prepared to shout a greeting and wave. However, a large farm wagon, loaded with vegetables, came to a halt before him. Walking past it and surveying the other pavement, he could no longer see him, if indeed it was the man.

Taxing his memory in an attempt to put a name to this hardly remembered face, one came to mind: Felton! That was it! John Felton, he recalled. The Lieutenant had been seeking urgently for a ship to take him on. He told a sad story of a dead father and a son's wish to make him some recompense. If it was Felton, then he was in the right place! George assumed that he had found a place in the Sablanceau expedition and was again ready for service. He must have been walking purposefully to disappear from sight so rapidly. Probably going to his ship and gathering his gear. "Good Luck to him!" he thought. "I expect we will come face to face unexpectedly somewhere, as these things happen. It's a small place, below the Bar. I'll keep my eyes peeled!"

That evening, the town was agog with the news that Buckingham had indeed arrived and had effectively taken over the Town house for his Headquarters Staff. The wind, by chance, was favourable for sailing and intense activity was in progress to ensure that he was not disappointed. Among his many qualities, he was known to demand perfection, and to vent his anger when frustrated by laziness or carelessness. The coaches and horses for his 300 chosen officers made great demands on the local hostelries, even fishermen's cottages were being requisitioned. George, his family and friends, celebrated with a fine dinner that evening, and many toasts were made for the success of the enterprise. Finally, the risks of an unknown future seemed to be opening before him: the prospect was one which created feeling of great happiness.

* * *

Next day, amid much activity, George decided to risk standing by the roadside, the better to seize any employment opportunity. Sir Francis, having paid his respects at The Spotted Dog, took his place in the window as arranged. The crowds grew and excitement rose as the words

"He's coming!" spread along the route. Sounds of fife and drum were heard as the small procession approached and passed, with Buckingham surrounded by his captains. The great man walked smartly, acknowledging the greetings of the crowd and condescending to offer a few smiling words to recognised faces. He was the finest gentleman George had ever seen, and an obvious leader of men. There was something of an aura about him, and George understood Villiers' strange magnetism which he had heard spoken of, but not credited. As he turned his attention to other individuals, they seemed under the spell of his presence, which rendered the most confident men strangely incoherent, and deeply grateful to have been addressed.

However, the group of captains following reminded him of his purpose, and he hoped to see among them one in need of a servant. A sudden movement behind and to his left, almost thrust him into the road, and he turned swiftly to see bystanders being jostled aside by a running man thrusting his way through their midst. He would certainly collide with someone unless he was stopped! George suddenly recognised his face, and an expression combining urgency and confidence. George was tempted to call his name- "Felton!"- but bit back the word, and exhaled silently as, within a moment it seemed, Felton had rushed forward to the Duke who saw him, recognised him, and brushed aside a paper Felton was offering. An attendant noticed the Duke's displeasure and stepped forward, elbowing Felton away. He staggered slightly, then turned, and was lost in the crowd.

* * *

The following morning Sir Francis was about early with the news that the fleet would sail that day, when the Duke was assured the tide was right. He would be walking from the Inn where he was sleeping to join the team of courtiers attending on him who would go with him to his ship. He suggested that George should find his way to the dining-room and join the procession: he should take the opportunity to be present on such an important occasion. George agreed but fell asleep again, waking to find the Inn silent. He dressed rapidly, realising that he might miss breakfast. Pulling his shirt over his head, he tumbled downstairs to find deserted rooms. In the kitchen, he collided with an attractive kitchen maid who told him that, if he was looking for the Duke, he had better hurry next door. The Duke was still at breakfast. George was prevented from rushing away, when she seized him by the arm to point out his shirt was tied crooked and forced him to stand still while she re-tied it. Peg was an attractive girl and George submitted, happy and docile, while she ran her hand over his chest to find the errant tie. Noticing that her bodice exposed well-rounded breasts, George stood, grinning with pleasure, asking Peg whether he could offer her a similar service. Laughing, she pushed him away and offered him a cheese pasty instead, for which he thanked her with a hug and a kiss, before she sent him on his way, although inviting him to come back to her when he had seen the Duke. She would have something for him to eat, she declared. George was now speechless, and she offered the information that the courtyard door was the quickest way to enter the Greyhound and the Duke's breakfast room, George, delighted at this future prospect, walked across, eating as he went.

"I'll have something hot and ready for you, in a few minutes!" she called after him.

Pausing at the door to swallow, George spotted his uncle standing beyond the Duke's seat, and the Duke gazed round, commenting about the excellent breakfast, and applying a napkin to his beard. Footsteps indicated the arrival of the messenger coming along the narrow passage to say that the Militia escort was ready. Their drums could be heard beating.

The Duke pushed back his chair to stand, reaching for his coat and refused to wear a breastplate, saying that his wife had embroidered a fine doublet for him to wear, and he wanted it to be seen. As he stood to display it, the walking man strode up to him, lowered a knife to table level, and drove it upward with great force and accuracy into the Duke's left breast. The Duke, startled, scowled, then put his hand to his chest and pulled out the knife, stared in apparent surprise and, shouting out "You villain!", coughed out a great mouthful of blood. Reaching forward, he gripped the table with both hands, clearly intending to issue an order, but his words were choked by a second gush of blood which scattered widely over those close to him, including George. His attendants crowded round, offering help or advice, which were shaken off, while the Duke staggered, coughing more blood, and allowed himself to be seated.

All this happened so rapidly that George, who was still chewing the final piece of bread, looked down the passage, where Felton had already reached the outer door. Without thinking, George followed him down the passage and out. No-one rushing to attempt an arrest, and Felton walked on, not hurrying or attempting concealment, through the gathering spectators attracted by the drumming. Reaching the marketplace, Felton paused, regarded the stallholders and housewives, then walked over to the Market Cross. Near it was a mounting block, for the convenience of riders. He stood on the top step, removed his hat, placing it carefully on the ground, took out his sword, and waving it, shouted loudly that "he had an announcement to make, which was of great importance".

Many paused to look, then looked away, though some stopped and stared. Felton repeated his statement to greater effect, and he began: "I wish to tell you that the Rabid Dog, Buckingham, is dead— and by my hand!" This time it was heard by several who drew the attention of neighbours to what had been said. Felton decided to wait until he was asked to repeat his words, this time the news was broadcast generally, and he continued to speak, loudly and clearly. Felton's claim then, and on many later occasions, was that this killing was "a Godly and patriotic act, and one intended for the service of the King and country." Trade came to a halt while he continued, and conversation grew louder by the minute. Felton paused, apprehensively it seemed, then a loud salesman's voice shouted: "Well done! He had it coming to him!" There was a murmuring of agreement, then a gradual wave of applause broke out.

Felton spoke again stating that killing the Duke was his intention, and he hoped he had succeeded. He explained that the Duke had maliciously ruined his family and that he could excuse him no more. He had served with the Duke at the Ile de Ré and had risen to a lieutenancy in the army and that he was owed £80 arrears of wages.

In later interviews he stated in the retreat from Breda, a sniper had Buckingham in his sights, Felton had protected him, taking a bullet in his leg from which he still limped. Buckingham had expressed gratitude and promised that he would receive a Captaincy at the next opportunity. Though he had respectfully reminded the Duke of his promise several times, he had been ignored on three occasions, the final one on the previous day, and that promise had again been broken. He went on to remind the crowd that Buckingham was clearly responsible for the present poverty they were experiencing, and the extravagances of the Court.

Most of that story was familiar to George, and he stood by still shocked by what he had seen and confused by the mixture of derision and support with which Felton's story was received. At last the parish Beadles assembled to make an arrest. They had been listening to the story and, as though reluctantly doing their duty, requested Felton to go quietly with them to prison to await the Magistrate. Felton offered them his sword and, carrying his hat with care, walked away with them as though walking with friends, stopping to tell of his action as he went. He made a good impression, it appeared, and many new friends. Some, George saw, were patting him on the back and offering their support if he wished to escape. No-one laid hands on him and he went quietly to await the appearance of a Magistrate. It was later revealed that he had made a written version of his public speech and pinned it inside his hat, to ensure that if he was prevented from speaking, there would be no doubt of his intention.

Standing there, stunned by events and tormented by conflicting emotions, George felt a hand on his arm and his Uncle suggesting gently that they should return to their Inn, sit down and that perhaps a small brandy was what they both needed. He allowed himself to be led to the door but was overcome by sudden nausea, which left him drained and unable to ask the many questions he needed to ask. Violence, he knew was evident everywhere, and the punishments for violent acts were performed on the perpetrator in brutal ways and led to public execution by hanging and sometimes quartering, but the strange behaviour of Felton was something completely beyond his comprehension.

He became aware that his Uncle was offering him warm ale which he at first refused but, listening to his Uncle, he was at last induced to drink. His Uncle insisted that they must both wash off the blood with which they were spattered and do away with his shirt. He recommended a sleeping draught to ensure that George would not lie awake going over the events he had witnessed. They talked long into the night however and George recounted the misfortunes that Felton had suffered because he lacked financial support.

* * *

Waking next morning he found his uncle and a man he felt he knew, standing at the bedside.

"I've brought a doctor to check you over, George. He says he knows you."

"Bore da, George. Ti'n iawn?"

"It's Dr. Jones from the Fair Haven! What are you doing in Plymouth, Gareth?"

"I see you have recovered from your shock. I expect you slept well after the draught I gave you. I am pleased to see you again, George, what are you doing here? Still searching for answers, I suppose. I'd prefer not to talk about the Duke: your father tells me you saw him killed. It must have been a dreadful shock to you. He was already dead when I was sent for, and there was nothing I could do"

"We'll talk about that after you have dressed," his father decided. "If your appetite has returned. I suggest we go down for breakfast."

George found that food was of some interest and intended to join them downstairs, eager to ask his doctor friend how he had come to work in Plymouth. He also felt an aversion to thinking about the Duke's death. His arm was seized in a firm grasp as he turned towards the dining room and, forefinger to her lips, urging silence, Peg led him away to a small but comfortable room containing a soft couch where she offered him care and sympathy. She cried at the thought of his dreadful experience and, seeing him staggering in with blood on his shirt, she had thought he was dying. Assuring her that he was well, the full horror of the previous day overwhelmed him suddenly and, tearfully, he fell into her arms where he accepted her sympathy and soothing caresses, to which he was more than eager to respond, feeling at last the burden of grief lift, that the pleasure and enchantment of life was returning. With many expressions of eternal love and promises to meet again as soon as possible, they separated finally, and Peg provided him with a large, hot breakfast which he consumed eagerly.

Jones told him, when they met later, that after the experience gained at sea, he had decided to spend his earnings on medical training and had spent three years at Leiden Medical school, where an increasing number of British doctors were being trained. He was working in Plymouth as a first spell in private practice and the town provided a good cross section of population and illnesses.

After further conversation, Jones asked him if he was ready to hear about the Duke. He would be grateful to hear news from Sir Francis, who promised to be brief for the sake of his nephew. Buckingham had died from fatal internal injuries about two hours after being stabbed. Later that morning a coffin would convey his body to London for an inquest, and witnesses had been easy to find. George might be asked for a written statement since many of those present, including Beadles, were assumed to be too ignorant to be reliable witnesses. George had the advantage of being a gentleman.

Courtney, the visiting Sheriff, was in a state of shock. A Deputy had been chosen to take the place of the Admiral then the fleet would leave as planned. Admiral Pennington would be in command. It was essential for Sir Francis to remain there to ensure all requirements were met. He went to make a brief written report for the King, as the senior civilian present. It was clear it was the action of one man avenging a personal slight. No-one else was involved, and the act had been committed in the presence of over three hundred armed soldiers and their officers, and Buckingham's entire entourage, while he was surrounded by the Military and civil officers of Southampton, and by his closest friends. The King's enquiries found that Felton had few acquaintances and his mother and sister were his only relatives. They had not seen him for several months.

Charles, attending Buckingham's State Funeral in Westminster Abbey, led the cortege though streets lined with jeering Londoners.

When Jones walked away to attend his patients, George enquired about the fate awaiting Felton. He was being taken under guard to London, his uncle told him, where he would be tried and sentenced for the murder of the King's Chief Minister. He had acknowledged his guilt, and accepted the inevitable death sentence with resignation, and a certain degree of satisfaction. He accepted that his action was evil and the possibility that only the Devil could have prompted him to act. Francis had shocked some family members, by declaring that, in his opinion, Felton had done the country a service. He was warned that he should not repeat it in public. George went for a long, solitary walk in the hills, turning the episode over in his mind, and returning just in time to see the last of the fleet disappear over the horizon. Francis Dowse's opinion seemed to have tacit support and he decided to see what the final conclusion was.

* * *

Before arriving in Portsmouth, George had thought how refreshing it would be to revisit Sark, where there was every chance that he would be able to join his friends in the water sports celebrated after the return of the fishing fleet. The best laid plans, however, often lie at the mercy of an employer, particularly if your employer is the First Lord of the Admiralty. Unexpectedly he was instructed to go to the harbour where his first command was waiting for him. When the order arrived, already late arriving, due to poor weather, he had already made arrangements with most of his close friends to sail for Sark in the near future. All relished the idea of the competitive events to come. He discovered months later that the event had taken place but had ended with bad

214

feeling for which the explanations seemed inadequate. He concluded it probably originated from competition for the affections of an attractive girl. George fully intended to make up for not being present in some way, but time passed, and his good intention was recalled at inappropriate moments, and was then set aside. It may have been the origin of misunderstandings which were voiced years later. Events which had happened during his absence certainly gave him more serious matters of concern.

While Buckingham's plans for military and political advantage were being put into action, and all that was involved being drastically altered following his murder, other matters were taking place. The King had met Buckingham briefly a few days before he went to his death, having seen the launch of his largest battleship. The Sovereign was a three decker, probably the first of its kind to be built, and far superior in firepower to any of the Dutch fighting fleet. The event passed largely unnoticed as it turned out. It would not undergo final sea trials for another ten years. In the same period of days, Sir Philippe Carteret bid a fond farewell to his wife, assuring her he would return in a few days, and set sail with a few seamen for St Malo to collect some goods held ready for collection. Halfway there, they were arrested by two Pirate ships, and made prisoners. The pirates were from Dunkirk, notorious as a base for piracy which was its main source of livelihood.

* * *

Their capture was a common happening, although the first time a Carteret had been captured. Once identified, his captors would offer to return him for a large ransom. These pirates recognised the crew and congratulated themselves on the capture of Philippe, whose antagonism to their trade, was legendary. Sir Philippe was welcomed with mock

215

courtesy and assured of a warm welcome when they reached Dunkirk! He was reminded of the executions he had meted out to their friends and promised a sharp taste of his own medicine. It would be reasonable to assume that despite the brave face he presented, he must have feared the worst, knowing that no-one would come sailing to his rescue. At worst, he knew he was faced with summary execution. However, they might have killed him immediately, and his men, if they had wished to do so, could have consigned him and others to a watery grave.

In Dunkirk he was immediately marched unceremoniously to the Court House and confined in a cell while his captors considered their next move. Philippe drew strength from the fact that summary execution had been delayed and hoped, although they might wish him dead, that, as a man of substance, and very well known, they might have an alternative. His family on Jersey might be asked to pay a generous ransom in exchange for freeing him. If that was to be the case, he must expect a lengthy imprisonment, while they decided whether he was worth the cost.

The States eventually received a ransom demand and deliberated upon the sum demanded and the raising of funds. There was no doubt that a ransom would be paid eventually. In the meantime, the Dunquerkers realised that their action had not gone unnoticed. On both sides of the Channel the feeling grew that the Pirates had gone too far on this occasion, and Port and Naval Commanders were instructed to come down heavily on them. Admiral Pennington and his fleet redirected their operations.

And so, time passed and uneasiness may have provoked a change of tactics. In the meantime, family anxiety in Jersey must have been intense, since there would have been no means of communication between legal authorities and irresponsible pirates, or hope of a rational resolution, no response had been made to the States' proposal. Those pirates charged

216

with negotiation ran the risk of rejection for failure, and face execution themselves. A rapid expedient was found, and Sir Philippe was hastily taken from his cell, probably fearing execution, and handed over to Officers of the Spanish Netherlands, who paid a large sum for his possession.

Some weeks had passed, but at least he was well treated as an officer and a gentleman, and the Spaniards had him to dispose of. The political situation in the Netherlands was complex, but treaties of peace had been signed between England, Spain, and France. Almost at once, Philippe was escorted courteously, to the Palace of the Governor of the Spanish Netherlands, and, knowing that his purchase price would have been considerable, he must have wondered what the Spanish would charge to release him.

The Governor was involved in a military engagement with a French province at that time and had delegated his powers to his wife in his absence. Princess Clara Eugenia was related to Philip IV and was a woman of political judgement and considerable personal charm. She had been an eyewitness of Charles's wooing of her cousin, the Infanta, and seemed predisposed to favour "English" gentlemen. Philippe, an experienced negotiator with difficult monarchs and their Ministers, established a warm relationship with the Lady, and a solution was reached.

The details are not known, but Philippe was released and returned to his family and economic agreements agreed, intended to benefit Jersey and the Spanish territories. This opened up new trading ports like Antwerp to Jersey merchants, and new exports for Britain, where the demand for fine, hand-made lace as a fashion accessory, was insatiable. A happy ending for all it seemed, and the reuniting of the family would have been a great relief to Elie and Gideon in particular, and the joy of his wife and children was still apparent when George reached home to

217

hear all that had occurred in his absence. He would have taken up his new posting, with renewed determination to punish the pirates of the Channel.

Chapter 17

A small rowing boat moved silently over the water as the tide attained the point of turn, leaving only a minute rim of sand and weed, among outcrops or jagged rocks of threatening variety. Avoiding the dangers, it found land, enabling a cloaked figure to step ashore silently, and in the darkness of the waning moon, hide himself from the gaze of any observer, had any been present on such a chilly night. The boat receded into the morning mist by which it was soon concealed, as if nothing had happened. The weather remained calm, the stillness unbroken, and the cove too small to be of use to fishermen, who prefer more convenient landing places.

Reaching firmer ground, the incomer waded through the tidal swell and, reaching the shore and a firmer footing, crossed a beach and vanished among the sedges, seakale and coarse grasses which characterised the coastline. The last glimmer of moonlight disappeared below the horizon as he set out.

Some ten minutes later a figure, moving at an unhurried stride, might have been observed on the track behind the coastal dunes where, beside the sedges, a desolate Etang spread beside the track into the distance, as he moved purposefully toward Palmyre. He might well be taken for a seaman searching for work on land, or sea, though it was still early in the year for either to be entirely credible. This was the impression he hoped to make when, arriving in the town, he mingled with other early risers, making the early hour an excuse for conversation, and made his way by instinct to a destination where others had already gathered for an early breakfast. The bread was fresh from the oven, and eggs, cider and thick fish soup, ready for eating. An observer would have found it difficult to separate locals from any visitor: a third of those present were probably, in fact "others", from places not far distant but where unemployment was rife. Our walker fitted this category well, as he ordered food with a nod of the head and a few muttered words of dialect, before taking his food to a vacant place on a bench among the crowded tables. There he sat and applied himself to eating, with every sign of enjoyment.

"Seaman looking for a ship, are you?" A voice from an anonymous speaker addressed him. A firm nod of the head, and a word of agreement was sufficient to provoke a rumble of negation, implying that he would be lucky to find anything there.

After a longer silence, broken by desultory opinions that luck was always a requisite, the stranger declared that it was worse further south, and was of the opinion that he might find La Rochelle more welcoming. A chorus of doubt and head shaking greeted this suggestion, also the remark that they needed only sappers and engineers there. Several said that they had thought of walking that distance themselves but had wives at home and it was too far to go back and forth daily. Later, as the company dispersed, the stranger placed coins on the table, nodded his thanks and, adjusting his cloak, struck out northerly, the only person to adopt this route.

Four days later, George reached St. Martin de Ré, after long hours of close observation and having gained valuable information under the guise of a man looking for work, There he took up a strategic place on the hill, where an officer on a ship moored safely off-shore and beyond the reach of enemy guns, might catch a glimpse of a flashing mirror, which he was anticipating, with the aid of a good telescope. Far downhill was a deserted beach. In fact, the very beach to which Buckingham had led his ill-equipped army several years before. There, a small rowing boat, Gaiches, one of his Jersey friends, would collect him, when he signalled that his task was complete, and take him safely to a ship, and on to meet Admiral Pennington, to whom he would make his report. He was surprised to be directed to a familiar ship, the Convertive, where after some time he was directed to one of a variety of different ships, under special orders, and as frequently, later, without ostentation, moved to yet another boat bound for a different port. George's imperturbability, and command of languages, was a useful aid in forming British sea patrols and intelligence matters.

* * *

The new Admiral of the Fleet, replacing the incompetent Buckingham, was Pennington, trained under Drake and an old friend of his uncles, Francis and Philippe. His uncle, he knew, had been promoting his name on every possible occasion, but he had not expected to receive any appointment in Portsmouth. He learned later that Pennington had plans for him.

The expected resumption of the French campaign suffered a sequence of delays. The causes were varied but could be collectively blamed on poor leadership and lack of money. It was becoming clear that decision-making was only given to those who were favoured by the King, shared his views, and had achieved high social rank. Such men must, it was assumed, be highly intelligent and, therefore, would make fine, natural commanders. Thus, they would direct operations, and experienced Captains would be compelled to perform the menial tasks they were given. Many campaigns foundered because a Captain refused to attack, not disobediently, but because there was no wind. Practical experience must always give way to orders from social superiors or from the King, from then onward. In time it seemed to become the way Charles chose to rule.

The other cause of delay was lack of money to pay officers or seamen or to build new ships and equip them with modern armament. Timber for shipbuilding was in short supply since the reign of Henry VIII, whose vanity projects, such as his constant war with France, and the cost of Mary Rose, had reduced the supply of mature oaks. Timber for construction had to be brought from France and masts from Scandinavia. Since a state of war with France existed, supplies were unreliable to say the least. The larger the ship, the longer, and broader the masts required!

Hemp for rope also had to be imported and ropes of a variety of diameters created to serve the complex needs of larger, new ships. English farmers were compelled by law to grow hemp on all their farms to supply growing demand. The King, unsupported by Parliament, could not afford these necessities, or pay officers or crew to sail them. Officers and crew sacrificed any right to payment if they left the ship before being paid. In consequence many ships lay idle in port with unpaid crew aboard, while the vessels rotted away under them.

Numerous letters went back and forth between the States in Jersey and Whitehall during the next two years concerning these matters with specific reference to the needs of Jersey. Sir Philippe Carteret wrote many letters asking for payment for materiel demanded by Whitehall and measures taken of necessity in emergencies for which payment was denied. Whitehall often questioned the justification for essential expenditure or demanded clarification, saying they had no wish to pay the same bill twice. These were clearly delaying tactics and caused anger. Small sums of money sometimes arrived, inadequate for paying angry claimants, and it was assumed that officials were embezzling funds. The King, who was assumed to have the interests of his people at heart, was charitably believed to be at the mercy of greedy counsellors. However, this trust was being progressively undermined. It was confirmed when Philippe de Carteret himself, with two of his ships, working for the King

222

under Royal Warrant, were captured by pirates and had to be ransomed. A claim to Whitehall for compensation, was refused. Events of this kind, in all aspects of national life, undermined trust in the King, with fatal consequences for his crown.

Conway, Manchester's secretary, was supportive of Carteret and invariably polite, but was embarrassed by the tone of some of the letters he was forced to write. On one occasion he felt compelled to state that he was not embezzling. In another letter, written to Philippe on behalf of Lady Faulkner, Conway requested the release of smuggled tobacco impounded by Carteret's officials. The range of services Carteret was expected to finance himself can be seen in his correspondence. George reflected that the murderer of the Duke was not a devious foreigner, but an Englishman, born and bred.

Having served Pennington well and acted as a spy on several occasions, as in the operation previously described, George commissioned as Lieutenant of the "Garland", a little fifth rater employed in "the narrow seas". His report to the Admiral on his return from his coastal reconnaissance, and spying, had been decisive. Ile de Ré and La Rochelle had new defence works constructed by Schomberg ensuring that an attack from the sea would end in failure, and a strong detachment of the French Fleet was in place to protect the natural harbour behind Oleron. His little fifth rater was ideally suited for shallow coastal waters. These secret operations were of great value and presents further insight into Carteret, as a man of action. George's ability to mingle and converse with Breton speakers, and his intimate knowledge of the Brittany coastline, and the natural harbours of its deeply incised fjords, which provided formidable, natural French Naval bases, was invaluable in preventing another pointless attack. An attack on the Normandy peninsular would also further alienate the Protestant population, among whom many English had strong family connections.

223

Barneville, Granville and Ducey were the original homes of George's English family, with Jersey remaining a refuge for them in times of persecution.

* * *

Espionage was in the air and, as always in wartime, the demand for Intelligence was increasing. Among the benefits produced was rewarding employment for men George could trust, and those who had been his close comrades in the trips to the banks formed the basis for a group of agents, able to pass with ease among the French. Dick Archer and Clement le Montais were among the most effective and resourceful in this dangerous enterprise.

King Charles, accepting that further attacks were pointless, abruptly made peace with France and Spain, and redirected his efforts to defending British commerce against pirates and asserting British claims to the ownership of the Narrow Seas. Recently, the Narrow Seas were being claimed as a British possession and renamed the "English Channel". Sir Philippe spared no effort to gain advancement for George, who became the most active and promising of the Carteret family, on whom the family future depended. When the Naval Secretary, Conway, was replaced by Sir James Nicholas, he was strongly advised that, "my Nephew, George" was the man to take command of the operations against the pirates. Shortly after, Philippe wrote another reminder "of the promotion promised to my nephew, George". His success in advancing his nephew represents the increasingly high regard in which George and members of the family were held by the King.

Increasing Naval operations came as a considerable surprise to pirates and licensed shipping alike. Any hope of regularity in patrols was, as always, at the mercy of the weather, but equally, subject to humiliating

224

retreats to a harbour for repairs. Masts, lines and food were constantly inadequate because of their poor quality. George often took the opportunity to visit his various family homes and was present at the Baptism of Sir Philippe's next two sons, named Gideon and Zouche. Much of his time at sea was spent on patrol duties, designed to enforce British supremacy in the narrow seas. Ships were to be arrested if they failed to lower their flag and topsail when passing a British warship. "We had Richard Eastwood, master of a Sandwich hoy, in the bilbos for not striking his flag," runs a report. It was not only foreign vessels who were arrested: even a Trinity House boat, on coastal duties, suffered the same fate!

George and his close associates made many reconnaissance surveys after the success of his first surveying trip, and compiled extensive reports on the ports of St. Malo, Le Havre, Honfleur and Brest, which Pennington and Philippe reported to Conway or Nicholson to be passed on to the King.

* * *

"I hear that the King's French Invasion plan has been postponed." Sir Philippe took an opportunity to speak to George in confidence.

"Also, unofficially, that you may have been partly responsible for the postponement by discovering how well the French have improved their port defences."

"I may have helped by supplying a little information. We've also managed to prevent their agents seeing the poor condition of our battle fleet, and I believe we may have better arms than theirs. I hope they don't realise we are in no fit state to fight even the briefest encounter," George responded with a grin.

"Don't try to tell me you played no part in the change of plan. I believe you may have been spying. Tell me George, is this true? I promise not to tell anyone."

"I must not allow you to believe anything so unlikely, Uncle. However, I may have suggested to Pennington that before attacking, we should discover the state of their defences. Nothing more." George claimed, "Though Pennington was reluctant, I made some discreet enquiries, and wrote a full report, which may have been helpful."

Noticing his Uncle's puzzled look, he added, "I can speak Breton quite well, without too much effort. Oxford University would have drummed my "regrettable" gift for dialect out of me."

"False modesty again, George! I only spent two months there myself, because of my father's illness, but I could never have attempted to pass as a Breton. You are my main hope for the future if our family is to play any part in national affairs, George, and your ability to dissemble may well be invaluable at court in days to come."

"It seems that I have some ability at spying, though it is fraught with dangers, Uncle. The excitement of successful deception is considerable, I admit, despite the dangers involved. After my first attempt I have been asked to investigate other French ports, including Avranches, on behalf of His Majesty. Of course, I have no desire to spend my life on secret missions, there are far too many risks involved"

"I'm glad to hear it! Apart from the perilous nature of the work, we need your help in the defence of Jersey. It's time I reminded Sir James that you are still waiting for promotion."

* * *

The following months saw many new and unpredictable changes to the way Britain was governed. The king ruled by personal authority at this time, with the aid of a small group of close supporters as counsellors. He had decided that trying to gain the support of Parliament was fraught with problems and caused needless delay. In the past, his father had tended to involve the Members in his policies and was able to blame them when things went wrong. This permitted James to be regarded as a cautious and detached arbiter, while his advisors reaped any criticism. Charles always wanted to have their constant and loyal agreement, and without it, decided to rule alone. Thus, he received all the blame personally. His personal rule created a situation in which he played an increasing role. The enforcement of his instructions fell directly on the shoulders of local County officials and wealthy property owners, all held responsible for organisation and payments. He would tolerate no opposition, believing that he embodied the God-given ability to choose what was right.

Charles appeared to have a mental condition that was making rational judgement problematic. He believed that he could not be wrong. He seemed prepared to ignore the sound advice his father in his book Basilikon Doron, that a good king should always attend to the advice of his councillors. By 1643, his rule was absolute, and civil and religious power to impose control, vested in the hands of Wentworth and Laud respectively. Each could arrest and punish those in civil or religious office for non-compliance with the will of the King. The first obvious problem which this created for Sir Philippe, only emerged with the death of Jermyn, the Governor. He had devolved his authority on Philippe but remained responsible in the event of a crisis. His son, Henry, who replaced his father, never visited Jersey, leaving his duties and responsibilities to Philippe. The religious policies of Bishop Laud created terrible problems in Jersey during the next nine years, and the anger they roused fell unfairly on Carteret, though it should have been Jermyn who took the blame. Amice de Carteret, who had retired to Jersey when his posting to Guernsey ended, died there in 1653.

* * *

George, with longer periods of absence, and with taxing naval responsibilities, was closely involved with a multitude of duties; as an escort, in countering acts of Piracy, and, at the same time attempting to keep his ships seaworthy and afloat. Any profits gained from fines imposed and cargoes impounded, and infrequent gratuities from grateful passengers, were rarely sufficient for the needs of his family. His close relatives had taken the family property, and as time went on, money was needed by Sir Philippe for the defence of the island. Each passing month brought George new challenges. One, for which there exists a lively account in his own words, concerns the intrepid pirate, Le Maigre.

He had succeeded in making himself a celebrity with his daring exploits and frequency of attacks on ships and small ports. Notorious also for his ability to side-step the authorities and for clever evasions of capture, he was a thorn in the side of the authorities. Information arrived that he had transferred his attentions to the Bristol Channel and might attempt to recapture Lundy as a base for his activities. Carteret set off in hot pursuit and heard that his opponent was hiding, anchored off Chausey. His prey evaded him, but astutely judging wind and tides, George caught sight of him off the Casquets.

"His ship being of 60 tons and a Flemish bottom, and a boat with him of 18 or 20 tons, I tacked about and stood after him."

The pursuit was fast and furious, but Carteret's ship proved equal to the chase. He piled on more sail in an attempt to stop and board the ship but, without warning, one of his masts broke, which brought down another, and Le Maigre escaped once more. Le Maigre was captured and killed soon after attempting escape.

George rearranged his confused mess of mast, lines, spars, and sails as best he could and limped back, defenceless, to Portsmouth. Pennington and others of the fleet congratulated him on his sterling effort and his report arrived on Conway's desk. There is no doubt that his skill and tenacity were noted and any doubt concerning either was dispelled.

* * *

The following day, Peyton, who had recently returned from London, called the extensive Carteret clan together. It was a good opportunity while so many were together in the same place. Since his wife was with him, he made a point of inviting wives to join the company, because they played such a vital role in the life of the island. Gratitude was offered to Elie, when they met for breakfast in the morning, for the fine restructuring of the Governor's Residence, which had increased its comfort and storage space.

"I have good news for you," he announced with a smile. "His Majesty is now the father of a healthy son and an heir to the throne! He and the Queen are delighted, and the boy has been baptised Charles. He is sturdy and there is hope that he will thrive."

"Excellent news," Sir Francis said. "If you intend to write a congratulatory address, your messenger must take one from me. Is there to be public celebration in London do you know?"

"I gather that selected Members of Parliament are to be recalled deciding what form it will take. I suppose the King will hope for a generous financial offering for such a guarantee of future security: there was some talk of a substantial sum to swell the depleted Naval fund. It may be offered with strings attached, of course."

229

"My nephew, Amyas, tells me that the pamphleteers are raging at the amounts wasted by the Court on masques, theatrical performances and the purchase of paintings and sculpture. New extensions to the royal palaces are being built to accommodate them, he tells me," said Sir Philippe. "He seems to share a taste for fantasy with his wife and, I believe, with Queen Anne, his mother. I suppose, as a King, he must be able to make a display of his taste for the finer things of life, to be their equal. He has attempted to show military prowess, I suppose we would agree."

"Now Buckingham is dead," Elie interjected, "he seems to have lost interest in our defence. I hope that he may try to repay us for defending his island and for the ships we are losing in its defence. Making peace with Spain and France does not stop pirate attacks."

"You men are all the same! Don't you agree, Anne? We are all wealthier than I ever remember, and it results from our own efforts, as it should. Why should a King be any different? He needs a comfortable home for his family, and entertainment for them when he has time to enjoy it. Wars and seizing the wealth of others is only a small part of life!"

Anne smiled and remarked, "Perhaps we could visit London with you when you have to go. I'm sure I would like to visit a theatre and see the King's tapestries. If you take his privileges away, he might stop being King!"

"Yes," agreed Elizabeth, with a severe frown, "we would both like to see what happens at Court to understand why so many find life at court shocking."

Entering a hostelry below Bar in Southampton, George was greeted by a fellow Lieutenant and was delighted to recognise James Hawkins in full uniform and exuding confidence. After hearty greetings had been exchanged, Hawkins declared that he would be honoured if George would be his dinner guest, which would provide time to exchange tales of their adventures of the past few years. James had been fortunate in gaining a Lieutenancy on the Bezan, a vessel charged by His Majesty to go to Genoa and bring to England valuable treasures. In answer to George's question, he confided that there were many decorative objects, one of which, he whispered, came unwrapped and revealed a bare-breasted woman welcoming a knight in armour to her tent! He was sure that George would have shared his horror had he been present. "The frame seemed to be pure gold," he reflected. "Melted down it would pay for a ship!"

They wondered whether His Majesty would send such a thing back to Italy, where Catholic Churches were full of obscene objects and partly clothed threatening women taking part in scenes depicting the life of Christ and his followers. Many of those who saw them thought them obscene and sacrilegious and were astonished that their King could permit such offensive material to be bought for him. George nodded a polite agreement and remarked that he and Admiral Pennington had escorted a number of ships flying the Royal Standard in the past four years, and that Petty and Derby were his leading agents and buyers at auctions in Italy.

Sir Philippe had told his family that the King was improving his palaces and needed modern paintings to fill the walls. George talked about his own ship and his role in opposing pirate raiders and that he had been asked on several occasions to carry foreign dignitaries to England or couriers to France. He objected to being absent from his protection work and was constantly worried by the thought that his ship might suffer a pirate raid in which he might be blamed for the death or kidnapping of foreign royals. Their feeding and comfort on board was always at his expense and he and the crew managed on short rations. Sometimes the guests were generous in tipping, especially if they had survived a rough crossing, but he often supplemented the crew's wages from his own pocket.

Changing the subject from dangers shared to the pleasures of meeting old friends, James Hawkins told of meeting Gareth Jones, the Welsh surgeon, when he took a crew man to have a nasty rash treated. He was well and had a growing clientele among the well-to-do citizens.

"He told me he had met you in 1628 when you witnessed the death of Buckingham: he hoped you had recovered fully from the shock, which was likely to disturb your sleep long after the event."

George confessed that he had awoken with heart pounding on many occasions having heard again the victim's cry of rage. It had not happened recently and was less frequent now. Jones told him about Felton's trial and execution at Tyburn the following January. James, to George's regret, asked whether he had spoken to Felton, as Jones had suggested. He wanted to know if Felton was the raving lunatic as was generally supposed. George told him that in fact Felton was no different from many, waiting for a berth as Lieutenant, though he was an army officer. He had been low in spirits however, since having taken an injury and thus saved Buckingham's life at Breda. He had been denied a posting and was, when George saw him last, about to make yet another polite request for one. He assumed that his violent reaction was the result of a final rejection which had disturbed his mind. James shook his head in silent sympathy and George admitted that either of them might have found their life's hope destroyed if they had been so rejected and wondered how he would have reacted. Should he have given Felton advice of some kind, or words of sympathy?

"On the Fair Haven I was beginning to think that I would never be able to afford the exam. Fortunately, Gideon Carteret asked whether he could help me gain promotion and I had sense enough to accept his offer."

"It was he and Sir Philippe who paid my board and lodging when I took my exam," George admitted." There must be many good seamen, who fail for lack of wealthy friends. I suppose all depends on chance and wealthy sponsors and we should be thankful if we find them!"

"Jones told me that after Buckingham's Funeral in Westminster Abbey, Felton's corpse was cut down and taken in a vegetable cart to Portsmouth where it is still hanging from the town gibbet as a warning to traitors. I was as shocked as Jones when he told me about it. The people of Portsmouth are furious, since it is a slight on their loyalty, and quite unjustified."

"We must hope that His Majesty finds better advisors in future," George agreed.

"He could start by listening to professionals when he starts naval operations, as he does when he buys paintings."

Chapter 18

" I heard that you were returned from London, Amyas. I want to ask you about the present state of affairs at Court. I heard an odd story about London merchants making an attack on Whitehall Palace. I hope it is untrue?"

Sir Philippe's face showed clearly the anxiety he was feeling.

"The merchants did not, in fact go out onto the streets, Uncle, they sent their apprentices, but they were so angry about the new tax levies on sales to retailers, they refused to provide retailers with goods to sell. Had it continued, Londoners might have gone hungry, or their warehouses attacked. The King ordered them to recommence trading immediately and, at first, they refused to obey unless the King withdrew the tax. He not only refused but ordered the London Militia and Artillery company to arrest a London Merchant, Richard Elliott, possibly the wealthiest of them all. He was arrested and tried by a new court, held in the Star Chamber at Westminster. Its hearings are held in secret and it may pass sentence of execution. The charge against him was that at a meeting of traders he had been heard to say, "merchants were in no part of the world so screwed and wrung as in England", and thus accused the King of tyranny, which was an act of treason. The merchants finally relented and the King, in a gesture of generosity, released

Chambers, another arrested man, Eliot, remained in prison. Though he was fined £2000.00 for challenging the authority of Government. Eliot, to the best of my belief, remained in prison."

"Fortunately, I have never heard you utter such a sentiment, Philippe," Gideon responded. "Of course, the king's laws must be obeyed."

"I shall try to ensure that the States don't hear about it, if I feel forced to complain. I hope that Government never attempts to force us to pay taxes not approved by Parliament."

"The merchants seem to be calmer now that trade with France is growing, but a number of them have fallen foul of an old regulation which the new Attorney General has revived, demanding that anyone with an annual income of £40.00 or more, must present themselves for a Knighthood. Anyone not applying before 1630 must pay a heavy fine for each year of non-payment. William Noy has also revived the sale of monopolies under the Treasury. Ship Money is to stay and be strictly regulated by County officials and must now be paid by every household nationwide and the poor will be reduced to absolute poverty as a result. The King asserts that in a time of national emergency, such as now, the King may impose such taxes as are necessary, with or without Parliamentary assent. Austerity is to be imposed. We shall have to wait and see whether this is permitted."

"I certainly hope that he does not impose it on Jersey. The States may refuse. One piece of better news, at least for us, is that Sir Richard Weston, the new Lord Treasurer, has found the money for a fine new ship of war and has given you Philippe, the task of building it. He understands the shortage of wood and that I will contract the work out to French shipbuilders, so freeing English yards for repair work."

"I must have free rein and I shall give it careful thought. I have already told Francis Windebank, Secretary of State, that George will

235

shortly complete a detailed report on the French Navy and seaports, and he will ask George to present it in person to the Lord Admiral, Manchester. This is very pleasing, and George will rise to the occasion, I know".

"I have a piece of news for you which I am sorry to report. At the end of the year I shall be leaving Jersey, with considerable regret," Peyton revealed. "Windebank has another in mind for the post. At the moment the favoured one is Sir Thomas Jermyn- although this may change. He is a wealthy, retired merchant and every inch a courtier, so I do not think he will bother you much with his presence. I believe it may be a financial gift from the King, for Jermyn's work in keeping the Queen's expenditure in order."

* * *

"Oh, George! You startled me! I didn't expect to see you here."

"Father, I've been living in your house for almost two weeks, treated like royalty by mother who plies me with food whenever she sees me. I've seen you passing through several times. I'm not invisible. You seem to be completely preoccupied. Mother is in despair."

"I thought you were going back to your ship to keep the pirates at bay. Where is your ship, by the way? The Garland isn't it?"

"Yes. It's in St Malo for new masts- both the fore and main masts snapped when I was pursuing a pirate and had all canvas up. You would have noticed me here if you had not been away from home so much of the time. Mother says she only sees you at dinner time, and not always then."

"I'm having to spend so much time settling trade disputes of one kind or another. It's good to have such a large increase in trade, but I shall have to employ yet another clerk before long."

"Are you doing anything constructive here, George? I'm told you had some experience of accounts in St John and I suppose with your skills you never need a bursar on your ship. I see you are not going to offer your help with the accounts. If you like, I would appreciate it if you would come with me to see the new fort I'm having built at Plemont and tell me what you think of it."

"Can it be tomorrow, father? My hands are stained black with ink, but I think I shall finish my report on the French Navy today. I'm just completing a fair copy, then I am at your service. Forgive me if I say that you should spend more time enjoying mother's food: you are looking thinner every time I see you".

* * *

"Good morning, Amyas. How was your trip?"

"Excellent, but I had to wait three days for a good wind. It's good to be back at Moore Court: I need a day or two before we set off for London. Have you seen Sir Francis; he wasn't in the stables?"

"He went into Romsey, but I think I can hear the sound of his voice, he must be back."

"I'll go up to my room. They have taken hot water and I need a wash and shave. Tell him I will see him when I've changed."

"Another crisis averted, thank Goodness! Was that Amyas's horse I saw in the stable?"

"He's gone to wash. He had a long time on board and looks tired."

"Very hardworking, Amyas. I don't know what your Uncles would do, without him. Congratulations by the way, I gather you are on your way to give Windebank your report. I think you are the first spy in

237

the family. You have provided us with valuable information if we find ourselves at war with France again."

"I hope not, Uncle. They have far too many fine ships for us to have success. Uncle- before Amyas returns, I would like to ask you to help me with a matter which is worrying me and would appreciate your advice."

"Of course, my boy- not about a young lady is it? I've heard that you are finding it difficult to make a choice in Jersey. You'll have a larger field of choice in London!"

"No, I can manage those matters myself so far! It's about the murder of Buckingham and its after-effects: there are some aspects I find troublesome and I would like to talk about them."

"Of course, my boy. The whole event worried a lot of us - still does, in fact. I think about it constantly and worry whether it is all about to happen again. I saw the effect it had on you: still having nightmares, are you? I'm not surprised. I think I may have upset you, but I feel I must know. Did you know Felton as a friend? Your reaction was one I have seen after a bereavement. If so, you have my sympathy, the death of a colleague is always a shock."

"Not exactly a friend, I suppose. I met him three times, first when in Southampton and then when I went for breakfast and recognised him as an army officer and saw that he looks gaunt with hunger. I was waiting to hear whether I had passed my test and knew he had succeeded, so I asked about the exam and interview. He started telling me and I was hungry, so I asked him to join me at breakfast. He answered my enquiries and told me he had served in the Breda campaign and was looking for advancement from Buckingham under whom he had served. He told me the Duke had taken him as a Lieutenant and now he had recovered, wanted to serve with him again. I had noticed that he had a slight limp when he walked. He had asked the Duke twice to remember

238

him and had been told that there was no vacancy though he had not given up hope and might speak to him that afternoon. I wished him luck and suggested we should meet next evening to celebrate his certain success.

"He did not join me that evening, and I hoped that he was celebrating with comrades. I think I caught a glimpse of him when I went for breakfast on the morning of the murder but felt that Felton was avoiding me or had not seen me. You know the rest, for you were standing behind me. You may not have noticed that he looked directly at me in the marketplace, and again later, when he was lecturing the crowd about his starving mother: he saw me there."

"You must not believe that you have anything to reproach yourself with. He may not even have been in any condition to recognise you. You must try to put it behind you, George."

"I thought I had, Uncle, until I met an old friend who told me about Felton's corpse being exposed to ridicule in Portsmouth. That seems to be an entirely despicable action on the part of the King or his Councillors, and I cannot understand how Felton's action could be seen as their responsibility."

"I must say how proud I am that you are my nephew and what a credit your words do you."

"I feel that my own promotion would not have happened if I had not been born into a well-known family prepared to support me and gain me favours I do not deserve."

"Again, George, I fully share your feelings. Felton had no supporters to support his petition. I gather that the Chancellor of Oxford University uttered a few rash words in his favour and was only saved from prison because of his high reputation. That is unfortunate, but perfectly natural. Buckingham was a man of very little talent, except for a persuasive manner and an ability to charm. Our masters select their Ministers from those they have ennobled for whatever reason, usually

239

financial, and many of our leaders are inadequate. What our family does is to try to reward ability with its support. You will, I am sure, do the same when your time comes."

"I suppose you are right. But I feel that Buckingham refused to accept Felton because he walked with a limp and did not want an injured man near him. It seems to me that His Majesty selects men as though they were pawns in a game of chess. He picks up a piece and uses it, then leaves it to its fate. If one man fails in an attempt to carry out his wishes, he is discarded and replaced by another. Even Buckingham has been replaced by others who are more ruthless."

"Possibly! He was brave, I hear, and very determined, but he made more enemies than friends and was certainly vindictive. I don't mind saying that many people I know were made happier by the news of his death, I hope the king chooses better councillors with his passing. You will meet some of them before long; Amyas will have made it his business to get to know them. My son, Thomas, is working his way up the ladder of the law and doing well, and you met Henry Paulet when he went to France in your boat to arrange the King's wedding, I believe. His father, Lord Winchester, is in great favour at present and the Royal Couple are frequent guests."

"When Felton was speaking to the crowd in Portsmouth, I heard him say that England would be better without Buckingham. It's sad that he did not know how many agreed with him. I believe he repeated it from the scaffold before he was hanged."

"Personally, I feel sorry for Courtney: a very kind and thoughtful man. He was beside himself with guilt after the Duke's murder, believing he could have prevented it. Apparently, he recommended the Duke to wear a breastplate before going to his ship, but the Duke refused. He told James that he wanted to display the beautiful doublet his wife had embroidered. James blames himself for not insisting, but the Duke disliked contradiction!

"The Courtiers suspected that there was a gang of plotters in Portsmouth, or that the local Militia were implicated. Nonsense, of course! It was in danger of becoming a witch hunt, but fortunately Felton insisted that no-one else was involved. You remember I burned your shirt and got you away as soon as possible in case someone thought you were involved.

"Poor James collapsed in shock later. It was nearly an hour before he came around. I doubt whether he will be able to continue as Sheriff, he had no energy. He had a seizure last month. Buckingham has brought misfortune on so many good people over the years. We must hope that King Charles looks for more useful qualities in his advisors that King James, his father."

* * *

"So, what do you think of this inn, George? My brother, Sir Philippe and I, often stay overnight on our way to London. You'll like it even more when you get some of their roast beef inside you. The road was surprisingly dry today. We may catch some rain tomorrow when we approach the Chilterns, and the road can be quite dangerous near the Devil's Punch Bowl, a favourite place for Highwaymen. After this we will probably stay overnight in Esher, a very pleasant town. Now, if you are ready, we will go down for a glass of ale before dinner: they keep a good Burgundy!"

"It is strange to see a stone building thatched, while the floors are paved, but it seems a welcoming place. Do you know the landlady well? I hope I did not seem impolite when I refused her offer to kiss me."

"Don't worry George! You made up for your hesitation in fine style. You will learn that it is polite to kiss a woman, and embrace a man, when you meet them in England. In Europe adults are more reserved than the English. The French are amazed that Englishmen expect their wives to be kissed. Jersey people are more like the French, I suppose, but you will have to get used to it!"

"I'm getting so used to the custom that I forgot *not* to kiss her when I met Rachel in St Helier and kissed her. She was quite embarrassed, but she has forgiven me, I'm pleased to say. She has quite taken to it recently! But enough of this: here is our soup!"

"I hope it is as good as its aroma. I enjoyed meeting Mr. Petty and his family yesterday. Am I right in thinking that he is a clothier?"

"Yes, George, and Mayor of Romsey, also. There is possibility he may be Sheriff when Francis ends his term, he might even have to pay the fine for not claiming a Knighthood. He is in two minds, I think. Being "Sir William" might sound impressive, but it creates certain expenses and he is making further enquiries. By the way, you really placed me in a difficult situation yesterday."

George gave a look of enquiry.

"Don't pretend you don't understand me. You forced me into a game of kick ball with his sons. I haven't done that for years and I've got a large bruise on my arse to show for it."

"You should be careful who you show it, Amyas. Try to avoid falling over so often, it is a sign of ageing!"

"Be very careful, George! I am your Uncle and demand due respect. Perhaps you would like to step outside where I can teach you a lesson?"

"I prefer to inflict more bruises, Amyas. Now eat this excellent dinner calmly as an elderly man should."

"Enough, George. You certainly made a big impression on William."

"William- do you mean Petty?"

"No, George, his younger son. Apparently, Francis has been entertaining the boys for months with gory tales of your fights with pirates, and swimming for your life from shipwrecks. He has ambitions to be a sailor. His father is very amused."

"I wish Francis would stop doing that. My young brothers keep asking me to tell them about the time I met a cannibal, and I have no idea what to say because he invented it. I try to invent a fitting yarn, but they keep correcting me because I'm changing the story."

"Wait until you have children. They will expect to hear the same ones, if Francis has his way."

"That's far into the future. I have to make my fortune and marry first. The family expect it!

"I believe they have the same expectation for you, Amyas!"

"And will it be Rachel for you, George?"

* * *

"Safely on land again, George. The river smelled dreadful today. These are the Temple steps, and rather slippery. It's the only entrance from the river, unless you want to enter a warehouse. The riverbank on our left is lined with the palaces of our wealthiest nobility. That enormity with gardens and a landing stage, is Somerset House where Buckingham used to hold court. It was built for Robert Carr, James' favourite- I expect you've heard the story. No? Well, he and his wife conspired in a murder. They knew Sir Thomas Overbury was going to reveal their part in the Mompesson scam and poisoned his food. The King refused to allow them to be executed and they spent twelve years imprisoned in the

243

Tower. They deserved hanging. It now belongs to the Queen. We'll walk from here and I will show you the newer parts of London, built in the last half century, which are still expanding. Most of the land belonged to the Church, but good King Hal sold it off to developers to fund his wars."

"I hope it is not as stinking as Southwark and the river!"

"We need a good storm to wash the filth away, George. You'll get used to it. Perhaps you need a pomander. Ah, I see you are puzzled. Perhaps we will see one for sale... This is the Temple, where most of the Judges have their Chambers. Francis has an office there, and so does his son, Thomas, but he lives further north. We will be crossing Holborn next, one of our most important streets and occupied by merchants. Broad Street is probably going to be the next fashionable street for the wealthy. I'm sorry about the stink caused by the Holborn stream which is choked with rubbish as fast as they clear it. Litter is thrown anywhere, I'm afraid. Behind these walls are the Inns of Court. Many were convents or monasteries, now occupied by lawyers. This next one is Staples' Inn and Francis has a house in the next street. You may remember meeting Henry Wallop when you were at Moore Court? I hear that he has just received a Knighthood for a voluntary loan to the King. Apparently, he has an agreement with Robert Oxenbridge to buy Hurstbourne Park. He was reading law at Thavies Inn before going to the Temple. You will spend a lot of your time here in London. Whitehall and Westminster are across those fields to the right and the City is over in the other direction, so, as you can see, we are in the centre. This street is one with several brothels. Many call it Sodom! It has a worse reputation than some of their other haunts. I warn you against the south bank punks, George. You may be attacked and robbed by their pimps before you know it!"

Chapter 19

"Thank you, Alice; we will have coffee in the sitting room. When you have cleared, that will be all for today. Breakfast at 8.30 please. Good night! Excellent couple, William and Alice. Been with Francis for years and his father too, I recall. I know you don't smoke, thank Heaven, but we must drink to your successful presentation at the Treasury. I don't wish to worry you but, to some extent, the family rely on you to make a good impression and I will be blamed if it goes wrong. I share the burden with the others you will meet and intend to introduce you to as many people as I can. In due course, you can return the compliment to another family member. So, let's drink- to success!"

"Amyas, this is a very fine burgundy. I think my report will speak for itself: I've included some plans of the defences which will give a very clear picture. I have some anxiety about my clothes, and whether I should have asked Mr. Petty to supply me with something better."

"Don't worry on that account, George. They know you are a successful sea captain and you've not had time to dress in your best land gear. They will not expect you to dress like a London fop- they might not take you seriously. If you have to stay in London, or return later, you can have something made for the occasion. I hear that Windebank is determined to make a good impression on Parliament and practice a new austerity, so your clothing should make the point."

"Will you show me to Windebank's office, Amyas?"

"Absolutely, though I have never been there before, and I may have to enquire."

"I suggest we agree a place to meet at three o'clock for dinner. If you finish early, you could go exploring by yourself. Whitehall is full of narrow alleys and little shops staffed by charming young ladies, and you could ask a guardsman to let you see parts of the palace in return for a few coins. In London you must take the bull by the horns if you wish to succeed in any situation."

* * *

"Ready for another of Alice's splendid meals, George? You look as though you have fought several battles. Perhaps I should not have walked you round Westminster after your interrogation. I gather it went well: am I right?"

"I was received politely by Mr. Windebank after a brief delay and saw that the two gentlemen present were poring earnestly over the plans which I had sent in earlier for perusal. They were much puzzled by what they saw but, taking the plan of St Malo as an example, I told them the old works were in black and the new works superimposed in rubric. I emphasised the impossibility of our poor fleet taking on the bombardment of the new works and they appeared to accept it with a good grace. At their request, I left my plans in their hands, and will be recalled when they have received thorough study."

"Then all is well, I suppose. I will make enquiries of friends as to their reception. They will recall you in due course. Were you wise to leave your plans with them, I wonder?"

"I have reserved a copy for reference."

"A wise precaution! It appears you will be my guest for some time to come then, and I have been considering how your time in London may be turned to our advantage. Gaming houses, brothels, and theatres abound, and may satisfy the entire needs of many, but since I

246

cannot meet with my legal instructor for another week, I will give you the benefit of my knowledge of the people and places which you must be familiar with. The three I have already mentioned, may at times be of great use, and I will not exclude them."

"Thank you, Amyas. I do not wish to cause you inconvenience."

"Of course you don't, George. First, however, I will tell you my plan which is a little like a military campaign, such as Elie would approve. As an introduction, before we set out, I have to make a few personal observations, which I hope you will bear with patience.

"Your dress will not pass in the City company you will meet, and your sword may be very suitable for clearing the decks of captured ships, but is not suitable for the street, or coffee house. You should leave it here and wear one of mine: I have several spare. In addition, I shall lend you one of my long coats in light woollen and a discreet shade of blue. Number three of the list. I shall introduce you as "Lieutenant Carteret". Your accent is pure Hampshire, which is fine, but try to avoid showing familiarity with French. In that way we all pass inspection without question and we never use the prefix "de" for the same reason."

"I accept your advice with gratitude, Uncle Amyas. Believe me, it is not the first time my clothing has been subject to criticism."

"Then let us prepare to face the world, George. Thank Heaven you were not baptised "Zouche"! He will need to adopt a more English name if he hopes for success outside Jersey. Perhaps it would be wise if you left most of the talking to me until you see how the land lies."

"I will try to follow your advice- and thank you for using a nautical metaphor to make me feel at ease!

"Beware impertinence to your elders, George!" His nephew responded with a rude gesture.

Chapter 20

“ That is St Paul's Cathedral. The enormous tower is where the Nave and transepts cross. We'll enter the north transept and leave by the south, which is more direct. All these shops and stalls run the whole length of the building, which I am told is the longest Cathedral in England, and probably in the world. This way! As you can see it's full of stalls and tables, offering almost everything you can think of. It's good for vegetables and fruit, but meat must be sold at Smithfield, which is close by. The Reformation has transformed St Paul's to the benefit of Londoners, since goods in open markets are ruined when the weather is bad: it's like the covered markets you see in France.

"That man wearing the black robe is an Anglican pastor dressed in his robe. They are a new uniform with two white preacher's tabs at the neck. The Protestants say it reeks of Catholicism; I think they are fussing about nothing. If you look left, you can just see the table at the eastern end with a silly fence round it to keep the dogs away. A new instruction says it must be called an "Altar": many consider that a name for a place where pagans used to sacrifice. Some, of course, find it difficult to accept new concepts. What do you think, George? I suppose people in Jersey may have strong reactions to the new practices."

"I know Dean Bandinel is inclined to favour adherence to the new order of services, but Sir Philippe is trying to ensure that any imposition of change may be tempered with caution. He is certainly anxious to avoid friction."

"We have to hope that Laud and His Majesty do not provoke the extreme reaction in London which they caused in Scotland.

"Come this way; it must be raining outside- people are running in, shaking their hats. Watch out for head lice! Some people are very thoughtless...."

* * *

"Now it's stopped, and we can go down to the River. I'm afraid the smell is no better. It's worse when the wind is westerly, which is why the rich live north or west of the city."

"I have never seen such filthy streets anywhere, Amyas. My shoes and breeches are caked with mud and muck and the smell is getting worse every minute."

"Then be prepared for a much worse stink. That is the smell of the fish sold in Billingsgate, just up from the fishing port. Thousands of skep-loads are distributed every day, and the filleted guts flung into the gutters. I suppose it may bring back memories of Newfoundland. The market cleaners cannot cope with it, and it gets washed down into the river eventually when it rains. Come this way now...

"That large building is the Admiralty. The sea lords work from there. Anyone seeking work, from deckhand to captain, has to make application every day to the clerks to show that they are ready. You will probably find yourself waiting in line unless you have influential friends. In fact, the increase in trade means that a new larger building is necessary with decent accommodation for the Lords of the Admiralty, but we may not live to see it. The Change is also too small for all the dealing that is conducted there. You can see how many men are waiting patiently in line, and many will return tomorrow. Down here is the Tower of London, still maintained as a Royal Residence, but not much used in the past century. Elizabeth and James preferred St James' or Whitehall, or a palace in the country. The church behind us is St Olave's, known as the

Mariner's Church. Seething Lane, where the Admiralty have their office at present, is just behind it. You know Church attendance on Sunday is obligatory, and you must be seen to attend. It is old and gloomy inside, as you will see, but it is where you will need to attend services. You will meet important sea captains in an informal setting, so you will have the opportunity to get to know them, by reserving a seat for them, or calling them a coach. After lunch at an Ordinary, we will go to Williams's Coffee shop. We will meet some of my friends who may support you to gain influence, and some may have nephews wishing to become Captains' Servants as the start of a naval career, whom you might be able to assist. You will also meet Jersey men of your generation who chose to graduate at Oxford before deciding on a career in London."

* * *

The plan outlined by Amyas bore fruit, and George soon gained new acquaintances with his readiness to take on a tab and was open in his appreciation of help and advice, and a good listener, able to give practical advice. George became familiar with the City and the Change, and was introduced to Whitehall and St Stephen's Chamber, where parliament sometimes met. He also listened to trials in Westminster Hall, where High Court Judges presided. Amyas introduced him to those making new careers and some who were influential and willing to share their experience. Having seen his father presiding as Attorney General in Jersey, he was impressed by the speed and firmness with which judgements were delivered in London.

Coffee House society was a strange experience and the drink seemed unpleasant, though he grew accustomed to its bitterness at last. Its main attraction was as a meeting place where men came, not to drown their sorrows, but for relaxation and make useful contacts in congenial company, enlivened by coffee and animated discussion. It was used by lawyers to rehearse the arguments they would later present before a judge, but it also served those eager to discuss issues from their study of natural sciences, or metaphysics. A number of those he met turned, after weather and actresses had been reviewed, to heated disputes about the ideas of Descartes and Bacon. Neither those names, nor their ideas were familiar to him, but he was astonished at first by the revelation that ideas he had always accepted as unchangeable, could be subjected to a kind of legal cross-examination, as though they were criminal suspects, attempting to impose their deceits and deceptive practices on honest God-fearing folk who, foolishly, trusted them. So many of his cherished ideas were, he learned, "a priori" and merited close investigation as to their merit.

These discussions shocked him considerably, particularly when they attempted to explain the differences between Justice and Law. His heart raced as he found that he could understand this new concept. Similarly, if blood circulated round the body, what purpose did it serve? If it was pumped by the heart, was the heart the main organ of the body or the brain? Why, above all, was it illegal to dissect bodies to discover how they worked? Did bodies wind up like clocks? Was God a celestial clockmaker? After a few days he felt it essential to question these assertions and was pleased to be told that he was perceptive when he provoked discussion. When one of his questions produced a sudden silence, he was horrified, but then realised that his intervention had led, not to mockery, but to more discussion. Generally, the evening ended on a cheerful note, sometimes with *a capella* singing. The landlord usually had a lute or cithern stowed away, and playing instruments seemed to be a common skill. Finally, Amyas took him to the King's Theatre where he saw that controversial issues were publicly aired without censorship. If the setting was an earlier age or a foreign country, matters of current relevance could be explored which would be prosecuted if published as a pamphlet.

He was amazed and delighted by the play of light and darkness which could be achieved and by the glitter of costumes and jewellery, and even more, by the beauty and skill of the actresses. These convinced him that they were indeed women of noble birth and the highest moral principles. "How could anyone believe that acting endangered the moral standards of the country?", he mused.

Some days later a lawyer friend, met by chance in the street, introduced him to his female companion who was clearly the worse for gin and whose language was suggestive, and verging on the obscene. "George, I'd like to introduce my dear friend, Molly Kemp." George responded politely and listened, astonished to be reminded how much he had admired the beauty and acting skill of "the Duchess of Padua" two days since. "You can make your compliments directly to Mrs. Kemp, for here is the object of your admiration!"

The woman came to embrace and kiss him passionately and thanked him for his kind words, adding that if he stayed behind after that night's performance, she would be delighted to be his guest for supper, if he had time to spare. His acquaintance, perhaps noticing George's confusion, murmured, "I believe George will be entertaining his fiancée tomorrow, but I am sure he will make a point of meeting you again."

Taking Molly's arm, he bowed, and led her into a dress maker's workshop.

* * *

George had received a salutary lesson in the art of acting but was by no means discouraged from attending other performances, and entertaining a number of other actresses to supper, and often to escort them to boisterous parties where drunkenness and assignations, in discreet corners, were the rule. Mrs Kemp approached him a few days later after a light comedy which was more to his taste than serious drama. The action was broken by opportunities for song and dance, and George soon selected his favourite dancer. Mrs Kemp arranged an immediate introduction, and Mrs. Jane York joined them for supper after the show. Jane became his frequent companion during his time in London, though not the only one to be favoured. There was also the appealing shop assistant whom he met while choosing gloves to present to Jane York and others. Glove giving was an indication that you hoped for a friendship or as a mark of gratitude. He had to remind himself that he had a living to make, and dependents to support: later when his family came to the theatre with him, Jane, his constant companion, became invisible to ensure he was never embarrassed. Seamen were reputed to have a wife in every port: George was finding it easy to follow that custom!

* * *

A week passed, and an acquaintance stopped him in Westminster Hall, and offered to go with him, if he was at leisure, into St James' Park.

"I'm Edward Knight. We met briefly last week on the tennis court here where Amyas had just played. You had arranged to play that afternoon. Did you enjoy a game?"

"I had never seen the game before, and it took me some time to get the way of it. I intend to improve with practice."

"Look, George, I wonder whether you have particular business. Amyas said you were eager to see London life and I hear that the King and Queen will be riding in the park today: I hear Prince Rupert has been challenged to a race, and the queen has placed money on him to win."

253

Amyas had only recently been introduced to the game of tennis, which gave him access to some about the Court, and he had a meeting in Westminster Hall to attend. Amyas went and George thanked Edward Knight and walked with him into the park.

"I expect the King's horse is being groomed for him. The Queen often rides with him, but I expect she will watch from her carriage. It may give you an opportunity to see the King at close quarters. Charles has memory for faces and it may be useful to have your face recognised, you may even be asked to speak to him. Some time, if you are here for some days, I could also take you into St James' and show you the private theatre where the nobility sometimes take to the stage. You will be impressed by the sets built by Inigo Jones. Buckingham introduced him to the King who thinks highly of his architectural plans and may employ him for new buildings at Whitehall, which lacks a large well-lit banqueting hall."

As they walked to gravelled paths behind the Palace, George commented on the welcome freshness of the air compared with the City.

"Most cities of any size have the same problem," Knight remarked. "It is perhaps a proof of the wealth and activity of a city that it should be redolent with the scent of money. If it is true that London is the greatest city of the world, then perhaps it is a merit."

"Even worse than the smell is the filth underfoot?" George asked. "I expect at any moment to slip into the gutters, which are either clogged or invisible. Worst of all is the Redcliff Highway where merchant ships are loaded daily among iron foundries, stables, drinking dens, and shipyards with all the rubbish they produce. The Steelyard is particularly fragrant and I wonder why it was given that name."

"I have only been there once and have no wish to go again", answered his guide. "It is a name given by its first owners, the Company of Hanseatic Traders. They dominated our overseas trade and controlled

254

all the major ports of Europe until Queen Elizabeth confiscated their property and forbade them the use of our ports, as a favour to our Merchant Venturers. We are just beginning to feel the benefit, though we no longer have any of the protection for our ships at sea that the armed Hanse vessels provided. Now, listen. I hear the sound of horses. It may be His Majesty's Guardsmen heading up the Royal Party. His Majesty is an accomplished horseman and may decide to compete in a race in the park. If so, we must keep clear."

Almost at once, shouts of command were given and the guards galloped past, ordering walkers and riders aside. Many gathered along the chosen racecourse, and, shortly after, two fine Arab stallions galloped past at full speed, ridden by men wearing hats, cloaks, and elaborate riding boots. When they had passed, in a cloud of dust, they remained waiting until a guided carriage, followed by a second, trotted up, coming to a rest a few yards away. The guards reassembled and took up stations at a respectful distance. Shortly after, the two gentlemen trotted back, engaged in loud discussion.

Laughing and talking, they rode to the first carriage where they stopped their horses and doffed their hats to the tiny lady seated among the cushions. She asked who had won and the younger man with long, flowing hair, bowed politely to the other who accepted the hand offered by the Queen, and kissed it. The Queen took a purse from an attendant, which he accepted with a deep bow. Equerries came to take charge of the horses, the riders dismounted, and other gentlemen came to offer congratulations.

One gestured to a member of the crowd to step forward, and spoke quietly to the King, who silenced him with a gesture, welcomed him by name, asked how he did, and whether his baby son was thriving. The King listened carefully with round unblinking eyes, then indicated he had heard enough before asking if there was another who wished for an

255

audience. A second was waved forward, was heard to make his plea, before kneeling in an attitude of prayer. The King placed his hand on the man's head, raised his eyes to heaven, and spoke the words intended to heal the man's sickness, the King's Evil. His ability as an anointed King, to cure illness was one that Charles took very seriously knowing that it enhanced his influence among the populace, and he rarely stopped anywhere without offering his blessing to any sufferers from scrofula.

* * *

George noticed how short the King was, although he seemed to have the ability to look down on others, whose height seemed suddenly to become an embarrassment to them. The supplicant rose, bowed, and was dismissed. George saw that the King's face lacked animation and that his eyebrows, eyes, and mouth seemed to droop as though expressing a deep and lingering grief. It was a face of great sadness, or regret, as though life afforded little joy. Was this the face of the man who had once impulsively planned to marry the Infanta?

The Queen, however, had an expressive face, reflecting rapid changes of emotion, and was always watchful of her husband. She had the appearance of someone younger that her twenty-two years. On an impulse, she gestured to the King to join her, and walked to her carriage, the King following. The carriage was driven away, she in animated chatter.

"I have not seen the Queen before," Edward remarked. "She is even shorter than he is and about four foot eight: the king is about five foot and always wears high-heeled shoes."

"Who was the tall, dark-haired younger man?" George asked.

"That was Prince Rupert of the Rhine, the son of the deposed Elizabeth, Queen of Bohemia, the King's sister. Now that the King has

256

a son, named Charles, Rupert is only third in line to the throne. He has a regal appearance and is a firm Calvinist. He has just been created, Duke of Cumberland and I suppose he and his brother, Maurice, will be staying in England while their parents remain trapped in Heidelberg."

"I wonder what I would find to say to the King?" George wondered aloud. "I am relieved that he did not notice me."

"You may be wrong. Though he looks absent-minded, he is constantly watchful, and has a retentive memory. His upbringing led him to be constantly looking for danger or slights: he does not tolerate criticism well. Before we go our ways, George, I must tell you your report has been well received by the Privy Council. You may be called to meet Counsellors wanting more."

"I wondered whether our meeting was as fortuitous as it seemed, Edward. Should I need to speak to the King, I will bear in mind your words as a friendly warning, though I doubt whether I shall have the opportunity."

"If you care to improve our acquaintance, George, I try to get to Will's at eleven most days. I think you would enjoy meeting James Harrington, an old friend with interesting ideas."

The following day, Amyas was to be given a *viva* by his legal principal. He claimed that George's questions had made him think more deeply about the legal torts he might need to elucidate and expressed his gratitude. They would meet, later at The Mitre tavern, for a meal.

"We will have to do something about your clothing, George, especially if you are to be seen in Court circles."

"I am not prepared to wear anything prinked out with lace and ribbons, Amyas!"

"It would not be expected of you, as Captain of a sloop. Something fitting you, in black with white linen, cuffs and hose, is what I have in mind. And good shoes are essential!"

257

"They will be ruined walking in the streets, surely."

"We have been walking solely to give you some idea how to reach the places you may need to visit. You should be able to avoid the worst mess and know where to take a carriage. The carriage drawing up outside is the one I generally use. Tom, the driver is steady and reliable. Come down with me and I will tell him to take you on as a "regular," as he regards me. When you need a carriage get William to send for him."

* * *

George had decided that he should get to know the layout of the Royal Naval Yards, partially visible when he had explored the Redcliff bank of the river. He took a carriage to the Temple Steps and engaged a waterman to row him over to the Southwark bank, planning to walk along to the Dockyard. The squalor of the streets and dwellings was worse than anything he had seen so far. The streets were running with sewage, and areas devoted to fishmongers and butchers were particularly loathsome and redolent with rotting filth and rejected offal. He avoided falling, by sheer good luck on several occasions, and almost lost a boot in one particularly glutinous mess, of which a dead dog seemed to be part. Girls were staggering under the weight of buckets of water carried to benches where strong-armed women, with pinched faces and lank hair, who wore grimy linen and battled with the filth around them, with little effect. Scantily dressed in rags, children ran riot among the loaded carts and barrows clogging the street, where drunken dockers, and old soldiers and sailors, with missing arms and legs, staggered uncertainly towards some welcoming hovel, or thrust a demanding hand in the face of passers-by. Whatever they were given, and this happened infrequently, the donor was thanked with abuse and foul oaths, as he hurried on his way towards the next vociferous beggar.

At almost every turning, gangs of apprentices or unemployed corner boys gathered to drink lethal, home-made gin, place bets, fight among themselves, sometimes stopping to abuse a passer -by or make salacious and audible remarks to a passing woman. Most appeared to be more than equal to the suggestions made, and replied with their own observations, to general approval. George was targeted on several occasions, but was accustomed to facing down such remarks, though he put his hand to his sword at a couple of instances of extreme impertinence. Occasionally tranquillity reigned, and he noticed that a vendor was attempting to attract customers, for whatever ill-made objects he was offering, to a public eager for cheap novelties. Even at this hour, women in need of money to feed children, or satisfy their need for rum, were offering themselves to passing men.

At an unexpected open space, where a building seemed to have burned to the ground, he came upon a larger gathering whose watchful silence was punctuated by cries of encouragement or abuse. Newcomers were jostling those at the rear of the crowd, and George's experience told him that a fist fight was under way. His curiosity aroused, he moved to a point where he might assess the state of play. He was not averse to such contests, which were a popular pastime everywhere, and also at sea. He paused to consider watching the match, however, thought better of it and, the entrance to the dockyard being in sight, made his way onward. There was a strong chance that the contest might continue until his return.

He walked along a broad quay where he saw the usual forges, timber yards and chandleries offering the supplies necessary in such places. He passed jetties where ships were tied up showing little sign of life and noted the number of others moored side by side further offshore. He assumed these were waiting for landing space. Some loading or unloading was taking place, the lightermen lethargic, and subject to the

259

friendly derision of others who had not been taken on that morning. In the dry docks, ships supported by gantries, apparently awaited repair. Closer observation revealed considerable work in progress, and small teams of men undertaking work largely of the patching and tarring kind.

The yard was sizeable, and he walked its length comparing it with those of St Malo and Brest and finding comparison unfavourable to Greenwich. Groups of unemployed men were standing about touting for employment whenever an authority figure appeared. Unexpectedly, he came upon a dock where several dozen shipwrights seemed to be working with enthusiasm. The vessel was sleek in outline, with fine open decking, elaborate deck housing, and seemed to be suitable perhaps for an Admiral of the Fleet. This was clear from the fixings along each side for two dozen oarsmen to stand to row.

George moved about to find a better vantage point and heard a firm and polite voice close by remark, "A very fine vessel, is she not, Sir?"

Turning his head, George saw that the speaker was as broad and strong as his voice. A formidable opponent, George thought. Fortunately, he seemed eager to share his admiration for the lines of the vessel, and he wore an expression of benign approval.

"Very fine indeed," George responded. "French built I would think, from the joints of her housing."

"I see you know your ships, sir. An officer, I believe? There are many seamen walking about hoping that the Royal Navy may find a place for them. There's a chilly wind coming in with the tide, may I offer you a comfortable seat and a warmed drink, Sir? There's a welcoming hearth just behind you where you can study her over a warmed ale."

"Thank you. I'm Cartwright- and this is your Hostelry, I suppose; it looks very comfortable! I'll accept your offer. Whose is that fine vessel? Do you know? Strangely enough, my mind was on ale when you spoke. I imagine it is comfortable inside to judge from its lines. It's certainly a cheerless morning and the walk here was as miserable as the weather."

"Come inside, sir, and welcome. We are very quiet these days, though there are some signs of improvement in trading, and I hear that there is money around again, so the Docks may regain their old glory. That's the Royal Barge, Sir. The old King couldn't abide water, but Charles is eager to get it afloat, it seems. It's French built, as you will have noticed. We don't have the timber or the craftsmen apparently. They've all found alternative employment if they're lucky, but I hope they will begin to drift back. Did you say you were looking for a ship?"

Finding the landlord, Jim Brewster, and the atmosphere congenial, George also noticed a very charming girl who had returned from some errand while they were talking, and was going about housekeeping tasks, and chatting to an older woman behind the dining area. Her activities brought her into sight from time to time as she passed though the room, and she was light of foot and singing while she worked. George heard the landlord speaking and asking a question. He begged his pardon for inattention and asked that the question should be repeated.

"I wonder whether I may offer you a steak, Sir?"

"Thank you, not today, but another glass of ale would be welcome."

"I'll ask my daughter, Jenny, to bring it to you. She is happy in her work, as you hear. I'm a widower and my sister, whose husband drowned at sea soon after they married, lives with us here. I know it looks unlikely, but just past the dockyard, there is real countryside, market gardens, country houses and all. Mr. Evelyn, a wealthy city trader, has a house there, and is planting a huge garden and a really big orchard. He wants to revive local cider production. Behind our house, of course, is the Port Admiral's residence. Buckingham used it from time to time when he was Commander, but it's shut up at present. It's a fine residence with fresh air and fine views up and down the river."

George responded with interest, at that moment catching the eye of the daughter, and found himself smiling and saying that, when he was free, he might return to see the barge completed.

"You'd be welcome, lieutenant, and I will mention that my daughter is a very fine cook. Many gentlemen come here for a meal."

Chapter 21

George made his way back through the squalid streets, surprised by the contrast within a few hundred yards and realising, for the first time, that London was, at heart, a collection of individual villages. He brought to mind Jenny's smile and decided that he would make a point of returning to experience one of her meals and perhaps engage in conversation. Pleased with the idea, he walked on. He was a little surprised to find that the fight, whose preliminaries he had noticed, was still in progress. Hearing the exclamations of shock and disquiet mingled with shouting of genuine encouragement, and deciding the end was in sight, he decided to see which of the fighters would win. He felt that the stevedore probably stood the best chance, and inserting himself in a suitable space, he was able to see that both men were almost dead on their feet. Only stubborn determination was keeping the contest alive. Bets were being laid on all sides and the odds were small, though some of the gentlemen-well dressed and wearing swords, were wagering large sums, having much to lose as they had sponsored the fight. Both fighters stood to receive a healthy proportion of the stake, provided they stayed the course.

The final stages of the fight were punishing and bloody to both men, who were now having to be pushed towards their opponent, so weak were their legs, so unseeing their eyes. It was a final unlucky swing from the seaman which caught the temple of his opponent and the stevedore collapsed, senseless, to the ground. The winner was lifted shoulder high by his shipmates and carried off to the next drinking den, while the loser was left to the mercies of a few friends who tried to rouse him. The dispersing crowd turned away, imitating the final moments to their friends and jostling though the crowd. George failed to avoid contact with a demonstration punch from a passer-by which glanced off his shoulder. A concerned voice urged him to be cautious: "There's a young villain trying to pick your pocket! Get away you rogue, or I'll wring your neck!"

The lad shot away making a long nose to show defiance and his new companion responded with a raised fist and a few choice oaths.

"Thank you, sir. I almost lost my balance then."

"You're lucky you didn't lose your money!"

"No chance! I keep a few pence handy for necessity, but crowns are stowed in my small clothes."

"I know you, don't I? You're Master Carteret, ain't you? Off the Kittiwake, if my memory serves."

"Yes! Why, I know you! You're Seaman Storace. Hion, if my memory serves me, formerly of the Fair Haven. What are you doing here?"

"Watching the fight, like you. But I really came to see the state of His Majesty's Navy, being in the merchant trade myself. I reckon you're a Captain, am I right?"

"Yes, of a Naval sloop, patrolling the Channel. And yourself?"

"I have my own sloop, trading for hire and getting more work than I can cope with at present. I am searching for another ship, if I can fit out one at the right price. I might have sailed by your boat without knowing it. I'm often in the narrow seas."

George was pleased to meet an old acquaintance; although he had encountered Storace two or three times on fishing trips to the Banks, he had not seen him for several years.

"Why don't we find a clean house and have a few drinks; you could tell me about Beauty, that dog you owned, and I can thank you again for your help."

Storace enquired if George had crossed by London Bridge, and allowed his old friend to hire a carriage, promising a ride to remember. Needless to say, it was indeed true, and George decided he would rather shoot the rapids between the piers of the bridge than cross again in a carriage. Laughing, Storace derided him, suggesting that a man who had crossed the Atlantic in storms could surely face the river crossing.

* * *

Storace selected a hostelry in a street next to Seething Lane and the Navy Office, and it was a good choice for food and more mulled ale. "So, now you are nearly 25, I assume you were searching for an affectionate young lover on the south bank; Southwark has always been popular for its biddable, but very Frail Sisters?"

"I suppose it was not your first visit then? I noticed there were several delights available, but before I could make a choice, I met you! On a return visit, were you, eh?"

"You do me the injustice of a lack of taste, George. In fact, I have a beautiful blue-eyed lover I should be seeing, instead of sitting here with you! I have little enough chance to speak with her, as it is! In fact, I'm preparing to buy another boat, my business is going so well. I thought I might get an ex-navy boat cheap, to do up, but there was nothing worth buying."

"Did you consider offering for the Royal Barge? The King clearly wants nothing but the best and employs French craftsmen."

"Did you see it today? You walked further than I thought. I wonder what name it will have. His large battleship is named "Royal

Charles". Perhaps it will be "Henrietta". I hear she makes all the King's decisions for him."

George realised that he had reached that conclusion when he saw them together. At that moment he was more interested in seeking information.

"Tell me Hion, what sort of goods do you trade in?"

"Mainly in goods from Cyprus, and ports like Coranto and Smyrna, and bring currants and dates and pistachios and, of course, sugar. There's a bigger tonnage of sugar than anything else, for the "Quality" Londoners like it above all. You'll notice they all have generously endowed wives to match their own fat bellies: they display their wealth that way, by eating sugar!"

"Does it all come to London? I thought there were problems in trading with the Levant."

"The French like sugar as much as we do, and they are trying to introduce it in the West Indies. If they succeed, Cyprus will be bankrupt, that will upset the Mussulmen, and we'll have to get our sugar from the French. I sell to the French and Spanish as well."

"Do the King's Councillors approve?"

"They have no reason to complain. They owe me a few favours. I'll say no more..."

"You told us you have never been searched while sailing in the Channel. There are two classes of ship we never stop: one is a privateer who has inside knowledge of Naval plans, or a great deal of luck; the other is any Captain who carries Lettres de Marque. Am I right? If it is the former, you realise this may prevent me paying for this meal, for fear I may incriminate myself."

"I see you have gained some useful insights while serving His Majesty. I shall exercise discretion and say that both are true: from time to time I carry letters and sometimes, Lord Arundel or the poet Potter,

266

who travelled with Charles to Spain. I hope you understand without more telling."

"Which reminds me: I was talking to one of the King's buyers and mentioned your family. He said he remembered meeting some of your people in Romsey -at Moore Court, I think he said. His name is William Petty. I see you remember him: he's an agent of Nicholas Lanier, who is probably helping the King to purchase more pictures for his galleries."

"I remember a Mr. Petty, who was a friend of my uncle: he had a son who was very clever- he was six and knew Latin, Greek and Hebrew, I was told."

"That will be him! He's recently qualified as a surgeon to Oxford apparently, but he certainly knows how to get a good bargain! Someone told me that the King is thinking of appointing him to another post with more responsibility. He seems a decent sort, for all his cleverness."

"Can I suggest, Will, that you carry on business for His Majesty and that other cargo carried need concern no-one else?"

"I would be happy to leave it there, George. I might say you are the public face of Royal Policy and I am its private face. Can we shake on that? Good! I expect you have heard salacious rumours of the King purchasing obscene modern art... Ah, here he is! Now, George, let me introduce you to an old mate of mine, who is in a similar line of business. Captain Carteret, my friend, Mr. John Ward."

"Good Day, Master Ward, I have heard something of your developing line of trade and believe I may have had one or two of your ships stopped and searched. I recall you presented letters of marque and were released."

"Captain Carteret. A pleasure to meet you. We see an increasing number of your ships in the Channel, and your assistance is valuable to traders with expensive goods on board."

"Ward carries much the same goods as I do, but his family have been in trade since his father's time," said Hion. "John is trying to encourage me to invest in a ship suitable for carrying slaves from Guinea to the Indies. I'm not sure the demand is there: I'm trying to persuade him to give me some figures to show increasing demand, but they are difficult to obtain."

"You should take my word for it, Hion. You must have noticed the coffee houses can't get enough sugar to satisfy their customers and all the London grocers are placing larger orders. It is the trade of the future, Hion, and I hope to be a rich man in a few years."

* * *

In the meantime, a messenger had arrived at Sir Francis' London house, requesting the presence of Captain Carteret at mid-day on the following day, at Whitehall. Amyas, concerned by the thought of George presenting a poor appearance at court, had alerted Tom Dowse to the dilemma and requested him to bring smarter garments, estimating that George, Edward and he were similar in build. The news was broken to George when he returned from Seething Lane, wanting nothing but a good meal, and a night's sleep, and now his make or break moment was upon him. Edward arrived by carriage shortly after, with Philippe de Carteret, his first cousin from Trinity Manor, whom he had not seen for almost a year. Philippe and Edward were both in Chambers, though Edward had not yet qualified. Both arrived with arms full of clothing and eventually, after lengthy discussion, George decided enough was enough and made a final and arbitrary selection.

Alice enquired whether supper was required and was asked for her opinion of George's outfit. Having studied him from all angles, she gave qualified approval, pointing out that the coat was too tight across the

268

shoulders, and that everything needed to be pressed with a hot iron, and should be set aside for that purpose. George experienced some feelings of apprehension but not enough to prevent him sleeping soundly.

* * *

"Philippe! You couldn't have arrived at a better time. I need all the support you can offer. I have worrying matters to discuss. It's been a very difficult day and I think we are in danger of being overtaken by events unless we can agree on the steps we will need to take."

"Of course, I'll do all I can to help. I saw they've sent the "Endeavour" over again: so the new Governor has arrived at last. The boys saw the great ship with the Royal Standard sailing in with the morning tide. They were full of the news when I reached Orgueil this evening. What do you make of Jermyn?"

"It's not Jermyn who has arrived. He's sent a Deputy, a Captain Francis Rainsford, with a detachment of Militia, and they moored at the Castle's sea jetty, unloaded and occupied the Governor's Residence, after firing a cursory salute. A Guardsman arrived later on horseback to ask me to attend the Governor at the Residence at mid-day. I feel that we have been occupied by a foreign power, Philippe, not by a normal Royal representative- and I felt even worse after meeting Rainsford!"

"I am surprised Jermyn has sent a deputy. Were you given a reason?"

"Only grudgingly: as though it was not normal practice to give explanations. I think we are being treated as inferiors whose reactions may be disregarded, Elie. The implication was that he was too deeply involved in other concerns of significance at present but wishes his deputy to report on island morale and prepare us for any necessary changes which we may be instructed to make. There are all these

269

documents which he gave me to "read, record and inwardly digest" as he put it. Damned rude I thought, and I said so!"

"It would seem that new brooms are at work and there are new officials demanding efficiencies and trying to impress the King. What did he say?", he asked.

"We should ensure that Jersey Government reflects the standards set out in the documents. His Majesty wishes to ensure that the highest standards are adopted and that our Government reflects those set down long ago but which had been permitted to lapse under the last administration. These are to be followed to the letter and enforced by all who conduct affairs of Church and State."

"Here we have been, congratulating ourselves on having achieved a considerable measure of material and governmental satisfaction, without any help from London," mused Sir Philippe, "I wonder what these new standards are and how we measure up to them?"

"That's the real question, Philippe. I've only glanced at them as yet. I suggest we sit down and read them together and decide what we need to tell the States."

"That can wait for a few days, surely: we have a full meeting listed in six days" time."

"That may be too late, I'm afraid. Rainsford has already sent copies to the Chairman of the States, and to all Churchmen. They are probably discussing the revised Order of Service at the moment! It is the only one to be permitted in future."

"What has His Majesty said that may annoy them?"

"It has not changed to a great extent. The orders of service which were optional are now to be compulsory and there are new ones for special occasions. These may not cause offence to most ministers, but they are also instructed to place a fence round the communion table and call it an "Altar". I think they might consider that a kind of heathen

270

Idolatry. Also, the Prayer Book is to contain the Seven Sacraments necessary for a Christian, and Ministers must not talk about political issues or matters of a local nature close to them but must confine themselves to explaining the meaning of the day's readings in simple terms."

"Surely a degree of leeway will be given?"

"It seems that would be seen as persisting in unsatisfactory standards. Officers are to visit churches to see that conformity is observed: in our case the Acting Governor will serve that function. Ministers in breach of the new practices are to be dismissed."

"Did I tell you, by the way, that Rainsford is to assume overall command of the Militias?"

"Is he indeed! This is an infringement of my authority; one I took on recently! I may have to relinquish all Militia payment to him if he wishes to take charge. He is welcome to that expense! Let us read these documents together. Perhaps they may not be as difficult to work with as appears at first sight."

"Surely these measures are contrary to our established customs, Philippe? They are expressed in such a confrontational manner; they may be seen to threaten some in the community. although others may welcome the forceful wording."

"Not entirely, I think, Elie. It was Peyton who passed the responsibility for the militias to me, to save himself money, and give us power to arrest and prosecute pirates. Not forcing us to refer to a higher authority made justice faster and prevented long imprisonment during the delay. That was a major step for us but reinforced the King's power. You may recall George asking us recently whether the King could overrule our decisions, and I told him that the King trusts us to do what is right. You look puzzled, Elie. Perhaps you don't remember: we had a discussion about signs that Charles might not be as trusting as his father? We must not jump to conclusions."

"However, I feel these new impositions may imply a change in their approach to us, possibly a resistance to negotiating change. If it re-enforces personal rule again, Parliament would probably refuse to accept it. It seems like another attempt to assert his personal power."

"We must hope a new Parliament to show more understanding and work with us as before. I see there is a document here called "The Eight Propositions": I've only glanced at them, but the King is obviously re-stating his claim to overrule Parliament, and any of its recommendations, whenever he feels they are undermining his authority. Here! See what you make of it."

"I suppose it needs further study and, as you point out, that last point is very worrying. It implies that he may impose increased taxes on all his subjects, even if it results in increasing the suffering of many of his subjects. The existing austerity is causing the collapse of many trades, and weavers and clothiers are already marching to demand local Sheriffs provide food for their children. Parliamentarians will surely have to offer mediation. Even the local militias are reluctant to disperse them."

"Is this perhaps why he has not summoned a Parliament for over four years? I wonder whether it may be for fear of being contradicted. I think we may come to look back on his father's rule as a golden age. We must give careful thought to any proposals to enforce religious reforms, as a matter of urgency. I gather that London congregations are furious at some of the changes. This will need careful discussion with the States and our Churchmen. I wonder how Dean Bandinel will react. He has always been in favour of Laud's revisions, but I wonder whether he will find the latest ones a step too far."

* * *

Sir Francis, having returned to London after a fortnight spent at Basing, asked for an account of George's meeting with the Ministers of State. He assumed from George's cheerful expression that it had gone well. George recounted the points made by Sir Richard Weston and Lord Bristol. All had read the report and had agreed on its potential. The King himself had asked how the information had been obtained, and Pennington's own report had confirmed that the research was thorough, and not a work of fiction. He had mentioned that young Carteret seemed to be very thorough, and detailed. He remarked they were in need of those who could bring reliable facts. The King "has regard for you", George had been told. The King mentioned that Sir Philippe Carteret, young Carteret's uncle, was building a fine ship, and he hoped to hear of early completion.

George had been conducted, next, to Sir Thomas Wentworth, who complimented him on his work, then ordered clerks to leave and close the doors. Wentworth told George that he had been selected to undertake new tasks of a confidential nature. This was by instruction of the King, and a great favour. The details would be fully explained to him by Rainsford when he returned to Jersey. He must remember that anything spoken under the starred ceiling must remain absolutely confidential. George agreed mentioning the possible danger to those he would recruit. That the King's reputation would be enhanced by the intelligence gained, was to be the first consideration.

Needless to say, Sir Francis complimented his nephew, and stopped short of asking question. Nevertheless, he had reservations: he was aware that ministers retained the services of agents who were to report on the actions and words of those of social importance, especially if their loyalty was questioned, and that an agent was always in danger. He decided to inform Sir Philippe, in view of his nephew's secret

273

commitments, that he might find himself in dangerous situations and should be always cautious.

George himself had certain reservations regarding Wentworth's commission. He was instructed to make himself known to those who frequented Whyte's coffee house and Gray's Inn, and attend Vauxhall, and routs, when possible. Someone would approach him soon with an offer which he should accept, and act on when he considered the time was right. George had asked whether it was with reference to his report, but Wentworth seemed not to hear. George's first thought was the danger to his closest friends, when involving them, which might endanger their lives. His new task, he hoped, would never force him to betray their trust. Fortunately, their lives were already fraught with dangers on a daily basis and how to deal with emergencies. He hoped that he would be working largely alone and, preferably, abroad.

He had never before met a man like Wentworth, and Sir Francis knew only that he had been a strong opponent of Buckingham and was deprived of his seat in Parliament for proposing his impeachment. In about 1630 he had been given the task of creating order in the North of England and performed his task with brutal force. He had heard that he was very much a family man, and Charles was very impressed by his firmness. Would Wentworth be recalled from Ireland to be Charles' chief minister for England, charged with strict enforcement of the Law? George felt the man's physical and moral determination, and strong intention to impose his will, backed by his intimidating gaze, might be highly effective.

Chapter 22

L ondon life was a source of continuing interest. The extremes of wealth and poverty were a constant and at times, dangerous reality. Those in carriages, chairs, and even on horseback, showed utter contempt for those on foot or grovelling in the gutter. George was generally able, by his mere presence, to discourage petty thieves or beggars, but sometimes needed to place hand on sword to warn off predators, even in daytime. Night-time was more dangerous, and Beadles were seldom seen, other than in the safest areas. Gin, from one of the many domestic distilleries, was available for a few pence, cheaper than bread or most foods. It was consumed to quell hunger, in adults or babies. Wounded soldiers and starving agricultural labourers made up the majority of the unemployed and were physically too emaciated for the press gangs to recruit them.

The theatres astonished him, and the fact that a man could pretend to have a personality entirely different from his own, intrigued him. He decided, ruefully, that his own exploits as a spy were not dissimilar. Later, he saw that a regal and imperious Aristocrat was, off-stage, merely an ordinary London barmaid. He enjoyed the comedians, dancers and acrobatics, but was surprised that the current political disputes were openly discussed, especially in historical dramas. In Marston's Play, "The Roman Actor", he saw a man portraying the finest attributes of "a good man" a scrupulous judge, dragged before his Emperor, who was a would-be tyrant with a strong desire to exterminate his opponents. The Emperor sought to know what the Good Man would do if faced by ultimate tyranny. The Good Man said that his survival would only be secured by the death of the tyrant. The Emperor had trapped him into a statement of treason and arrested him and he and all his friends, were executed.

No moral needed to be stated, but George saw at once the relevance to his Uncle's dilemma. A similar situation of importance was being aired. Was it not best to speak out against injustice? Pamphlets were available on the streets advocating varied solutions to problems which George was unaware of, some religious, some political, and pamphleteers were often arrested and imprisoned or placed in the pillories to face public humiliation. Nevertheless, their pamphlets were eagerly sought and read, some of the most popular written by an ex-lawyer named Prynne, who had the temerity to criticise the king for indecent foreign paintings, and allowing the Queen to flaunt herself on stage, indecently costumed as a Greek Goddess. She was lampooned for immorality and heresy, deserving public rebuke.

Prynne had been punished, disqualified as a lawyer, and been branded with an "S" for sedition. Would this silence him finally? Everywhere George heard violent views expressed on religious issues, largely content of services, although often these were spoken of as though they were moral issues rather than doctrinal ones. "Enthusiasm", a name used as a term to disparage the expression of strong beliefs, was condemned, although it seemed that rational thought itself was considered pernicious "Enthusiasm".

George was never able to see for himself, at this stage, Her Majesty and the little Princes taking part in Masques, written by Ben Jonson and performed by Shakespeare's company. He saw only one of his plays, where one Scottish king killed another, and was killed by a third. It seemed pointless, though exciting and bloodcurdling. He also went with Philippe, his lawyer cousin, to the Savoy, the London home of the Queen, which had its Chapel adapted for Catholic priests to perform

276

Masses for the Queen. He understood much of the Latin, and Philippe explained the actions. He found the music very discordant. Afterwards he expressed disappointment not to have seen the Queen. Philippe said that she was the little person dressed entirely in black who had been served, while kneeling, with bread and wine. Nothing like that ever happened in Jersey, or Newfoundland, on Sundays! It seemed to him merely another example of acting performed on a glittering stage, and given the choice, he preferred the Scottish Play!

In addition, he attended an execution at Tyburn where six criminals were hanged. Two of them, both traitors apparently, were also quartered. The crossroads was crowded with carriages, horses and pedestrians, and the usual apprentices, who seized any opportunity to avoid work. George found that their crime was Heresy, and thought quartering was excessive. Consequently, he took a poor view of the proceedings. He had no problem with capital punishment as such and hoped Jersey folk would continue to be executed for the crimes of witchcraft or piracy, as tradition demanded. However, to punish men for their thought, was a step too far, as he had agreed with Gideon years before. Smelling sugared cinnamon buns for sale nearby, he ate one with enjoyment. Later someone remarked that the sugar cross was superstitious. Clearly innocence of action and words could no longer be relied on as a defence.

He became well-known at Whyte's, which his uncle frequented, and drank coffee to excess and tried smoking, but decided he would ration himself to inhaling the smoke others exuded. He listened carefully and learned something of the complexities of the new stock market, and betting on future gains in value of material goods. Traders made money betting on the possible scarcity or availability of goods. Wind and weather, it seemed, had financial implications. George had known this from an early age but had not thought it could be a source of income!

For fresh air he walked in St James' Park, or on the hills of Greenwich. He used a carriage for safe travel and made a point of stopping at Brewster's, the hostelry by the royal barge, after first inspecting the Shipyards. Progress there was slow but thorough, and he got on chatting terms with one or two of the shipwrights, drawing upon his own experience. In general, they seemed to believe that life was improving under King Charles. Brewster was a well-known figure about the dockyard and offered to escort him to see the ships being built. The Ship Money Tax, though unpopular, was reviving the activity of the graving docks considerably, though the work had to be shared between the three English yards, at Deptford, Chatham and Portsmouth, each of which had its own rules and customs. Brewster was an excellent cicerone, and George saw that the Unicorn and Vanguard were almost finished, and two new ships laid down, to be called Leopard and Swallow. He expressed surprise at their overall length and, by coincidence, Phineas Pett, reputed to be England's finest shipbuilder, happened to be on site.

Their unusual length was apparently a modification to Pett's plans at the insistence of the King. Pett had been reluctant to take instruction from anyone but realised that the King had made effective improvements in the past. One example was the Sovereign of the Seas, its keel laid the previous year and expected to go to Chatham for completion. Charles had insisted it must be lengthened, and Pett, who retained strong reservations, had also undertaken to fit two-gun decks, which had never before been attempted. The King made frequent visits to all his dockyards, to see that money was spent wisely and, on every visit, made a thorough inspection of the work done. Before the last two ships were launched, His Majesty had spent several hours inspecting every space, from holds, to cabins and lockers. The King was on board and sailed down the Thames, on their maiden voyage, climbing from ship to ship as they were put through their paces. His Courtiers were exhausted by his energy and Pett learned that he was meticulous in everything he attempted, and worked long days at his desk, drafting plans, or hunting, or whatever task he had set himself.

* * *

There was a warm welcome from Jim Brewster, Jenny, his daughter, and her Aunt, Jemima, who always stopped to talk when regular customers were involved in dominoes or chat. As he was leaving late one afternoon, Jim mentioned casually that, if he was intending to visit next Tuesday, his Hostelry would be closed. He was eager to give the whole public area a thorough clean, and had engaged a team of men to scrub, whitewash and repair, for the benefit of the new customers beginning to arrive. As a regular customer, George would be welcome as usual, but would eat cold meats and tarts, and then Jenny and her Aunt could take him on a pleasant stroll along the bank to see the gardens and fields: his sister had promised to visit an old friend who had a surfeit of plums she wanted them to jam. George readily agreed and hoped he would have an opportunity to get to know Jenny better by spending time in her company.

The next few days were full of fresh experiences and Tom Dowse and he, hired horses to ride northward from the city to the Wells, where there was a popular food and entertainment area, not smart and expensive, like Vauxhall, but where low-paid lawyers, and respectable clerks and their families, could enjoy the countryside. There were inns with Gardens, and walks by small lakes, and some good rides were possible.

With his uncle, or Tom, he attended a rout or two, which were occasions for the wealthy to open up their gardens, and new houses, to an invited selection of their friends and acquaintances. The main object was the ostentatious display of their wealth and good taste: also an opportunity to make new, and advantageous, contacts, or to find marriage partners for sons and daughters. If possible, there would be an important guest invited to grace the occasion, if possible, a Royal Personage, although a Duke would do.

This formed a talking point on the following Tuesday, when the trio set out for the riverside walk. Jenny had been to the Wells once, with a friendly family, and her aunt. George, unaware of this, had bought a little porcelain spaniel which Jenny had seen at that time, but had not been able to afford. Georges" unrehearsed gift of the model was a great success. He mentioned the rout he had attended at Chiswick, and Aunt Jemima wanted details about the fashions in vogue, the carriages, the fishponds, boats on the river, dances, important guests, and the music. He did his best to wrack his memory for tantalising information and found he had an eager audience as he conveyed the extravagance of the proceedings without letting the women feel they would have been outshone.

After some time, Jemima announced that, if they had no objection, she would visit her old friend, who saw so few people that she would be driven to distraction, and never speak a word. She suggested they should walk on and return to their usual picnic place under the willow trees, where she would come to find them when she managed to tear herself away.

"Don't let Jenny do anything silly, George!" Jemima commanded. "Somehow she always gets her dress soaking wet: she's a terror for the water."

George promised to do his best, Jenny demanding to know how he proposed to stop her and, bickering and laughing, they went on their way, happy to be free. The size of the Royal yards was an effective barrier to further development, and beyond them remained low-lying meadow, and agricultural land where villages remained largely unchanged. Then

280

the land rose to form the foothills of the North Downs. Their highest point was some twenty miles further east. They were content to climb the slope of Greenwich Hill and admire the view of the river. Finding a bank in the shelter of trees, they sat talking about their childhood, and early friendships. Her father had been a Thames waterman and had saved enough money to buy their Hostelry, after the death of his wife, as a security for his sister and daughter. She was a country girl and knew little about London and its ways, and George fascinated her with tales of the New World, and of life on Jersey, a place she had never heard of.

Below them lay the Dockyard and the glistening water of the Thames, thronged with vessels, large and small. Almost ahead was the Tower and its defences; to the left, St, Paul's, and further west, the Abbey and Whitehall. The air was clear that day, and the sky blue where they sat in a fond embrace, and Jenny expressed the hope that she would always be a country woman and marry a farmer. George, she supposed, would never settle, but roam the seas, fighting England's enemies, and bringing his ship safely home. He explained that they must certainly part in a matter of days, since a ship was being prepared to take him to Portsmouth, but he would make every effort to return to see her and her family. He promised to consider farming as a career, but doubted whether he could take to it, even for her sake. She said, sadly, he would always be welcome to visit, and rising, challenged him to race her down to the river, where her Aunt must be waiting. They sat on the bank there, throwing twigs into the water and talking, until she arrived, laden with vegetables and fruit, and a dozen eggs in a string bag. Each carried a share of the spoils and they returned to the house, which smelled strongly of soap and fresh paint, where George and Jenny made their farewells.

Walking on his way to re-join the main thoroughfare, George began looking about him for a carriage, when he was hailed by a familiar voice, and saw Storace waving him over. Greetings completed, George had a folded paper pressed into his hand and broke open a small stamp in wax showing an elaborate W surrounded by oak leaves.

"I can see that you are surprised to have me acting as postman, George. Our meeting that day was not entirely by chance, and Wade and I have been trying to catch you alone ever since. I trust you had a rewarding time with your young lady."

George shook hands warmly but asked who had told him to deliver the letter.

"Edward Knight waylaid me this morning, I thought I might find you here on a Tuesday! This is the letter you have been expecting, I've carried several, sealed with that crest before. I won't tell you the name of the writer, though you have met him and been approved. If you are leaving London in a few days, and the weather stays fair, I hope your lady friend is not expecting to see you soon! Wade is waiting with a carriage over yonder and, while we drive back to Gray's Inn, we have more to tell you, in confidence. I know nothing of the contents of the letter, of course."

Over a drink, the three discussed the possibilities of making money with private trading contracts. A ship generally had space for a little extra cargo it seemed, and Wade had plans for it.

* * *

Reading the letter in the quiet of the sitting room later in the day, George learned that he was to return to Portsmouth, where he would serve under Pennington as Captain and Commander of the "Mary Rose", one of the first Ship Money vessels. For the next two years, as it happened, he was kept very busy carrying secret messages and important items to France, and sometimes beyond. His natural skills as a linguist and mimic stood him in good stead and saved him from more difficult

282

situations than it caused. His promotion was rapid during this time, and Mary Rose was not always his ship: there were frequent changes of ship, to confuse anyone intent on taking advantage of regularity. Ships required constant repairs or new masts, but some of these changes were a means of concealing his spying exercises. His changes of ship were carefully managed to cloak his surveillance activities by making him invisible, often for months at a time. Normally a regular letter writer, he was forced to be more circumspect.

George had always known that he had a natural facility for languages and was a quick learner. His mother tongue was Jersiais, which was closely related to Norman French and which made the increasingly standardised French of the court easy to use. The fishermen catching cod on "le coté", spoke many languages, including low German and Spanish. His fluency increased with age and practice, and he enjoyed conversation in most situations. Engaging with the interests and concerns of others, made him a welcome companion. Possibly as a result of living in a household of strong women, accustomed to daily farm work, and the management of their workers, he was at ease with women and children, and perfectly happy to dance or sing when the need arose. These abilities were to prove of great value in the coming years.

One of his naval duties was to lend active assistance to ships engaged in bringing home His Majesty's acquisitions, not only of paintings and sculpture, but also of talented foreigners, some of Dutch who would construct sea and river defences, and engineers to extend farming land in England by draining marshes. The Dutch were often protestant, and therefore non-controversial. Nicholas Lanier, a protege of Buckingham, was now, with Lord Arundel, a principal buyer and negotiator, assisted by Daniel Nijs and William Petty. George had met William as a small boy when visiting Sir Francis and later, William had studied medicine, Mathematics and Astronomy at Oxford, and joined the Oxford

Philosophical club with Hobbes, Locke, Newton, and other luminaries of the new sciences. Inigo Jones, of Flemish background, and Wenceslas Hollar, and Jan Komenski, from Bohemia were both refugees from the pogroms waged against non-Catholics in central Europe. Hollar was a skilled graphic artist and engraver who made maps and panoramas, and Komenski had written a new curriculum for children to learn languages from early childhood. The Thirty Years War had destroyed his schools in Bohemia and his family had been massacred. Charles hoped he would create a national education system to the economic benefit of Britain. He was optimistic that even parliament would support such a worthy enterprise by lending financial support.

The cost of financing these projects was not touched on explicitly, until Ward unexpectedly began to explain how their operations were being financed. He was aware that Carteret and Pennington often exchanged captured seamen with other ships' masters in need of crew. Such a practice avoided a cost to Jersey in terms of food and lodging, but often the exchange was in part financial. Although their work was to rid the seas of pirates, it was preferable, once they were captured, to sell them on. Ward had taken on the mantle of Sir John Hawkins and Sir Francis Drake, each was in turn Admiral of the Fleet, and Knight of the realm, who had originated the Three Way Trade, by which products from Europe were shipped to the Spanish and other American colonies and exchanged for an increasing flow of black slaves, obtainable from West Africa and eagerly sought by the European settlers. Thus, Colonists grew rich on exporting coffee, Slave traders and African tyrants grew rich by selling their "enemies", and British merchants gained more than anyone else.

To George, most of the King's ideas seemed fanciful. Whether or not England had more land under the plough, and children who could read or write, seemed of little practical interest or use. Ridding the seas of

284

pirates and extending the possibilities of overseas trade would bring prosperity to all, which was a sound prospect. It seemed a logical way to proceed, and George knew that slavery brought wealth to many countries and was of long standing. The King, by adopting this practice, was not penalising those in Jersey or England, who would otherwise be taxed to pay for ships and weapons. There was unlikely to be opposition to this practice, since the British could not be kept as slaves in their own country. Of course, the utmost secrecy must be observed, but George was content to comply with the plan. Further meetings would be convened in the following months for operations to begin in the spring.

* * *

George prepared for departure, Sir Francis having already left for Southampton, having heard of the death of Courtney following a second seizure. Thomas continued with his legal studies and Philippe, his near relative who was about to join the Bench, informed him, with some pride, that he had been accepted by the Honourable Artillery Company, whose H.Q. was close to the Inns. He had served in the Jersey Militias and was eager to support the King's re-formed regiment to quell street riots or possible invasion. It had its origins in the reign of Good King Henry, and he was pleased to have been invited. "What a family we are!" George reflected in an idle moment; the whole family were strong in their loyalty to the King. Of course, he knew that this was not a recent development: Carterets owed their success to their rulers from the 12th century, when in 1100, Guy, "le Ouiseleur", was awarded lands in Normandy and France by Duke Rollo: their motto was "Devoir Loyauté" and so it seemed to him, it should remain. George found that Philippe was knowledgeable about Military matters; he had enjoyed

285

issuing orders from his early childhood. Now he was expecting to be made an officer in a week or so.

George had been told that Bunhill Fields had the best views of the whole of London and when in need for quiet reflection, he often went there. It was generally deserted, though at times children came there with their mothers seeking fresh air, and the quietness never available in the City. From time to time he thought about the course his life had taken. As Storace had pointed out, he was in his mid- twenties. He had begun to ask himself what he had achieved in a quarter century. What was he other than a postman delivering unknown goods across the Channel and, sometimes, passengers on mysterious missions? What did he possess? All that he owned was contained in a sea chest. What did he have to show for his endless seafaring? Did his life have any purpose or was he one who would always be dependent on other for instructions?

He could not find an answer. He began to consider the lives of other friends and relatives. Many were successful farmers and landowners, reaping the rewards of their labours, and with children to inherit their goods. Others had rejected that life and passed smoothly from success at school to academic rewards in Saumur, Coutance, or Oxford, where the States had created Scholarships at Magdalen College, available for able students from Jersey, who were now Sergeants at Law or merchant traders. Some islanders continued to send sons to Saumur in accordance with tradition: The States were increasingly angry that they received instruction based on Catholicism and might find themselves out of step with Jersey Protestantism. Where would he find a secure living, lacking learning, qualifications or even military experience? Surely all he had achieved was due to the influence of family members who had misguidedly allowed him to have his head and rush off on a random path of his own choosing, leading him apparently to no significant achievement.

His depression increased as he considered William Petty. Storace had told him of William's success at Oxford. He had been an infant prodigy combining a gift for languages and a love of adventure. At the age of fourteen, perhaps inspired by George, he had become a cabin boy and broken a leg on his first trip at sea. He was set ashore in Normandy and spent his recovery teaching English and applying to Caen University with a Latin application letter. There he had acquired a mastery of Latin, Greek, French Mathematics, and Astronomy, and was now employed by the King as a buyer of valuable objects. He was bound for success!

It was inevitable that George would meet William Petty, since he was often called on to escort the King's treasure ships though dangerous waters. Petty was, despite his accomplishments, a good humoured and entertaining companion, and they established a lasting friendship in spite of Petty's comparative youth: he was born in the year George made his first voyage to Newfoundland. It even survived the fact that they were on opposite sides in the Civil War.

Even Pierre le Sueur, his close companion in Newfoundland, had found growing success in France in the workshop of his uncle, and was becoming a sought-after caster of bronze figures.

Perhaps he could learn from Storace. He found there were two kinds of trading, one legal, the other "unofficial". Legal trade was bound about by legal restrictions and caveats. The Nobility were given Monopolies and permitted to trade only with merchants who would give them a percentage of their profits in exchange for naval protection. Every product, from paper to brandy, was controlled by Monopolists, and they in turn made payments to the King, whose Treasurers inspected all the transactions. Tight controls like these gave the King money to buy his treasures and govern without Parliament.

Harbour masters however, at the main ports, took their agreed share of profits gained, from both merchants and captains, and shipowners.

Storace was owner of two ships and George suddenly realised that he had been offered an opportunity which would bring profit his way. Storace did not use the main ports, preferring ones without customs officials, or ports where trade was poor and officials would ignore formalities, and accept a share of the profit. Surely Storace would take him into partnership if some of the Jersey boats were placed at his disposal. He was not unaware that some of his countrymen had always been privateers: his old friends from spying expeditions would enjoy the thrill of illicit trading.

He found Storace without difficulty at the inn in Seething Lane and, after hard bargaining, handed over a reasonable sum of money to equip a new ship for a trading voyage to the Netherlands, where precious fabrics from the east were available for purchase. The enterprise went smoothly, and George made a pleasing profit to be invested in his next venture. He had joined the age-old company of Merchant Venturers, but in a private capacity. He was following the example of his heroes Greville and Frobisher and, of course, he was following the example of the King.

FOOLS MATE

The Remarkable Life & Times
of George de Carteret
1609 - 1680

The second book of the Royal Chess series.

Coming 2021

Printed in Great Britain
by Amazon